telling tales

D0723391

CHARLOTTE STEIN

sourcebooks
casablanca

Published by Sourcebooks Casablanca, an imprint of Sourcebooks, Inc., in conjunction with Xcite Books Ltd.
P.O. Box 4410, Naperville, Illinois 60567-4410
(630) 961-3900
Fax: (630) 961-2168
www.sourcebooks.com

Originally published in 2011 in the United Kingdom by Xcite Books Ltd.

Library of Congress Cataloging-in-Publication data is on file with the publisher.

Printed and bound in the United States of America.
VP 10 9 8 7 6 5 4 3 2 1

To the Terrifying Person of Great Importance,
for making me believe I could be a writer.

Chapter One

IN MY HEAD, I fucked him the first opportunity I got. I didn't wait for some perfect time, some perfect place, some perfect convergence of events. I just kissed his sweet mouth right in the middle of him telling me something funny or ridiculous, like—peas are green because they ate too much spinach—and then when he couldn't quite gather himself after something like that I took his hand and pushed it between my legs.

Or maybe in this dream scenario I could have taken my hand, and pushed it between his legs. I spent so many nights in college, thinking about how his cock would taste and feel. It doesn't take much to shove my imagination into a slightly different sort of area—one where I unzipped his jeans and licked long and wet over the length of him, while he sat back and simply…let me.

That's all we were missing, after all. Him letting me. I mean, it wasn't as though I ever asked or tried to fuck him or any of that stuff, but it was always in my head. That I would make a move on him and he would knock me back, and then I'd lose that bubbling bright friendship between us forever.

Funny how I seem to have lost it anyway. I didn't even try, and I've lost his friendship anyway. It's been five years, for God's sake. It's been longer, according to Professor Warren's letter, and for a moment I'm just so lost on a sea of trying to remember Wade Robinson's face.

I'm lost, thinking about things that never happened—his mouth on mine in the back of Kitty's old Ford Escort, fingers sliding slickly through my ever-ready cunt. How many girls did he do that with? Too many to fucking count, but never to me.

No—I got to sit up front and pretend I couldn't hear him making out with Tammy or Candy or Veronica, while Joan Jett blasted out from the radio and Kitty shouted at me that we should really actually pick up some boys sometime.

Instead of letting ourselves escort Wade the make-out machine around.

Of course, Kitty soon got into the swing of things. She was my little cloud of blonde loveliness, and she floated through the rest of college on a tide of too-happy. And I was happy too, I was. I really was. We had a great time together—me, Wade, Kitty, and Cameron.

So why am I looking at this letter with dread?

—◦◦◦—

I look at it with dread all through breakfast. And then all the way through lunch too, while simultaneously trying to think of a way to make knitting sound interesting. The magazine wants the article by the seventeenth, but something in me says I'm not quite going to make it.

I'm not even sure what knitting is, really. Something to do with wool, maybe? Possibly a little bit about making jumpers that no one wants to wear with two pointed sticks? I can't build an article on those things—I know that much. I might as well write what I really want to, which goes something like this:

And then aliens invaded Earth and blew up all the knitting in the world.

But instead I look at the letter again, while pretending I'm not doing anything of the sort. The letter mocks me with its weirdness and its reminders of everything I don't have anymore, and it makes me think strange things like: *I wonder if Wade ever did become a screenwriter. I wonder if he's still as funny and amazing and handsome, with his gorgeous electric-blue eyes and his mean, mean mouth and his look of something wolfish, as though he might just bite you at any second. God, why did he have to be so attractive? I would have loved him if he'd looked like something that dragged itself out of a drain.*

And I know that much is true, because when the phone rings and it's suddenly Wade's voice crawling out of my past at me, saying things in that yawing Canadian accent of his like yeah, no time has passed at all, everything in me goes still. I can't move for a second, just sitting there staring at the answering machine like it's suddenly caught on fire.

While he says perfectly normal, ordinary things like *How've you been, Allie-Cat?*

As though no time has passed and I'll just understand it's him, immediately. He even has the nerve to demand I *pick up pick up pick up*, because of course he knows I'll be here; I have to be here—I've just been sitting in one place all this time, waiting for him to grace me with his presence.

I'm almost ready to kill him with the force of my own resentment, when a touch of the old Wade sings out at me from a million miles away. A million years ago:

"So are you up for the Mystery Machine or what?"

Because, let's face it, that's what this is. For reasons unspecified, our old professor has left us his rambling house—the one we used to go to every weekend and rattle around, telling stories by candlelight because Lord, how spooky it was, even back then—on the condition we spend a month within its walls. "Renovating," the letter says. "Restoring," the letter says. But Wade knows the score and so do I.

The professor wants one last bump-in-the-night story. One last hurrah for the Candy Club, and all those nights we spent telling tales we now can't remember—or at least, I can't remember. They're all at the bottom of my desk drawer and the bottom of the drawer under my wardrobe and the bottom of everything in my apartment ever. They're spilling out and coming to get me through the dearly departed spirit of Professor Warren, and his house with the corridor of stepping stones and that one room with the little round boathouse window and the doors that sometimes went to nowhere.

I close my eyes and I can almost *see* Cameron putting the flashlight up to his face—reluctantly, because Cameron was always reluctant about goofy stuff like that—and saying in his gun-metal voice, *Mwa ha ha, we're all going to die in here*. Those eyes of his like a storm at the bottom of the ocean, always, and the flashlight making his dark eyelashes seem like shadows, deep shadows.

The machine beeps and I jump as though I've been pricked with something, and then it's just me in my apartment. Just me and the knitting articles and the letter that says, *Come and play Scooby-Doo and the Haunted Mansion one last time, Al. Come and see if you can figure out if it was old man Withers all along.*

But I don't think I can. I know what the house is worth—I've looked it up, of course I have—but even £750,000 split four ways doesn't seem like incentive enough. In fact, it feels like a pretty poor payoff for too many memories and too much pain and this low thrum I always get when I think about his face or his mouth or the way he used to grab me all the time.

He didn't understand what it did to me. His hands on me, I mean. He didn't understand that when he fell asleep with his long body curled around mine, I lay awake aching and unfulfilled, wondering what it would take for him to touch me in the way I needed to be touched.

Like now, when just hearing his voice has driven my hand to the top of my thigh—almost at my slowly pulsing sex but not quite. I won't give in just yet, not yet. Instead I shove the letter in the top drawer of my desk, and stare long and hard at the knitting article that's blinking away on my laptop.

Then I go one further—a really desperate move, I have to say—and open the bottom drawer. The one crammed with writing, most of it smutty and some of it probably about Wade, and then I grab a wedge of it. Just to, you know, distract myself.

Only it doesn't distract me. Of course it doesn't. The story on top—actually handwritten, ink almost disappearing, corners curled—is the one about the girl who comes back from the grave and haunts the man who didn't love her.

And it's embarrassing, Lord is it embarrassing. I can hardly stand to look at it, it's so obvious. I've even given the hero a mess of blond hair and those bright sparking glances of his, and there are so many psychosexual Freudian undertones that calling them undertones is like calling a mountain a sinkhole.

It actually turns me on, reading it. I imagine the girl in her dress made out of mist and fog, spreading herself over the hero's body until her non-flesh sinks all the way into him, and all I can think about is fucking, fucking, fucking. I think not about Wade but about this supposedly faceless and nameless hero, about him over me and under me and inside me like something I always want but never get.

And then I put the heel of my palm over my aching sex and ache harder, stronger, sweeter.

My clit feels huge beneath the press of my hand, but I resist the urges it thrills through me. It says: *Replay the answering machine message.* But I ignore it and think about the story instead, the story I once read out to my former friends, without shame or worry or any of the things I'm feeling now. He must have known I was writing about him, but back then I didn't care.

I just care now, as I try to pretend I'm not sliding my hand under the waistband of my panties, to get at my slippery pussy. And it *is* slippery, because Wade always got me that way and even if he hadn't, six months of neglecting myself in that regard has definitely put a spike in my libido.

I'm suddenly thinking about what I can do to make it better, make it hotter. There's a vibrator in one of those many bottomless drawers of mine, but it's probably still in its wrapper. The batteries inside it have most likely melted. I barely even know what to do with things like that, but just thinking about it buzzing against my clit or filling up that great empty space inside me is almost too much to take.

I can hardly remember what it's like to get fucked, and my fingers just aren't enough. They slide around in all this wetness I've somehow produced, glancing over my too-sensitive bud until I'm shaking against the hard wood of this chair and on the verge of doing something stupid.

Something like calling Wade up to ask him to talk dirty to me, while I fuck myself on something I don't know how to use.

Of course, I do know. I've written stories about it, so I do know. I've written stories about girls masturbating with cucumbers on trains, for God's sake. I've written about girls fucking machines, girls fucking each other, girls fucking guys who can go for hours. It's just that I've never actually *done* any of that stuff. It's all fiction and none of it's fact, not even in the tamest, stupidest, slightest little sense.

Not even a girl getting herself off against a sex toy, because everything in her head turns her on but nothing in reality does the trick.

I think about Wade. I think about the hotter stories I wrote in his honor but never actually read aloud to any of the Candy Club, about the great and terrible land of Hamin-Ra, where the Queen rules over her harem of sweat-glossed men and my imagination gallops and thunders and tells me the most wicked things.

In the story, there's always a line of men. A huge long line of them, one after the other, and none of them can look at the Queen but all of them feel the urge to. All of them are naked and some of them squirm, pricks stiff and backs too straight, trembling with the effort of being so perfectly obedient.

But none of them want her really, she knows. They want the idea of her, they want her crown. They want to stand at her side and rule Hamin-Ra, and so she teases each one with a finger on their cocks or a raised eyebrow, and passes them by.

Until she gets to the One. He doesn't have to pretend, or feign desire. He stands there so seemingly insensible of her presence, with something smoldering and burning beneath eyes so quiet and still. And when she runs her hand over the heavy length of his slumbering cock, he seems to despise the thrill of desire that charges through his body.

Though I've no idea why. I've no idea why this one story turns me on so much, either, or what's so compelling about his resistance. It hurts, that Wade so indifferently rejected me. Why do I give this one man Wade's face and have him turn away from my Queen, even in so silly a fantasy?

But I do and he does and my clit thrums beneath the busy slide of my finger, all of me eager to hear the rest, the best parts, the scenarios I've replayed over and over in my head. Like the ones where the Queen tests him by tying him to a bedpost, then makes him watch as some other man licks and licks at her creaming sex.

Or maybe one of them—some big burly guard with grasping hands and a stone-like face—fucks her and fucks her in ways my resisting hero knows are wrong. He knows she'll never come on her back like that, with her legs in the air and the guard's little prick shoving in and out of her cunt.

How he longs to please her, my best hero. How he wants to fight the ropes around his hands and get at her with his stiff, swollen cock. He's in agony—I know he's in agony—but worse than that, I truly understand the fantasy for the first time ever. My cheeks burn with shame and I fuck two fingers inside myself, knowing that I'm this ridiculous creature who wants someone to want me *that* badly, and oh there's nothing I can do about it.

I try to slow everything down, to just feather those strokes over my bursting clit, but it's like striking a match. It's like rubbing my face against the coarse grain of someone's stubble, even though I can barely recall what that feels like. In my head the hero doesn't care about my shame or what the subtext of this fantasy is. He just tears his way out of the bonds that restrained him suddenly, full of all the fury and lust I've never seen on a man's face in real life.

And then he does all of the disgusting, perverted, insane things I've always secretly wanted. He fucks her face with his steely cock, hand too tight in her hair and body rippling with that delicious tension. Or maybe I go worse and weirder than that, and have him force her to fuck *his* face, cunt pushed so tight against his mouth that he can't breathe or move or do anything but moan.

Oh yeah, yeah. I like that one. I like it when he gets her on her front and fucks her ass, oil running over her thighs and her hands twisted up behind her back. I like it when he makes her suck the guard's cock as he takes her, or maybe, God, maybe *he* sucks the guard's cock as he takes her.

It doesn't matter. It all amounts to the same thing—me moaning aloud in an empty apartment, my head full of all the stories I never dared to tell, and then God, God, Wade's face flashes up behind my eyes and I'm coming, I'm coming, and I'm making so much fucking noise it's almost enough to drown out the phone.

Almost, but not quite. In fact, I'm still right on the edge of it— little shocks of pleasure still shuddering through me—when I hear another voice on the answering machine, as familiar as Wade's but for different reasons. Wade I know because of all the things we shared together, because of everything in me that longs for him. Cameron's voice is recognizable because it's like liquid metal, pouring out of that accursed masturbation-interrupting box.

"I don't know if this is you," he says, while my cheeks flame red for reasons better left untouched. I mean, it's not like he can see me, right? It's not like he can see me with one foot up on the desk and my knickers half down and my fingers inside, still stroking over my wet and swollen folds.

And even if he could, what would it matter? It's only Cameron—Cameron with his liquid metal voice that isn't really liquid metal. It's just deep because he's massive, and it's cultured because he comes from one of those snooty American Harvard-going families even though he didn't go to Harvard and his family has no money now and, to be honest, I don't know when he last lived in America.

But he's on my answering machine anyway, talking and talking.

"Or if you remember me," he says, as though I could forget. Why did Wade assume I'd know it was him, when Cameron thinks I'd forget him so easily? "But I just wanted to call and say I've missed you, Allie. And if you come to this…whatever it is…it'd be nice. It'd be good to see you again."

I think it's the most I've ever heard him say in one go. He was never big on talking, Cameron. And if he did talk it was always about something that bored most people to tears—computers or rowing or something that once happened that no one else is interested in. Man he was beautiful, but *man* could he clear a party.

And his stories…so strange and mechanical. Wade wrote things full of life and pizzazz, people pogo-ing across the universe in space-ships filled with magical robots from the planet Neptune. Whereas Cameron, well…he wrote about spaceships filled with robots too. But then later we'd all find out that he'd intended to write about living, breathing humans, and only ended up with weird, emotionless automatons by default.

That was Cameron. A weird, emotionless automaton by default.

"Oh, it's Cameron, by the way," he says, and it's strangely those words that touch me. Wade's message was all bolsh and Kitty's was all *Oh my Gods,* but Cameron doesn't even think I'll know it's him.

Funny, that it's this very thing that makes me decide to go.

Chapter Two

THE HOUSE IS EXACTLY as I remember it. More so, in fact. The driveway seems longer, the surrounding grounds bigger. Nothing has encroached on it—when I'm standing on the neatly shaped gravel semicircle in front of the entranceway, all I can see is a grassy veld that slopes downward into trees, and then more trees, and then nothing but farmland and quaint little villages and the mist of the morning rising up over everything like a veil.

It's beautiful. The house itself is beautiful. There's even more ivy all over the front and it's the same squat, deceptively large gray building it always was, with the thickly varnished blue front door and the actual bell instead of a buzzer.

I almost don't want to go in. What if it's not the same inside? The letter said it needed some work, so naturally my head is full of images of walls that have fallen down and squatters living in fireplaces and God knows what else.

But when I get in—the key the solicitor gave me unneeded, because it's open, creepily—everything looks so…familiar. The great staircase standing between the kitchen on the left and the living room on the right. The living room still stuffed with those leather wingbacks and the big red sofas and the painting over the fireplace of the stag with the terrifying stare.

They still follow you around the room, those eyes. And the colors are still a mess of vivid and impossible greens and reds, as though any second the whole thing is going to come alive and chase you into another dimension.

That was what this house was like. Another dimension. Everything else about university—the mundane classes, the mundane people, the sense of being alone even when actually in a room full of people—was a great swathe of nothingness, apart from this. Apart from the Candy Club and Professor Warren and the weekends we spent, talking until 2:00 a.m. under the watchful gaze of the Evil Stag.

Most of the time Warren just left us to it. It was like our house anyway, in those days—but I think of him now, even so. I think of him in one of these great old chairs, falling asleep thinking about the students he must have loved, and then just one day never waking up.

I wish we'd known. I wish I'd known. I miss him, standing in this plush room, with everything about him all around me and the best memories I've got swamping my mind. He gave me those memories, after all. He made me come to this place, and he made me write, and he was the one who said to me: *Don't ever give up.*

Real sorry about that, Professor.

I swipe at my eyes and shake myself, suddenly bristling with a new kind of discomfort because is that another set of bags, by the bureau? Those are definitely someone else's bags, and if the unlocked door wasn't enough of a clue to my ridiculous brain, this sure is.

There's another person here already. And judging by the assortment of sports bags and rucksacks, it isn't Kitty. Kitty works as a model now, I know she does, and she was always one for the finer things anyway. She'll be carrying Louis Vuitton, and if I've got my Kitty right, she'll have bagged a room already. No dumping her stuff in the living room for her.

So that just leaves Wade or Cameron. And odds on it's Wade. Wade was always the sloppiest one, the one who never packed properly and wound up having to borrow some socks from Cameron that resolutely would not fit him because Cameron's feet were the size of boats.

Which means that any second I'm going to bump into him.

I'm just going to turn a corner and see him, and then the bottom of my stomach is going to drop out of me and find the floor. Hell, I wouldn't be surprised if it found the basement. I feel sick just thinking about him awkwardly hugging me or even worse—what if he goes for the equally awkward handshake? What if I'm not worth a hug?

What if I throw up on his shoes?

It's then that I know why it was Cameron's voice that persuaded me to come. It's because Cameron is calming, his very being is calming, and I'm never scared of what he's going to do next because he's as steady as a rock. He doesn't do wild, unexpected things. He's insular and strange and silent, where as Wade is big and funny and never without a wisecrack. I can't predict him, and that's a hard thing to realize when most of me was sure I knew him so well.

Still, I take the hallway past the staircase—the one that still has the stepping stones set into the glossy floor—and make my way to my favorite room. Wade will be in the study if I do actually know anything about him at all, and I'm building up to it.

First, the boathouse room. The one that has nothing in it—not even a carpet—except for the one round window with the glass like melting butter, and the light coming in to fill it up in a way that no other place in the house does. Everything is dark here, everything is heavy and plush and like burying your face in crushed velvet.

But not this room. This room is like suddenly being on a boat in the middle of a golden ocean, and when I press my face to the heavy glass it's just the same. I can see almost nothing and imagine it's almost anything, out there. A whole world of high seas that I get to explore.

Though more typically it was Hamin-Ra I got to, through this portal to another world. I wrote about it a thousand times—me lifting the latch, and pushing against the glass, and then the golden beauty of my sand-strewn land would spread before me and—

"Allie?"

My heart hits my mouth. It chokes me—and weirdly it's not because I know it's Wade. It isn't Wade, and my heart wants to kill me anyway. Apparently, all four of my once-were-friends have the same effect on me, which is to say they make me want to run and hide.

Maybe by pushing through a portal to another world.

I brace myself and turn, and sure enough it's Cameron. Of course I knew anyway—that *voice*—but it's still a kind of electric shock to see him so close after all these years. He doesn't even look any different, either! God, how I must seem to him, with this cardigan on that I shouldn't have worn and my hair all massive and curly like this and the glasses, oh no the glasses, oh no I totally forgot how much of a dork Cameron makes me feel, with his bigness and his jockish hair and his smooth, perfect face.

And then I remember that he's a complete nerd—one who fumbles over his words on a daily basis—and it's OK. It's OK.

"Hey," I say, only it has about four extra syllables. And I can feel my face cracking, like it's made of clay and he's just set a blow-dryer on it.

It's just Cameron, it's just Cameron, I think, over and over, but my brain can't remember him being this…immense. Was he this big before? I think I kind of knew he was, but with him filling the doorway like that it's a different matter. He looks like a giant. He looks like he killed the beast that ate Jack, then devoured the beanstalk too.

And he looks a lot more jockish than I remember too—though maybe that's just because I'm seeing him fresh. He hasn't spoken yet, or spent hours not speaking, or bored some girl to death at a party he didn't want to go to. I vividly recall putting a baseball cap on him before we went to the Christmas blow-out over at Missy Taylor's, when he'd asked me how he could at least *seem* cool and approachable.

Smile more, I'd told him, because he'd always appeared to

find it a strain. His parents had been very don't-smile-old-money-be-composed sorts of people, and though I always knew he didn't want them to, those qualities had rubbed off on him.

They're all over him now as he stands in the doorway, obviously wanting to hug me or something like it, but completely unable to. I can see the hint of a smile peeking through too, but it's only because of those neat little incisors of his.

"Can I give you a hug?" I ask, and it's weird how easy it comes. By God, I'd never ask Wade. I'd never ask Wade anything. Pass the peas seems like too much, with him, but with Cameron it's suddenly and oddly easy.

I try to think back—were we close, Cameron and I? So close that I didn't mind being the one who suggested, asked, persuaded? I don't think we were, and yet I can picture a lot of me putting hats on his head or shaking his big body back and forth to loosen him up or asking him if I could read stories he'd hidden somewhere.

Usually he rolled them up and stuffed them down the back of his pants. I have no clue why. Why bother to bring them to class or to the house if you were just going to pretend they weren't there?

Until I found them, of course. I always coaxed him out of his shell.

"Yeah," he says. "Yeah, yeah—sure."

And I guess maybe then I know why it's easier with Cameron. Because although he's probably better looking than Wade—he's so good looking that it's blinding, for a moment—I somehow have this weird little inkling…this little feeling that he won't say no. Like maybe he understands that I don't ever expect anything to happen between us, so he can be open with me. Or maybe he just…maybe he's just like that. He just wants to be hugged, probably.

Even though I'm sure I've seen him bend away from a pat on the shoulder, before today.

He doesn't bend away from a pat this time, however. I put my arms around his middle—just like that, easy as anything—and I feel his huge hands spanning my back, so warm and good after all this time. He even smells the same, like that airy aftershave he always used to wear, and then all I can think is how odd it is that I can remember Cameron's scent.

"It's so good to see you, Allie," he says, almost directly into the top of my head. Mainly because he's six-five and I barely graze the *Pembroke* on his old and very worn university hoodie—but then it's not his height I'm thinking about.

Instead I'm flooding with heat, remembering when I last heard him say something like that. On my answering machine, as I…did stuff. With my legs all over the place and my hand inside my knickers and ohhhh, there it is. There's discomfort and embarrassment, my old friends!

I pull away from him too quickly and he looks…startled? I'm not sure. Sometimes it's hard to read the expressions on his immense face, and it gets even harder when he says things like this: "You look really…great. Just very…pleasant."

Because I remember how often he used to search for words, as though the real, normal, sane ones eluded him. As though his brain constantly wanted to put weird things in there instead, like *You look really pumpkin. Just very bicycle.*

Odd, that it only makes me want to leap in there with all the casual conversation I don't usually have, and that he resolutely cannot provide.

"So do you—I think you've gotten even better looking, somehow."

Which is absolutely true. His mouth looks even plumper, and softer—Jesus, that lower lip like something out of *Hot Blowjobs Monthly*. And he's cut his copper-hinted dark hair so that it kind of swirls all over his head and swoops over his forehead and looks much lazier than he is and oh God, why is he staring at me like that? Am I staring too long at him?

It had seemed easier to do, at first, but now it's getting harder.

"I think the others might be here," he says and then I definitely know I stared too long. He's going to think I'm hot for him or some other nonsense thing, which is completely not the case. Even if my face feels like it's burning and there's this funny, tingly ache between my legs as though *really*? I'm horny *again*?

Usually it's once a month and even then I'm pushing it. So what's going on here, exactly? Is the thought of Wade really such an aphrodisiac?

It must be, because little weird sparks prickle the length of my spine when Cameron puts a hand on my shoulder. Like he wants to steady me as we make our way back down the hallway, like maybe he knows that my heart is hammering and my legs don't want to keep walking—even though that's impossible.

Cameron never knew anything about me, least of all this.

He doesn't know that I can hardly bear to look Wade in the face, not even when we come to the entranceway and Kitty's giggling her ass off, camera in hand as usual, snapping away like there's no tomorrow. And then there's Wade, my Wade, just standing there with his back half turned as though this is nothing at all, really.

"Allie!" Kitty screams, and I see how easy this is for her too. I see her in slow motion, tiny arms out, charging toward me—oh, she was always the one who never let me forget she loved me, with postcards from far-flung places and ridiculous emails about swimsuits made of ham—but it's Wade I can't stop watching, Wade who turns in that said same slow motion while my heart tries to eat itself.

He looks older. And then my brain kick-starts and yells at me that *of course he looks older, people with masses of handsome stubble generally look older*. At which point I have to process that he has masses of handsome stubble and dear God I can't let it slide. I just can't! It's all over-styled and too practiced and he's gonna get it, now. He has to.

"Did something *grow* on your *face*?" I ask, and oh I'm so grateful for the great chunk of incredulity in my words. I'm so grateful that it all floods back into me—the way we used to talk, like nothing could ever be serious. Nothing could ever hurt.

And he grins that shit-eating grin of his through the great mess of hair all over his chin, as though to tell me I'm right.

He's still him and I'm still me. I haven't lost him forever, my best friend in all the world.

"There's something on my *face*?" he says, with a real and perfect slice of panic in his electric eyes, and then he just throws his arms around me. Just like that. Nothing to it. Cameron's hand slides right off my shoulder and I'm hugging Wade as though no time has passed at all.

Makes me wonder what I was worried about, really.

———

It takes three boring conversations about jobs we all do now—Kitty models, of course, Wade mysteriously works in real estate and Cameron now does something to do with software I've never heard of—and around two bottles of the terrible wine Kitty found in the back of the fridge—Cameron drinks more than I remember, Wade drinks less—before we get around to stories.

Of course, we all know it's coming. I can feel every tale I ever told right on the tip of my tongue, and when Wade congratulates me on staying true to my dreams I can't stop myself. I have to start us down this path—the one none of us have actually taken.

"It's not real writing, what I do. I just…" I start, but Wade cuts in. Of course he does. I can see he's been raring to go ever since that stubble crack in the entranceway. He looks so bristling and spark-eyed, with all his hair slicked back and his new, gorgeous man's face.

"So it's fake, then. You write on air with a magical unicorn hoof."

"I don't—"

"They print your articles in *Non-Existent Monthly*."

Gah, him and his stupid fake magazines. I make them up myself, but it's only because of him.

"No, it's not fake. It's just…not what I always wanted to write."

He raises his glass to me.

"Hey, it's still more than any of us managed, kid."

I kind of hate him, for saying that. But then Kitty stretches out on the couch beside me, and curls an arm around my scrunched-up legs, and puts her head in my lap. She's already half-cut, I know she is, but I also know why she then says: "We could all still manage, if we wanted to. People don't ever run out of stories."

I expect Wade to interject then—with something about rejection, probably, or losing the will to or any of the things I've felt myself a thousand times—but it's Cameron who gets there first. I'd almost forgotten he was there even though he's just to my right, in Professor Warren's old wingback. Sitting at the head of the room like a tombstone, still and quiet and far more comfortable than he'd looked two hours ago.

I guess maybe he's a little cut too.

"Apart from me. I think I ran out before I ever even began."

And then everyone laughs, of course they do. Funny, that I don't really feel like it.

"I always loved your spaceship story," I tell him, because that's the truth. I did. It's not a pity party I'm throwing here.

But he looks at me as though maybe I am.

"Ohhhh no you didn't. I stopped writing years ago anyway," he says, and then he runs on before I can push at him again. "But I did always want to hear the end of "Hamin-Ra." Did you ever finish that one, Allie?"

I think I go a little cold then. Not because I couldn't remember ever reading it out to them—after a moment, I vaguely recall reading the tame, vanilla beginnings of it—but because it's so fresh in my mind. I think about the answering machine and the lurid list of bizarre scenarios, prancing through my head. I think about the window in the boat room, just waiting to open and let me through to another world of joy and pleasure and beauty.

Not like this world of leather and drinking and designer stubble.

"Yeah," Kitty mumbles from my lap. "I want to know if the Queen ever found her heart."

And now I feel slightly less disconcerted. It's better when it's not just Cameron remembering this one weird story I wrote, as though it had some special meaning or even worse…as though he somehow heard me through a fucking answering machine.

But it's still odd. I can't even recall writing that part of it, about the heart or whatever it is Kitty's blathering over. The whole and original thing is in one of my bags, but I'd stuffed it in there without looking, while the majority of me pretended I wasn't doing it at all. After all, it isn't as though this month is really going to be about ancient writing we did three hundred years ago. We aren't really going to share stories just like before, and God knows I'm not going to share "Hamin-Ra" even if we decide to do just that.

I only brought it because…I brought it because I brought other stories too. I brought it because I grabbed a bunch and shoved it all in, and there's nothing more to it, really. Just as there was nothing more to Cameron shoving rolls of stories into the back of his pants as though yeah, none of us were ever going to find them. None of us were ever going to say come on, come on, where's your tale, Cam?

"Probably," I say, but Wade laughs, then, and says, "Oh, she knows. She knows for sure, she's got it with her!"

And I hate him for that too. Now they're after me to read it and no, no, no, I can't, I can't, and then I have to tell them why and it's mortifying somehow. It's like pulling a tooth. Out of my vagina.

"The ending's smutty, OK? No no no."

It's more than smutty—it's downright pornographic. But I don't say that and I'm glad, because even something as tame as the actual word I used has made Wade touch his tongue up to one pointed incisor, and I can see Cameron sitting up even straighter, on the periphery of my vision.

Plus Kitty starts giggling like an idiot into my lap, spilling wine from the glass she should no longer be holding, while she's sprawled all over me.

"Great. Great, guys. Laugh it up."

But Kitty goes one better than that.

"I always knew you wanted to write porn," she says, in between hilarious, hilarious laughter. "All those stories about ghosts that wanted to have sex with people but couldn't."

Oh, *Lord*.

"I didn't really want to write about porn, OK?" I say, but then Wade has a go too.

"I think you kind of did."

And then even worse: "I *do* remember a lot of sex-ghosts." Everyone turns to look at Cameron immediately. Mainly because he just used the words sex-ghosts as a term, and he didn't even have to spend a lot of time searching for it. He just blurts it out and then, when we all stare at him in amazement, he takes a massive swallow from his wineglass.

Definitely half-cut.

"See. Even Harvard over there thinks so," Wade says, and of course Cameron rolls his eyes in reply. Sometimes Wade would call him Yale or Dartmouth, but the result was usually the same.

"We *went* to the *same* university!"

"Yeah. Yalevard."

"There's no such place."

"Harvale, then."

"That's even less existent than the other one you mentioned."

Ah, it's like no time has passed at all. They can go like this for hours, every word hinging on Wade's ability to be intentionally ridiculous for long periods of time, and Cameron's almost death-like insistence on the literalness of things.

Though he has grown a slight hint of sardonicism, right at the back of his words. It's very faint but I can hear it, and there's something about the gaze he lays on Wade that seems…cold, almost.

It makes all the hairs on the back of my neck prickle, at the very least.

"But anyway. Back to the sex-ghosts," Wade says abruptly, as though maybe he spotted the glittering cool beneath Cameron's steady stare too.

Sadly, this only puts me in the spotlight again. I feel like a Vegas stripper, only without the feathers. Or spangly nipple-covers. Or skin.

"I really have absolutely no idea what you guys are talking about."

"Your stories were always like that, Allie," Kitty says, because she's a goddamned traitor. "But it's OK, 'cause mine were too."

OK, maybe not a traitor, exactly. Maybe more like a really evil partner in crime who drags you down with her, into disaster. In all my many dreams of how this reunion would end up going—minor explosions, someone killing someone else, nervous breakdowns—none of this ever featured in even the tiniest, remotest sense. I didn't even imagine myself ending up in bed with Wade, really, because whenever I let myself want something it almost never happens.

Did I do the opposite of wanting this chat about sex stories?

"Yeah, also guilty," Wade says, and I rack my brain trying to think of where they crammed all this boiling lust into tales about being a pig who could fly (Kitty) and a cyborg from the future (Wade).

Maybe the pigs and the cyborgs had a lot of sex I just don't know about.

"It's OK, Cam, you don't have to put your hand up for this one," Wade adds, and my brain automatically makes an odd little dinging noise. As though it's decided to tally up all the little digs Wade's going to get in about Cameron, for no apparent reason. "Everyone knows that you're not a part of our dirty perverts club."

Seriously. Were they like this before? Because that last part seems even meaner than the first bit, as though Wade would like nothing better than to slice Cameron right out of our group forever, for some end I can't quite see.

I can't see it so much that I'm compelled to say something in too big and too funny a voice, as though I can just smooth everything over by being ridiculous.

"Hey, how do you know he's not a dirty pervert? You seem really perverted to me, Cam, I swear."

By being *really* ridiculous. Because in truth, there isn't a person on earth who seems less sexual than Cameron. I'm sure Mother Teresa was more adventurous with her lovers than Cameron is with his. In fact, now that I'm thinking about it…I'm not even sure I've ever seen him with someone I could loosely term a "lover."

He probably has constant, epic sex with the robot girl he's built.

Annnnddd…*now* I feel mean. Especially when he then says: "Thank you, Allie. Your faith in my perverted-ness is very…welcomed."

He actually does seem heartened too. When I look at him he's getting really close to smiling in this strange, almost-definitely-drunk way, and after a couple of long, weird moments have ticked by I find my mind rolling back and back to that word he used.

Welcomed. And the pause he had before it, as though he had a couple of other contenders before he settled on something so mundane. Though for the life of me, I can't think what other word he could have slotted in there. What replaces welcomed, easily? Pleased? Sweet?

And then my brain throws up *arousing* like an insane hiccup, and I move along quickly.

"OK, so, maybe I liked to occasionally write about sex-ghosts,"

I say, but it comes out less funny and more wounded than I intend. And Wade spots it, which is weird because he never used to. He never used to know when I'd taken a mortal hit and was down for the count.

"Hey, what's the big deal?" he says, and there's this creamy, smooth note of conciliation in his voice that sounds weird. Weird, but not exactly unwelcome. "We're all grown up now. We can be perverts if we want to be."

"I didn't care about being a pervert before, quite frankly," Kitty says.

Of course, my mind flicks to her bonking the living daylights out of Martin Carruthers in the bed next to mine, in our tiny dorm room. Though I'll admit, my mind sometimes goes to her bonking the living daylights out of Martin Carruthers when I'm busy plunging the toilet or waiting for a kettle to boil, so it's no real commentary on the things we're talking about now.

"So where are the stories, Kit? The dirty stories, about something other than magic balloons that get lost?" Wade asks, and Kitty *heys*!

Then tries to hurl a cushion at him and fails, miserably.

"I wrote loads more than kids stories, you doof. I wrote fabulous tales of rip-roaring sexual adventures the likes of which the world has never seen."

I can well believe her. One of her postcards just had the word "five-way" on it in big letters. Is five-way even a word? I'm not sure and largely felt too afraid to ask.

"Yeah?" Wade says.

And then he does something that makes my stomach kind of flip-flop. As though maybe I'd just thought this whole conversation was going down a path to nowhere, and any second we'd start talking about the same cool, literary stories Professor Warren always used to encourage, with everything sexual about them stuffed firmly into the subtext. The subtext that's now, apparently, cracking under some weird pressure I didn't even know was there.

It's not there, is it? I mean, none of us fancied each other, or anything like that. Unless you count me fancying Wade, which is pretty linear and only in a single direction. I mean, it's not as though you can write a postcard to someone with "one-way" on it in big, fancy glitter letters.

"Like this story?" Wade says, which isn't the thing that makes me flip-flop inside.

No. It's him leaning over the side of the chair he's sitting in to the satchel bag resting at its side, to whip out his usual scrunched-up bunch of semi-clipped together pages. Pages that could well have text all over them, and none of it subtext.

Kitty squeezes my legs and squeals: "Ooooh, he's a magician!"

Because she's bonkers. Only Cameron and I are sane, adrift in the sea of weirdness this whole night seems to be sinking into.

"You're not *seriously* going to read a dirty story, are you," I hear myself saying, but it's from very far away and the tiny section of me that's cool is staring at this very far away person with a sneer on her face.

"Well, it's not as though Warren's here to tell us off for using the word *fuck*," Wade says, and though it's mean and Cameron interrupts with *Hey, man, he just left us a house*, he's got a point. The Professor didn't even like to hear the L-word in fiction.

And the L-word's *loose*. So you know. The *craps* and the *damns* didn't stand a chance.

"Why do you think he did?" Kitty asks, and we all sort of freeze in position, then. Not because it's a little jarring in the middle of a discussion about smut that was starting to get...let's say...*heated*— though it is. Jarring, I mean. The weird tension I can feel pushing against the nape of my neck and under my arms doesn't dissipate, but it does start tapping its foot, waiting for us to go back to whatever Wade's got us moving toward.

But no, it's the question itself that makes us freeze. As though we all know we've been kind of avoiding it, and maybe we wanted to avoid it a little longer. I can hear Wade shuffling the pages of his probable hellfire and brimstone story around, as though he just wants to get back to this, *this* is the point of us being here.

Sharing what we never shared before.

Though when I think about this idea, my stomach stops flip-flopping and drops out of me entirely.

"Because he had no one else," Cameron says, finally, and though Wade starts blathering on about Scooby-Doo and Kitty wants to know why he wanted us to stay here for a month first, then, if it was just about him being a lonely old bastard, I think Cameron's right.

I think we were his family, once. And maybe he just wanted his family to come back together, in some sort of wildly eccentric and completely inadvisable fashion. One that makes Wade say: "There's a curse on the house, and a month is what it takes to possess us all and make us kill each other."

This time, Kitty manages to hurl a cushion at him. She even kicks one little leg out at him, and misses by a country mile.

"You dick! I'm already not going to sleep tonight, thinking about people watching us."

"People *watching* us?" I say, and Kitty turns her head almost 360 degrees to shoot the weirdest look at me. It has nothing to do with the content of my words, though, I know, and everything to do with the fact that me and Cameron say said words at exactly the same time. We even use the same incredulous tone—or we would have, if I had a gun-metal voice like his.

"Well yeah. There must be people watching us. Checking that we're staying for the month, you know? Making sure we're doing the 'renovations.'"

"The place doesn't even need renovations," Wade says, and he would know. But Cameron's still stuck on this idea of being watched.

"No one is spying on us. The solicitor even said to me that a clause like that wouldn't hold up—that we didn't have to stay if we didn't want to."

We all go silent, then. Though I can practically hear what everyone's thinking, anyway—*so why are we here?* What are we all doing here, if we don't have to be? None of us have jobs that we need to rush back to, and there's a nice healthy provision been made for us, but even so. Even so, what are we doing in this old house again, reliving old memories?

"So," Wade says. "Back to my story?"

I can see he's just raring to plunge right into it—which makes my palms inexplicably sweaty and puts my heart somewhere up around my throat—but Cameron pulls him up short. He points out that none of us have any candy, and I'm almost certain he does so for the same reasons I would, if I'd have thought about it.

To stall Wade from reading out the Story of Probable Depravity.

But then he comes back too quickly with a bag of actual red licorice, the staple story food of the Candy Club, and then I'm not so sure. Plus he kind of looks at me as he passes by to the kitchen, and there's something about his expression, something hazy in his bottom-of-the-ocean eyes, as though summer heat has hit the water and everything is melting away.

And then Wade starts talking, and I don't know whether it's Cameron's strange smoky stare or the words of this obviously filthy story that make me feel suddenly warm and liquid between my legs.

Though I think the latter has a running start.

"He thought about licking her cunt when he brought the pair of panties to his face, even though he didn't want to. He wanted to think about nice things, cute things, because she was a real lovely girl. Her eyes only ever laughed at him kindly, and her sweet mouth seemed to have no edges. She did nice things, like slipping an arm around him when he felt down—despite the fact that no one else ever seemed to know if he was down or not.

"But she did. And now he was in her room, going through her things. All of her panties and bras and other stuff besides that he'd never suspected she'd have. She had something that looked like a see-through teddy, and when he rubbed it over his cheek it felt liquid-soft, like maybe it would melt if he kept doing dirty things to it.

"Even so, he ran it over the stiff ridge of his erection—plainly visible through the material of his jeans—and thought about doing that same thing with her inside it. She'd be all spread out on the bed with the silk clinging to her curvy body, and he could get on her and slide his cock over every inch.

"The thought alone made him sweat. He could feel his stiff cock pulsing against his zipper, and longed to take it out. But then the door sounded down below, and a new kind of feeling sprang through him"

I know just what Wade's perverted character means. A new sort of feeling is springing through me too. Wade pauses to snap off a bit of red liquorice, but other than that he seems completely unfazed by all of the cocks and cunts and, oh my word, I don't think I can take the heat in here. I think I need to get out of the kitchen, even though I'm not actually in one.

Where has he *gotten* this stuff from? Is this real? Something about it sounds it, but I can't imagine Wade sneaking into some chick's bedroom to sniff her panties—and especially not this new Wade, all smooth and creamy-voiced and too-slick.

In truth I can't imagine anything at all, because the bottom half of me has been dipped in warm honey and I can't seem to breathe out. I keep breathing in, but nothing's going back out again.

And he continues! Kitty is kind of squirming on my lap and I dare not even look at Cameron, but Wade only goes and carries on.

"Fear. She'd come back early from the poetry recital. Any second, and she was going to climb the stairs and find him here, lurking in her most private space.

"He did the only thing he could: he opened the door to her adjoining bathroom and slipped inside.

"However, this action presented a slight problem. Once in there, he had the urge to shut the door tight and lock it—maybe he could tell her he'd desperately needed to go, or something like it—but by the time he'd thought of it, he realized two things. One—an excuse like that wasn't going to fly. And two—he couldn't safely shut the door right to without her hearing and knowing he'd gone in there only a moment before she arrived home.

"It just wasn't watertight. Which was how he found himself in her bathroom, staring at her through a crack in the door, willing her to leave before anything worse happened."

I don't want anything worse to happen. Kitty has a hand inside her blouse—I know she does, without even looking down. But I don't blame her because my own nipples feel like two great big glaring points, sticking right through my jersey for everyone to see. I wish I'd worn a thicker bra, but really, who could have predicted this?

Does he somehow psychically know I'm this horny? Can anyone else feel it, vibrating off me in waves? I'm sure I can sense some kind of strange heat emanating from Cameron, but maybe that's just because he's so massive and I'm so turned on.

God, I'm *this* turned on before he's even gotten to the good stuff.

"It was almost a slap in the face when she stripped out of her clothes before doing anything else. Of course he tried to look away, but it was useless. Here was the object of his lust in just her bra and panties, and both items barely hid a thing.

"When she turned he could see the groove between the rounded, glorious cheeks of her ass, just visible beneath her plain white of her underwear. His mind went automatically to the most lurid thing he could imagine—stroking a finger over that shadowed crease, or even filthier—sticking his tongue there and licking and licking until she begged him not to stop.

"And then she turned around, and that warm pulse of arousal he'd felt while stroking her silky things over his body became a sharp kick. A warning—if he didn't do something soon, he was going to spurt in his jeans just like that.

"She looked more amazing than he'd ever imagined. He could see it now—the clothes she wore were too shapeless. They hid the full, perfect curve of her hips and the neat way they nipped in at her waist. The slight swell of her belly looked smooth and warm and infinitely caress-able, and though her legs didn't have a lot of length, there was something about them—something sweet and inviting.

"She'd barely be able to get those things around his big body, and the thought was exciting. As though she was both solid and real, easily grope-able and always promising a soft sensuality, but also small and quite fragile.

"The contrast made him want to groan, and he put a fist to his lips. She'd started taking off her bra and any moment he was going to get to see her breasts—the object of many of his fantasies. He'd often imagined covering her in something slick, then easing his swollen cock between those two soft mounds, but the image was so much clearer, here. It was so close he could almost taste it, but he resisted.

"He didn't move, or make a sound. Not even when she suddenly slipped a hand beneath the material of her panties, and rubbed slowly over her almost visible pussy."

He looks up from the story, then, but I can't look back. Mainly because I've covered my face with my hands and am only watching through the cracks between my fingers. Of course, I still know he's grinning. He's grinning underneath his stupid designer stubble and, when he continues, he sticks his tongue, lewdly, into the hollow cup of his cheek.

Then Cameron interrupts in a suddenly heated tone, and I don't know what to think anymore. I'm starting to lose my ability to make sense of things.

"Maybe you should tell a different story, Wade," he says, almost like a warning, but Wade just kind of winks at him and carries right on.

"She was wet. He could tell she was, because even from all the way over in the bathroom, he could hear the slick sounds her fingers made as they parted things he wanted to part, and did things he wanted to do. The urge to open the door and just go to her went through him, but he held it in check. She'd never forgive him, if he revealed himself now.

"Not now that she'd spread herself out over her bed, fingers busy beneath the thin material, free hand on one plump, gorgeous breast. From this vantage point, he had a complete view of the place between her spread legs, and when she frigged herself a little more vigorously or slid two fingers inside her tight pussy, the strip of material covering her mound slid to one side to reveal little tantalizing glimpses.

"He couldn't help sliding a hand over the pulsing ridge of his erection. At first he went with something small and unassuming—the heel of his palm pressing down hard and almost cruelly. But once she started moaning and squirming on the bed, those little glimpses of glistening flesh getting clearer and clearer, he couldn't stop himself.

"He'd never particularly thought of himself as a sexual person—he rarely felt anything above a mild arousal and masturbation wasn't top of his list of fun things to do—but the heat coursing through his body was undeniable, irresistible. It was as though a strange force had gripped him, and was inciting him to slide a hand inside his jeans and stroke over his stiff and swollen cock."

I swear to God, I jump right out of my skin when Cameron interrupts this time. Even Kitty jolts a little, in the middle of doing whatever it is she's doing—that's how loud he suddenly is.

"I really think you should stop now, Wade," he says. But Wade doesn't.

"It took only the slightest touch—just his thumb on the slippery tip—to bring him off. He felt it like an avalanche, like something breaking inside him, uncheckable pleasure jerking upward from his straining cock to some place low and deep in his gut. Great spurts of come covered the insubstantial cup of his hand and then flowed messily outward, to stain the inside of his jeans. He could feel his body straining, strung too taut, while all of her cries of pleasure echoed every sound he wanted to make.

"It was only afterward he realized these sounds had made him bite down hard enough to draw blood, on his still-clenched fist."

He puts the pages aside, but nobody says anything. It's as though he hasn't finished, as though there has to be more, despite the buzz of relief that seems to be going through all of us, to have heard it come to an end.

And yet when Kitty sits up quite suddenly—blouse partially unbuttoned and blonde hair a mussy halo around her head—and says: "So did she catch him?"

I'm echoing the sentiment inside. It's the first thing I want to know, and it feels weird to understand that this is the only time I've ever been so desperate to get to the end of something Wade has written. As though all of his other stories somehow pale in comparison to this—whatever *this* is.

"Tune in next week to find out," he says, though I'm sure he's lying. There are no more words left on the page. He's drained them all dry and left us wanting more, even though I'm clenching my nails into my palms with the weird awkwardness of all of this and Cameron is bristling to the right of me, somewhere.

I glance at him and he looks…I don't even know what he looks like. Pissed on Cameron isn't the same as pissed on anyone else. He doesn't frown or grind his teeth, though I can see he's pulled his lower lip right into his mouth in this mean sort of way. And I think his cheeks are a little flushed, even though that seems impossible.

I don't think I've ever seen him blush—so I guess that's it. He must be embarrassed, in some fashion. I've never heard him talk about sex frankly, and he certainly doesn't seem to want to talk about it now. In fact, before Kitty's even done pressing Wade for more, Cam has gotten up out of his seat and left the room entirely.

And I can't help glancing after him, as he goes.

Chapter Three

OF COURSE I CAN'T sleep. I try, but it's impossible with Wade's story on my brain, and then in the kitchen, later on, him hugging me from behind. Him whispering in my ear: *Did you like the story?*

I felt like saying *Nooooo, I hated it. I wish it would die a horrible, untimely death, and then I could just stop thinking about it forever and ever, amen.*

But instead I had just gone all hot and cold like an idiot, feeling his much-bigger-than-they-used-to-be arms around me, and smelling his rainy days smell as though no time had gone by at all. Only the thing is, back then he wouldn't have whispered something like that in my ear. No—I don't think he would have.

Because…and here's the kicker…it was definitely suggestive. There was something suggestive about it—I can't deny that fact. His breath had been all hot and moist against the side of my face and my throat, and his voice had held a little burr of something delicious right down low, right from the deepest darkest place inside him.

My clit had jerked to that sound before I'd even had chance to process it. His hand had spread over my chest—so achingly close to my right breast—and he'd pulled me so tight against him, so tight I could have rubbed my ass into the curve of his body and maybe felt something else that possibly maybe could have been there.

It was there on Cameron, I think. I don't want to face it too head-on because there's this weird barrier in my mind, this weird urge not to embarrass him any further even though he's never going to know I saw something just as he passed me by. But he's a big guy, and, well, it's not as though sweatpants hide a lot. And neither does kind of bending over and moving fast.

Christ. Why the fuck am I thinking about Cameron's possible erection in the first place? I've got sex on the brain. I've got sex on top of me and all over me and in the tiny grooves between my higher thought processes. Wade has poisoned me with his stupid, ridiculous story and now all I can think about are cocks and sweatpants and maybe getting up and going to Wade's room.

A blush storms my entire body whenever I let myself entertain the notion, but the notion is there nonetheless. I mean—that's what he was saying, right? He was being suggestive. He was suggesting I get up and go to his room in the middle of the night—or maybe slightly earlier than that, because I'm sure he didn't imagine it would take me three hours to stew over all of this—and maybe talk for a little while. You know, about old times.

And then after all the talking: fuck his brains out. Just fuck and fuck and fuck his brains out. Hell, if he wants me to masturbate on a bed while he spies on me from the bathroom, we can do that too. I'm feeling loose-limbed and lax and up for anything, even as the neurotic side of me tries desperately to cling to my teetering mind.

He doesn't want you that way, the teetering side says. *He was just being friendly.*

Only I know there's something new here, now, and it isn't exactly holding hands and sharing tales of happy pigs. I don't know what it is, exactly, but it's almost as though I can feel it charging through the walls of this house—between his room and my room and probably Kitty and Cam's rooms too—when I put my hand on the smooth, cool surface above my bed. Like we're all connected down this great red hallway we've picked as our living space, every buzzing molecule in our bodies breathing life into the Professor's weird old place.

It's even something weird—like the thought of the lush crimson carpet out there, gathering between my bare toes—that urges me up, and out of bed, and down toward Wade's room. His is the fourth door on the right—mine is first, then there's a bathroom, then comes Cam's room, and Kitty's picked one of the rooms opposite—and I know before I even get to it that it's open. I can see a slither of blue through the crack, because Wade's room is all navy curtains and swirling sky-colored rugs, though it's not those things I'm paying attention to.

No, God, no.

I'm paying attention to the sounds of people fucking. Obviously, vigorously fucking. And for a long, long, frankly pain-stricken moment, I'm not sure what to do. I could keep going toward the door, clearly, and uncover exactly who's doing the fucking in question. But that just seems like asking for heartache, because really there are only two options.

Either that weird tension between him and Cam was actually intense sexual attraction and they're both in there doing each other in the ass, or else it's the far more likely option. Kitty snuck across the hallway well before I ever even considered it, and now she's in the middle of a marathon sex session with the object of all my hopes and dreams.

God, I hate that he's the object of my hopes and dreams. I hate Kitty for one bright, burning, selfish second, because she's brave and I'm not, and she's lovely and I'm not, and she doesn't have to be a eunuch for the rest of her life, and I somehow do.

And then I get to the door with my mind this boiling cauldron of stupid ideas—like how I'm going to barge in and accuse Wade of cheating on a girlfriend he doesn't actually have, or accuse Kitty of betraying a friend over something she doesn't even know about, or have some kind of ridiculous meltdown where I say words that aren't even really English, just the blind tumbling result of my stupid heartache—and I just can't do any of it. I can see them through the crack in the door, and I have to simply stand there and watch my hero twisting into some pretty incredible shapes with a person who is not me.

I have to watch him lift both of her legs over his shoulders until she's almost bent double on the bed, and then pound into her as though sex is going to disappear tomorrow. Whoever invented fucking is going to revoke everybody's license, and from then on we have to spend our days shaking hands or violently waving.

I wish I'd done more than that in the short window of sex we all had. For one far too long and not-quite-agonizing second, I find myself gazing at them with my mouth actually open. Heartache falls by the wayside in the face of this, because by God I've never seen a man flip a woman like that. He just gets hold of her hips and somehow she's on her front, even though I'm sure such a move should have dislocated her hip.

Of course, I've seen things like this in porn. I'm aware that most people have more athletic sex than I've ever had. But even so, it's different when it's close up. It's different when it's only inches away from me, and I can see the look on Kitty's face when she turns it to one side and bites at her own arm.

She looks like someone who *realizes* there's going to be no more sex tomorrow. She looks desperate and blissed out and she's making this noise—this *ah ah ah* noise—that I can hardly stand to hear. It forces unwanted feelings through my body, and I know they're there because I just have to squeeze my legs together against them.

God, what must it be like to feel that way? To have someone pounding into you over and over again, so hard I can see her little cupcake breasts bouncing beneath the curve of her body, and when I dare to flick my attention to Wade I can make out every muscle in his tensing stomach, all ab-tacular and hard as anything and fuck, fuck.

This is too much. Did he look this way, before? He had a good, strong swimmer's body, I know that much. But I can't recall him being so hairy or having those ropey, muscular arms or those actual high, firm pecs. He looks so *rippling*, so hard-bodied—though I suppose the overall effect is added to by the sheen of sweat all over him. It's as though he slid out of the pages of *Men's Health* only five seconds earlier, and I'm not ashamed to admit I can't take my eyes off it.

Though maybe it's partly because I don't want to look at the two most obvious eye-magnets: his cock, and his face. If I look at his cock or his face, I swear I'll die. He's saying some pretty dirty things— *Take it, take it, you little slut,* among others—and that's enough all on its own. It's enough to make me press my legs together tighter, tighter, and I can feel I'm sweating through my pajamas, I know I am, I know any second I'm going to touch myself like the guy in Wade's story.

And then I look up at his face—just as Kitty says something disgusting like *Ohhhh yeah, fuck my slick cunt*—and of course he's staring right at me. Of course he is. He's staring right at me as he fucks her, this look on his face like something the Devil would do on realizing he's corrupted another innocent soul, and I back right up in a hurry until I crack my shoulder blades against the wall.

I realize I'm breathing hard. Probably hard enough for Kitty to hear, if she takes a second in between ordering him to *Fuck her pussy harder, goddammit.* I almost laugh hearing my little pixie girl being such a bossy-boots in bed, but then my mind flashes on Wade's grinning, mischief-lit face again and I'm too shocked to get the sound out. I think I'll be too shocked to make a sound tomorrow, actually. In fact, I think I'm too shocked to ever make another sound from now until the end of time, because God I don't know how I feel about any of this.

I can't even find bitterness, anymore, which seems very odd

indeed. Instead I just seem all juiced up with too much sex, and when I try to walk back toward my room all I can manage is a kind of vague slide along the wall.

Of course it's only once I'm tucked back in my bed, staring at the ceiling like a ghost of myself, that I actually dare to admit what I wasn't sure I'd seen before.

He beckoned me in. He jerked his head in the universally accepted gesture for "come on in, the water's fine." And then he winked, and I broke my back against the hallway wall, before slithering back to my room like the proper little eunuch I am.

Of course, the sleeping situation is even worse now. I catch myself staring at the alarm clock I brought with me—the one I've perched, incongruously, on the ornate dresser in the corner of the room—watching the neon numbers flick by, one at a time. 4:36 a.m. 4:37 a.m.

Jesus, what a nightmare. So typical, too—of course he's fucking Kitty! Of course he is. I come here hoping for one thing, and get a face full of that instead. With possible weird threesomes thrown into the bargain. And then in the insane aftermath I get my body humming like an overheated tractor, everything between my legs all swollen and heavy and obviously soaked.

In fact, I think I've soaked through my pajama bottoms. Whenever I move everything feels wet down there, though I don't want to move because when I do my clit sparks and my pulse beats slow and heavy all the way through my sex and the urge to masturbate is just incredible.

But I won't, I won't, because I'm heartbroken. And because it's weird. And because I'm going to keep telling myself those two things until I utterly believe them.

God I wish I wasn't so horny. And so thirsty too. A night of pacing in my head has left me dry-mouthed, and while horny's worse, thirsty means I'll have to get up and pass the dreaded room of sex again. No doubt they're still going at it, only this time the door will be wi-i-ide open and I'll have to see him perpetrating other insane things too, like doing her in the butt with a dildo while he fucks her pussy with his cock.

Oh, there's no end to the depravity my mind can conjure up. It conjures it as I'm passing Wade's closed door, by telling me that it's only closed so he can nail her up against it. And then when I get to the bottom of the stairs and hear sounds from the living room, it tells me they're doing it on the sideboard.

The faint noise I can hear? Plates rattling.

Even though it sounds much more like papers being shuffled. And then someone gives what sounds like a little muffled cough and I almost jump right back up five steps all at once, because apparently I've turned into this nervous nelly and every little thing makes me want to jerk right out of my own skin.

It's the house, I think. It's not just the sex and the weird feelings and the meeting up with old friends. It's the house, which seems so dark and coated in shadows even with the upstairs hallway light on, and the faint glow coming from the living room.

There's no door to it—just an archway—so really that glow should be more than enough to comfort me. But instead I find myself peering around the arc of the stairs to the passageway that reaches down, down toward the boat room and the stepping stones, as though any second a sex-ghost is going to leap out at me and drag me into the walls.

It did that in my story. Dragged people into walls, I mean. And now I have to think about it while creeping through the house that doom built, too afraid to go forward and too afraid to go back and just desperate for a fucking drink. I'm dying of thirst here, while Kitty and Wade go at it in every available room as though fear is just a wacky concept some nerd invented one time.

Of course I get to the very edges of the archway and then realize

I'm not going to be able to get to the kitchen. If I do anything but press against this wall—if I do something mad like cross the hallway to the kitchen's arch—whoever's in there is going to see me. And seeing me once was quite enough, thanks all the same.

Especially as it's not actually Wade and Kitty. Though for some mad reason, I'm holding my breath anyway. In fact, I hold it so tightly and so quickly that for a moment I'm sure I'm going to burst. I clench all over like a giant fist, everything in me rushing to some core I didn't know I had, because he's not just sitting on the couch, casually coughing and reading *Boring Things About Computers* while sipping tea.

Oh, of course he's not. Why would he be? This is the night of insane shenanigans, like we actually are in some episode of *Scooby-Doo*, only it's a version that's really inappropriate for kids.

Because he's…well. He's gone through my stuff, for a start. I left my bag full of writing down here, and Cameron—strange, closed-off, always polite Cameron—has actually rummaged through the thing and is reading some nonsense load of old bollocks I wrote about a thousand years ago.

Or at least, he was probably reading it at some point. Now he's just got it half-crumpled in one white-knuckled fist, and for too long a moment it's this that I focus on. I can't take my eyes off it. His hand is just so big, and with everything tensed in such a way it looks as though he could punch through brick. And for some reason that's all I can think for a good while—about him punching and punching something until his knuckles turn red and a great hole appears.

But then I'm forced to look at other things, as though I've somehow been transformed into a perverted voyeur over the course of one night. Someone's erected a pane of glass between me and my friends, for reasons unspecified, and now I've got to walk around with it between us, watching them do weird things I never thought they'd do, my face pushed up against it like a kid outside a candy store.

I don't even know what the candy actually is, in this simile. I don't even know what's going on—was there ground-up tiger blood and ten tonnes of oysters in that wine we all drunk? Or am I just in the middle of the most crazy sex-dream of my life? Because God knows I never thought I'd live to see Cameron Lindhurst doing anything like this.

Kitty and Wade was bad enough. This is just…overkill. He's twisted sideways on the couch, long body spread out like a great diagonal slash, still in the clothes he left the room in earlier on. Which I suppose should make the scene before me seem less lewd, somehow, because it's not as though I can see a great deal of skin. He's got his jersey ruffled up and I can see the hairy and solid expanse of his stomach, and the sweatpants are tugged down enough to give me a glimpse of the almost coppery fur down there, but other than that he's completely covered.

Though I confess it's not the idea of naked that's exciting me. It's the hand he has, between his legs. I can see it, even through the barely there light. He's got a hand underneath the material of his sweatpants and he's tugging and rubbing at the second shape I can just make out, and whenever he gets just a touch too frantic with it he presses his mouth into the leather of the couch and, oh God, he *moans*.

I can hear Cameron moaning. Cameron. Moaning in sexual ecstasy. It seems impossible but he's doing it, and then even more shocking he suddenly takes that hand out of his sweatpants and *licks over his palm*. Before returning to the furtive dirty stroking he's doing, faster this time, fiercer.

I think he might actually be close to coming. He's rocking his hips into his own touch and he's practically biting at the couch, and now when that hand slides downward beneath the material, his whole body shudders.

"Ohhhhh God," he moans, and that's it. I don't know who this person is. This person apparently reads a story of mine and then masturbates in a place he could easily be caught in. None of it even remotely seems like Cameron, and the more he moans and gasps and seems almost tortured by desire, the more my paradigm shifts.

Has he done this before? Masturbated where someone might catch him? I think of the story Wade read out, of course I do, but then I realize with a little jerk that *I'm* the pervert in this particular scenario. I'm the spy, watching him fuck his own hand and moan and strive frantically for his orgasm, which is going to be utterly glorious when it comes.

I'm practically on tenterhooks waiting for it, like the true dirty little fucker I am. Is he going to tug his sweatpants all the way down before he does it, come into the cup of his hand, maybe? The thought is enough to send arrows of pleasure directly to my groin—as though I'm going to meet my orgasm just by standing here, watching him be this amazing and lustful and disgusting.

Because it seems like all of these things, when he does it. Wade didn't even seem that disgusting when he winked at me and beckoned me over. But Cameron doing this is beyond the pale; it's deliciously decadent, it's too much to take. I can feel my clit swelling and begging for my touch, but the tense feeling it provokes isn't just localized to that one area this time. It spreads upward through my body, burning as it goes, and the urge to masturbate, to join him, to just go there and suck his cock into my mouth is so overwhelming suddenly I'm stunned by it.

He hasn't even beckoned me over, but I realize with a start that he doesn't *need* to beckon me over. I just want to go to him like some sort of lust-starved maniac. I want to slide down on that cock he's so desperately stroking, but more than that I want to see it, taste it, touch it.

I can't stop wondering if it's as big as the rest of him. It looks it, even though I can barely see more than a ridge beneath the material. When he starts working his hand over the head, licking his hand again before he does so in such a lewd and wanton way I can't stand it, I can see the heavy line of the rest of it pressing heavy against his sweatpants.

It's unbearable. I feel like I'm standing on the edge of a precipice with him, just waiting for him to swell and push into his hand and let go of all that pleasure. And then he does and I almost feel myself go too—a great wash of sensation runs through me, as though someone licked between my legs. As though I'm finally getting what I've been needing all night long, just from hearing him groan that he's coming, he's coming.

Just before the grip he's got on himself gets audibly slicker.

It takes me a moment to realize it, but then it comes to me.

He's working his own hot liquid down over his shaft. Like he just wants to draw it out and can't quite bear to have it finish yet. Like he needs more and more and if he just keeps writhing and rocking into it, he'll get it.

I almost moan with him. It's the strangest, hottest thing I've ever seen, in a night when I also watched my best friend fuck my other best friend. That fact alone seems remarkable, but it's worse when I get back to my room on shaky legs and realize something insane:

I don't want to masturbate right now, and think about Wade. I want to masturbate right now and think about Cameron.

Chapter Four

WHEN KITTY COMES AND joins me at the breakfast table in the kitchen the next day, my face doesn't go red. I think she knows—she gives me a very pointed, "Did you sleep well?"—but it's not as though it's unusual between me and her. I've seen her fuck before. It's no big deal.

It's not even a big deal when Wade comes in and he's sort of, you know...pretending he and Kitty are like business partners now. How are you today, weather is fine, have you seen last night's stock reports, etcetera. It's all very clinical and normal and I don't even find myself blushing when he gives me this mischievous look. Eyes narrowed just ever so slightly, almost-smile touching his lips, all of him just quivering for a reaction from me, I can tell.

But somehow, bizarrely, I *do* blush when Cameron comes in. I more than blush, in fact. I feel it right to the roots of my hair, this King Kong mega blush from the planet beyond. I don't even know why, either, because what he was doing was far less than what they were doing, but somehow it's worse even so and then he says, "Hey, Allie," and I mumble something back, into my cornflakes.

For the barest of seconds, I'm sure he looks hurt. Not hugely, or anything, but something definitely passes across his face. As though he's used to me being silly, sweet Allie and now that I'm suddenly not being, he's sorely sensible of the change.

It makes me wonder if he's thinking about last night, and suspects something. It's the first thing I'd think of if someone's demeanor changed toward me—that I did something wrong and now I have to pay for it. And although what he did wasn't wrong, exactly, I'm pretty sure someone like Cameron feels it is.

I mean, he masturbated after going through my things. That's almost as bad as Wade's story, and it gives me a little shiver thinking about how close we both were to mirroring those fictional events. He went through the stuff, and I played the voyeur. He masturbated, and I thought long and deep and hard about masturbating.

I didn't do it, however. I felt the way I do now: electrically embarrassed. Kitty watches me slosh my cornflakes and eventually asks me if I'm OK, but I can't deal with that right now, either. It's obviously starting to dawn on her that maybe I'm not quite OK with her fucking Wade, but it's the least of my concerns right now, it really is.

Instead I look up at Cameron, now he's sitting down with his eyes on his own breakfast. What's going on in that head of his, exactly? Why was it my stories he was going through? I feel almost as though I've caught a thief, but I can't confront him about it because the thief is way too nice and kind of weird.

Plus, what if his answer is something bizarre, like: *I have a fetish about people being sucked into walls*? Maybe my sex- ghost story affected him more than I've ever suspected, and he's just been waiting all these years for another chance to read it. I mean, there's not much else it can be, realistically.

It's not like he's going to be secretly in love with me, or anything. I glance across the table at him and see the way his eyelashes curve so darkly against his cheeks when he blinks, as though everything is in slow motion suddenly, everything is so brilliantly clear. Did I notice before now how beautiful he is?

I don't think so and yet I can't escape it, right in this moment. His lips are so perfect—the lower one barely there and the upper like a soft bow, like a woman's mouth in a face that's otherwise so masculine. His face is heavy, I think, as though he held a lot of baby fat when he was a kid and suddenly shot right out of it, and now that he's older and taller and handsome, he doesn't quite know what to do with any of it.

And then he looks right at me with those eyes of his—such a different shade of blue than Wade's—and I forget everything I was just thinking. I forget about Wade and the night before; I forget all my fears of coming here. I just stare at Cameron like I'm seeing someone for the first time, and all the sound in the world boils down and down into nothing, as though I've found myself in a long tunnel beneath the ocean, all the waves crashing above but none of them reaching me—

"Allie! Jesus Christ. Are you alive?"

I jerk to Wade immediately, and out the corner of my eye I see Cameron do it too. Somehow it's like we were both caught with our hands in the cookie jar, but I can't think what, exactly, the cookie jar is in this scenario. It's not as though we were fondling each other or kissing or any of that stuff, after all—and not as though I actually *want* to, either, because you know, I don't. I've never even thought about Cameron that way, and have no idea why I'm thinking of it now.

"I was just saying," Wade continues, and there's something steely in his voice. Something he's grown since college—an insistence about himself. Like the night before when everyone had to look at him and hear his story. Like the night before when he seemed so sure I would come into the bedroom and do fuck knows what. "Maybe we should all go down to the lake today. Have a swim."

It makes me want to say to him, weirdly: *You don't look like you swim anymore. You look like you run. You look like you* power *run.*

Though I'm not sure why he does, exactly. Something about the way he slicks his hair back, maybe? Something about the way it looks almost dirty blond now, as though he dyes it, though I'm not certain he does. I just remember him saying to me that he hated being so cute in a family of big dark-haired men, and it seems awfully convenient that now, he's almost a big dark-haired man. He's slick and efficient and bristly, and he's just waiting for an answer.

"Sure," I say, though I wish I hadn't.

~~~

The trouble is, we always used to come down here in our clothes. In the night. Never in broad daylight with everybody suddenly half-naked and me looking like a prized idiot because I've got three jumpers and a pair of dungarees on.

And OK. Maybe not that bad. I've got a swimsuit on underneath these shorts, I swear to God.

But the swimsuit is absolutely gargantuan compared to Kitty's swimsuit. Hers isn't even a swimsuit, really. It's two specks of cloth over her nipples and one speck of cloth over her vadge and I must really be an old lady inside because all I can think is *Dear God it's March. She's going to die in this freezing disc of gray-blue water.*

I'm dying already, just looking at it. I mean, it's as beautiful as I remember it being—surrounded by misty open fields and clumps of trees here and there, the sun just skating its surface—but I can almost see ice forming, in places. The grass around its banks has frost on it.

"I think we're going to die," Cam says, but then I have to look at him, so really dying is the least of my issues.

God, he's big. Just really, really big. I even see Wade casting a weird look at him before he takes his own shirt off, because I'm pretty sure Wade was expecting to have the body, you know? He obviously goes to the gym now and everything is just as bumpy and firm as it was last night, when he put on his little fuck-show for me.

But somehow he's not quite as…immense as Cam. Cam is… huge. And not just in a freakishly tall, six-foot-five sort of way. His shoulders look heavy and substantial, as though he spends his days with a yoke over them, climbing up some never-ending hill. His chest is broad and weighty, muscular but not in a gym-bunny way, like Wade's is.

This is more like…I don't know. I want to ask him what he's been doing to get his body like this, but just the idea of posing the question makes my face heat. Asking would only suggest that I'm looking and that I *like* what I'm looking at and both things seem impossible, suddenly.

I might have said it before—*Whoa, hey there stud*, something like that—but I can't now. Not after…he did that thing. I can't, I can't.

Unfortunately, however, Kitty *can*.

"Jesus Christ, Cam—get *in* me. Wow."

I do not like the fact that, when she says this, I have the sudden urge to shove her in the lake. No, I do not like this feeling *at all*. Where is it even coming from? I didn't feel like pushing her in the lake when I saw her fucking my one true love. Thinking it now is just weird and insane and then I glance at Cam and his face has gone bright, bright red and he's fingering his T-shirt like…I don't know. Like he wants to put it back on maybe?

Yeah, he looks like he wants to put it back on. As though she's being sarcastic, or something, and he should cover up quick before anybody else sees the rest of his grotesquery.

Makes me want to put a hand on his arm and say something good and reassuring like *I've never seen a better body on any actual person*, only I can't. I can't because it would be the absolute truth. He looks better than I've ever seen any other person look, and thinking about it makes my face flush and my body go all weird and, Jesus Christ, I'm turned on again.

"Come on, you doof," Kitty says, and grabs his arm, and even though I can see she's trying to make up for whatever weird discomfort she caused him, I feel that little flash of something again. That urge to shove the girl I love best in the whole world right into the lake.

"Why can't we just use boats, I need a boat," he says as he trails after her to the water's edge, and I find myself thinking: *Is that how you do it? Is it the rowing that makes you all big, do you still row after all these years, do you still stand around in a boathouse somewhere in those tiny Lycra shorts that show just about everything you've—*

"Hey. Earth to Allie. Seriously, what's going on with you? I talk, you're off in some other world."

I manage to tune back into Wade again and I don't know. I guess I'm expecting him to be half-laughing or not that bothered. But when I actually look he's kind of pissed. Yeah, there's definitely something angry in his expression, like before when I thought about him being *insistent* somehow.

Was he this way before? All I seem to recall is me begging for *his* attention, me feasting on the tiny scraps of his laid-back love, though that's not what I'm thinking about right now. Instead I find myself wondering just what his expectations were for this little get-together.

Everyone pledging undying sexual allegiance to him, maybe?

"No, I was just…" I start, but then I stop. Mainly because the words coming to my lips were definitely going to be about Cameron, and they were going to be something along the lines of *Did Cameron ever talk to you about my stories? About maybe liking them a whole huge lot?* And I realize I don't want that. I don't want Wade to know what I saw, or how I felt about it, or anything of the kind.

Which is weird, when you really think about it.

"Nothing. I guess your story last night really threw me for a loop," I finish, though it's no better than what I was going to say, in all honesty. It sounds as though I'm talking about something else altogether, and when he grins I know he's thinking that.

"Yeah?" he says and I brace myself. I know what's coming. Or at least I kind of do until he does it, until he gets right up close to me suddenly and breathes all of his hot breath on me and murmurs in that husky way of his. "Well I thought *you* were going to come to my room last night. And maybe if you had, I could have told *you* a story instead."

Ugh. Ugh. When did he become this Master of Seduction type of guy? Was he always like this? Did I always like it? Because I'm liking it now even though I don't want to, and my body feels all hot and my face feels all hot and this close up he's *so* good looking and so wolfish. Predatory, I think, even though I always used to consider him gentle. Kind, and gentle.

"Oh yeah? Is that the one about the amateur gymnasts in the middle of the night?" I say, only I mean it to be confrontational and aggressive and it comes out like I'm flirting instead. Like I want him to lean even closer toward me and whisper in my ear about all the stories he just can't wait to tell me.

I won't deny, it makes my heart speed up. I mean, I have no idea if he's serious or not—in truth I don't even know what we're really talking about anymore—but I can feel myself leaning in to him, anyway, and though the morning mist is making goose bumps prick out all over my flesh, I'm syrupy warm inside. I feel like I'm glowing, like you could see me all the way from Scotland.

And I kind of hate myself a little for it. Not in a huge way, but it's there nonetheless. He just walks right up and talks all low and seductive to me after I've spent years agonizing over all the things we didn't do and how much he didn't want me back in college, as though it's all just that easy.

Why wasn't it easy before, huh? Why couldn't it have been easy all those years ago? It seems almost like a kick in the face that he seems to find it easy now. I want to ask him, really loudly, what's changed, but the truth is—I'm afraid of the answer.

"I'm gonna go swim," I say all in a rush, and then I dash down to the water like a massive galumphing idiot. Though I suppose this technique would have at least worked—it's a great way to avoid awkward, sexual tension–fraught conversations to just suddenly jump in freezing cold water in the middle of them—if he hadn't followed me.

He actually follows me.

Though what's stranger about this is my reaction. God, I would have *killed* to have Wade follow me, back in college. I was always the one splashing or running or tripping up after him. But this time I wade away from him into water that sets my teeth on edge, ploughing on determinedly even as the cold gets its claws into me, sinking right into the murky depths when it gets deeper and stroking out in my own clumsy fashion. And I'm not even looking back at him, particularly, as I do all of this.

Instead I scan the lake, looking for Kitty and Cameron. And when I see her not a meter from us facing our way, while Cameron is off toward the center somewhere, swimming like a seal…I don't know. I feel…satisfied, somehow.

I can concentrate, now, on the matter at hand: Wade chasing me until I feel like shrieking at him to just *fuck off*. Just don't, don't. I've never liked being chased at the best of times and right now—with the freezing cold water and my clumsy swimming skills and him like some kind of Olympian—it's worse.

And I have to admit, the suddenness of his sexual, flirting whatever-the-fuck is only contributing to this feeling. So much so that I actually shout back at him, "Don't."

But he just laughs and asks me what exactly I think it is he's doing. Good question. I have no clue. Could you maybe put your answers on the back of a postcard, Wade? Could you not keep chasing me like this so I can think for a minute?

Only when I turn back, he's not there anymore. I spit out a mouthful of probably panic-swallowed lake water, tasting weeds and that weird new-penny tang I remember so well. It's in my eyes too, so I give them a swipe, trying to slow my breathing and acclimatize to the deep freeze as I do. There's something about this lake's coldness that isn't like ordinary coldness—it's a bone deep, silvery sort of thing that never goes away, not even in the height of summer.

My teeth are starting to chatter. We probably really are all going to die in a second.

And then Wade quite suddenly bursts out of the water, so close to me he could have run his tongue over my skin as he did so, and I think: *Did I say die in a second? Because I actually think I'm going to die right now.*

I almost drown. At the very least I splutter and flap around and do my very best to get away, but all that makes him do is get me into a lifesaving sort of position. Which also happens to be—very conveniently—a take-you-from-behind sort of position.

He loops one arm around my shoulders—just above my breasts—and pulls my back to his front, and the minute he does so my treacherous brain stops thinking *What an asshole* and starts thinking *Oh Lord, he's so warm.* As though warmth is a state that promotes perpetual forgiveness, somehow.

"Just relax," he says, as though I'm struggling. Much to my embarrassment, however, I'm actually not. I just lie limp in his arms like half a pound of soggy seaweed, extremely aware of every little part of him like the dark hair on his forearms and his bicep squeezing hard into my shoulder and his breath all hot against the side of my face.

There's also something I think I can feel when I cycle my legs through the water. Something I don't really want to think about too hard because it's both explosively exciting and somehow… not right at the same time. I mean, he did have sex with my best friend last night. And even if he hadn't done, it's Wade we're talking about.

He shouldn't have an erection. He just shouldn't be hard against the curve of my ass and, even if he has to be, I know he shouldn't be rubbing it over my body. I can feel him doing it and, though it sends an answering tingle of pleasure through my sorely neglected sex, it doesn't seem like a good idea.

Can't we admit some sort of long held but silent crush, first? That's the way things should be done. He has to get down on one knee and weep and tell me he's sorry for never telling me how much he loved me, and then I swoon. And *then* we get to the sex part.

Though even the above seems appallingly unrealistic. This is just…out of the realms of sanity. He's rubbing his cock against my ass, for God's sake. And he doesn't stop there either. No, no—after a moment of very obvious and very heated rubbing, he whispers in my ear:

"Why didn't you come to my room last night?"

In this crooning, pleading sort of voice. For a moment, I'm sure he means *Why didn't you come in and have a threesome with us?* and my mind briefly explodes, but then he continues down a different route altogether.

"I was just waiting for you, Allie-Cat. And then Kitty came along and…well…"

I want to shove him away at that. I really, really want to. But then he slides his hand down over the bit of chest just before the swell of my tits, and I forget what words are. I can't even think straight—what is he saying, exactly? That he wanted me but made do with Kitty? Pretty gross whichever way you look at it and yet somehow I'm not finding it gross. Or at least, my body's not reacting as though it's finding anything gross.

My sex swells against the tight confines of my swimming costume, and when his hand passes over the upswell of my left breast, I have to fight not to moan. How long have I dreamt of something like this happening? So long it's like a constant thrum through my pathetic, too-weak body.

And yet, when I close my eyes and drift into the feel of Wade's touch, I see Cameron behind my eyes. I feel his hand sliding over my back as he hugged me and his eyes burning into mine as though he had something to say, something really important.

But worse than that I think about him jerking off, desperately, and sensation gushes thick and strong between my legs. My nipples are stiff when Wade finally, finally brushes over one of them, and I don't think it's because of the water. I'm not even sure if it's because of Wade.

"God," he says, when I can't help pushing into his touch. When I can't stop the little sigh from escaping my lips. "Why didn't we ever fuck in college? You're so hot, baby."

He's pinching my nipple now. And then even worse he slides his hand underneath the clingy material, over the slick, cool flesh of my right breast. I won't deny—it feels amazing. His hand is somehow scalding hot and the contrast is like touching a live wire.

Plus there's the utter *rudeness* of it. We're out in the open—Kitty and Cameron only a few meters away—and he's cupping and fondling my bare breast. He's rubbing his cock against my ass and whispering in my ear and oh, I can't help squirming in his arms. It's not my fault, though—I just need to come so badly! I should have done it the night before, I know I should have, but now it's too late. I just need to come here, now.

And the need gets stronger when he says: "Is this doing it for you, huh? You like it?"

Because all I can think of is all the things I do like, and none of them are Wade. Instead I think about Cameron coming all over his own hand, making a slick and dirty mess that I just want to lick up. In fact, I go one step further than that—I imagine Cameron doing it all somewhere dirtier, like all over my face, while Wade keeps right on stroking and pulling at my nipple.

And it's so good I'm sure I'm going to come. Just from that little shred of stimulation. Just with him moaning in my ear and the idea of Cameron somewhere to the left of us—so close I could probably see him if I just opened my eyes.

"I have to go back to the house."

I blurt it out without thinking, but once it's there it feels right. I need to get away from him; I need this to not be happening. If he wanted it to happen so badly he could have waited for me to come to him the night before.

It's too late now. And though the thought makes a dart of pain go through me, I can cope with it. I can cope with it so hard that when he shouts after me *Allie, Allie* in this confused sort of voice, I just keep right on going. I swim for the shore and then I climb out of the water, not even bothering to wrap a towel around myself in any sort of reasonable don't-die-of-flu fashion.

The house isn't that far anyway. Though when I get there I realize three things automatically—I've got mud streaked all the way up to my thighs, my lips have turned blue, and Wade did not follow me.

I'm not sure which of these is the most troubling. The blue lips, probably, though they disappear after five minutes in the shower. And the mud goes easily enough too, which just leaves the thought of Wade not following me—though this alarmingly seems to fade as quickly as the other things did.

Instead I find myself standing in the middle of the beige-y room I chose, with the pleasant but bland seascape above the bed and the window that looks out onto nothing, thinking about the Mystery of Cameron. Which I suppose is understandable, really, considering that it is an actual mystery. I didn't just put mystery before his name like some dumb joke Wade would make.

He just *is* one.

And it's this thought that makes me go down the hall and stand in the middle of his room, instead of my own. I'm sure it is. It's not really anything inside myself, because I'm not a spying sort of person. Honestly I'm not. It's just the thought of a mystery making me, as though this isn't an episode of *Scooby-Doo* at all. *Scooby-Doo* is too tame and PG for the likes of this. This is an episode of *Poirot* with real actual bonking in it, and we're all here in the country mansion to figure out who secretly tried to kill Cameron with some sort of sex drug.

Because reasonably, that's the only explanation for what he was doing. I mean, just look at this room of his! He's given his bed hospital corners. He's set up some kind of immense computer station on the mahogany dresser by the door, complete with books perpendicular to the corners of this makeshift desk and eleven monitors and everything humming like the machine out of *The Fly*.

He's just not a very sexual being. He doesn't give off a sexual energy. He gives off the energy of someone who has twenty computers and lines up his trainers by the door to the walk-in closet as though there's an invisible barrier preventing them from moving an inch out of skew.

I feel dirty just sitting in front of the flickering monitors, in only a towel. I feel illicit, like I shouldn't be in here, inside his inner sanctum. His books have titles I don't understand, like *Operating Parameters of a Twelve-Bit MDOS* and *Bits and MDOS Ride Again*, and the corners of them are all curled as though he's devoured their pages many, many times.

This is the stuff he's avaricious about. Operating parameters. MDOS. Control, Alt, Delete. I mean, the keyboard in front of me is missing the letter "A," for God's sake. He's spent so much time hammering at it that the letter "A" has actually rubbed off.

I have absolutely no idea why I imagined he has some kind of secret sexual inner life. Clearly whatever he was doing the night before was just a one-off, a little letting off of steam after hearing Wade read out that filthy story. He's probably actually gay for Wade, and his immense computer-bashing brain just couldn't take hearing the object of his lust talking about willies and fannies and the like.

In fact, the most prevalent image I have of Cam is him sitting in front of a screen, the blue light backwashing over his strange, still face. Everything around him dark and cave-like, as he performs some miracle of computing that I can't even comprehend. Kitty says he mostly designs websites and things like that now, but I know he invented something too. Some kind of interfacing site or programmable network or, Jesus Christ, I don't know.

I also don't know why I've never asked him. Of course, there's that clichéd idea of him, that image of him boring girls to death at parties with all of his see-DOS-run talk, but the truth is I can't remember ever finding Cam dull.

He's not dull, at all. I mean—just look. He's got a copy of my favorite book, buried underneath the stack of tech manuals. *Tehanu*, by Ursula Le Guin. And it's all worn with the ridiculous swirling purple right-out-of-the-seventies cover, just like the one in the library at Pembroke.

Only then I realize it *is* the copy from Pembroke. The exact one. I open it up and the spine creaks and the pages almost fall out, and there's my handwriting on page two hundred-something, in the margin after Tenar has told Ged that she's loved him from the first time she saw him: *There is a secret place in my heart for you. It's with my secret name, the one I will not tell you.*

I flush red, thinking of all the stupid, childish poetry I probably wrote back then. About how many people have seen my stupid, childish poetry and my ridiculous thoughts, in the margins of a book about freedom and feminism. Here it is, right here: evidence that I always latch onto some idiotic notion of love, rather than anything more important or interesting.

I'm lost in a love that doesn't exist. That will never exist.

It doesn't even exist in this story I'm holding in my hands, this beautiful but brittle story by a real storyteller. I flick through and it's just as amazing as I remember it being, and I can still recall exactly how it made me feel, when the dragon came and Tehanu made everything all right again. Tehanu being the heroine, all along—just a little girl, really.

I flick right to the end pages to read it over again, but I don't get to the words. I don't get to the part when the dragon comes. Instead, I find what Cam has sandwiched between Ged and Tenar almost dying and Tehanu saving them. He's put a picture in the book—he must have put a picture in the book, because I never left one in it. And he has the thing now, so he must know it's there.

Of course he knows it's there. It's his handwriting on the back of it. I recognize it after all this time—all those big looping letters, as though he had to put on the page what he could never be in real life. He couldn't be big and extrovert in reality, so he had to be in his writing.

And he is, he is. Because it's a picture of me—one I have no memory of—and on the back he's written *Tenar*. He's written *Tenar*.

Chapter Five

OF COURSE, THERE ARE a million things this could mean. There are a million things catching him jerking off to my story could mean. There are a million things standing in front of an oncoming train could mean, but really, when you think about it, only one possible answer makes sense.

I just don't want it to make sense. I want the person to be standing in front of the oncoming train because they accidentally superglued their feet to the tracks. Not because of the obvious, reasonable answer like *Cameron is totally in love with you—you're the Tenar to his Ged*. Because that would just be weird and it's making my armpits all prickly and so I just close the book with the picture inside and put it back on his desk, underneath several manuals.

It seems like the best plan for everyone. After all, the idea that Cameron likes me enough to keep a picture of me in a book I loved is just too impossible to comprehend. I'm probably imagining it. My head is full of Wade and it's making me drift on a sea of nonsensical love thoughts—so much so that I have to get the book back out again and just check that the picture is really me.

Yeah, it's really me all right. I think it was taken when we all went to Whitby that one time, and the wind on top of the cliff had blown my hair into an untangle-able mess. It's all crammed in a curly heap on one side of my head, and I'm laughing as though I know it, and by God I can't think why anyone would want to keep a picture of something like that.

I look ridiculous. I look…happy. Lord, was I ever that happy? My eyes are as bright as buttons and I'm wearing something of Wade's I think—a big black cable-knit jumper sort of thing that can't possibly have been mine.

And then I realize with a start that it was *Cameron's*. It was his jumper—the one with the hole in—and he gave it to me after I got soaked by a wave, walking by the insane ocean. After we'd bought fish and chips and eaten them in a hurry under the shelter of some shop awning, and then I remember being filled with a burning warmth when Wade put an arm around me and rubbed my shoulder, as though sensible of how cold I must be.

Of course it occurs to me then that Cameron has very different memories of this day than I do. I think of Wade and how he made me feel, but Cameron obviously thought about his jumper, me laughing, me running away down over the grass toward the old church. I can see it all now so clear, like a video-recorded version of real events. Everything hyper-real and too bright, me looking back at the person filming, hair flying. Sleeves too long for my arms.

Jesus Christ, I think I'm crying. I don't even know why, either, because it's not as though there's something particularly sad about finding an obviously well-loved picture of yourself in a friend's book. Only there is, there is, because he's written Tenar on the back and I didn't know. I had no idea.

God, why didn't he ever say anything? Why did he have to be so quiet and strange and unknowable?

The question makes me furious, suddenly, and before I know what I'm doing I'm flicking through the pages of his other books, looking for answers. And I don't even feel bad about it, either, because he went through my stuff. He went through my bags and read stories I never intended people to see, and he deserves this. He deserves me riffling through his drawers, finding only socks and more computer manuals and other stupid stuff, because he's stupid, he's an idiot, I *hate* Cameron Lindhurst.

I hate him even more when I find his stash of handwritten stories, underneath a mess of meaningless paperwork and folders full of nothing. My heart is kind of rattling in my chest by this point and I really have no idea what I'm thinking, but I remove the elastic band he's put around this great green hardback writing pad anyway.

I have to. He said he'd stopped writing, but he was lying. This thing is new, I can tell. I've filled enough books with my own writing to be able to tell. And then my palms tingle and my armpits do that prickly thing again, because I realize something a little disturbing. Or maybe not disturbing, exactly…more like… not quite right.

Because he's this big computer guy, he's so much of a computer guy that he's worn the "A" off his keyboard, and yet he's filled this nice green hardback book with handwriting. He's used a pen, with good, thick blue ink, as though he wanted to really feel the words coming out of him.

I realize with a little a start that I can hardly wait to see what he's written. It's prying and it's wrong and of course I know it, but all I can think of is that word *mystery* again, and then I'm flicking through the pages like some sort of furtive maniac.

Certain words jump out at me immediately. Mainly because his "Cs" are these massive scything things, so it's hard to avoid the "cocks" and the "clits" and the "cunts." And he hasn't skimped on them, either, no matter what he tried to claim—the books are filled with nothing but.

It's the second revelation I've had about Cam that I don't know how to deal with, and all in the last half hour. I look up at the bedroom door and see myself coming in here only a short while ago, with one completely formed notion of Cameron in my head. Sexless, distant Cameron who did not take pictures of his friends and keep them forever, and who did not write dirty stories that I feel almost too embarrassed to read.

Though I know I'm going to do it anyway. I couldn't resist watching him and I can't resist this here, now. It really is like an episode of *Poirot*—like unraveling a thread I didn't know existed, and on the end is some sort of mythical beast. A unicorn, maybe. A dragon, perhaps. Or possibly some kind of unearthly hybrid of both, because the first story is called "Bad Girls" and it is so the opposite of the Cameron I thought I knew I don't know what to say.

A secret crush on me was shocking. This is…unbelievable.

But they like him enough to pin him down and fuck him like some loose little slut, I read, and then I have to stop. I stop, and close the book, and try to pretend it doesn't exist. Did he really write the words *pin* and *fuck* and *slut*? About a *guy*?

Though really when I think about it, those words aren't the most shocking part. No, the most shocking part is that this story he's written, this apparently filthy story—far filthier than I've ever got down on paper—is actually really, really good. Far better than anything he ever read out in class. The robotic weirdness is almost completely gone, and what's left behind is this:

They smell like summer when they walk through the door, and he can just make out a hint of the lake too. As though they'd been swimming in the barely-there clothes they've got on, though he knows they haven't. They've been swimming in no clothes at all, because the ones they're wearing are hardly damp and now they're in here, giggling and murmuring things he can't quite hear.

Like let's *and* fuck *and* with Ben.

Only it's the strangest thing, because the more he thinks about them fucking with him, the more he can't focus on anything else. His mind fills with elaborate scenarios before they've even gotten anywhere near the couch he's pretending to sleep on, and when they finally walk over it's almost like a relief. As though he knew it was going to come to this sooner or later, and now that it has he can breathe out.

"I think he's hard," one of them says, and he knows it's Lydia. Lydia with her mess of dark hair and her almost-green eyes, gazing down at him like he's something that needs devouring.

He wonders, idly, if she knows he wants to be devoured.

"Definitely hard," the other one says, and when she giggles he feels an odd little trickle of fear run down his spine. As though cool, indifferent Lydia could be cruel, but her little blonde friend could be crueler.

Much crueler.

"Touch him," the blonde one—Mindy—says, and he hears Lydia make a soft, noncommittal sound. As though she can't decide what's best, in this sort of situation. Should she wake him, and ask him if any of this is OK? Or should they just plunge right into whatever dirty things they feel like doing?

For one wild, unbearably free second, he hopes they're going to go with the latter. Go the whole hog he thinks at them, but then a hand goes around his obviously stiff cock, quite suddenly, and he wishes he hadn't been so rash with his thoughts.

He isn't wearing much—just a thin pair of shorts—and the hand is rough and jolting. Whoever it is squeezes, hard, and yet another delirious thought shoots through his mind—the hope that it is Lydia rather than Mindy, grasping and groping him through his clothes.

But then Mindy squeals that he's really big and stiff, and that strange and unwanted hope is dashed. It's Mindy squeezing him, and then Mindy stroking him, and finally it's Mindy actually jerking him off through his shorts.

Although when he finally dares open his eyes, it's Lydia he sees. And it's the sight of her—eyes burning down at him, breasts almost visible through the thin material of her vest, skirt showing too much creamy thigh—that sends a strong current of pleasure through his body.

"Have you been dreaming dirty dreams, Ben?" she says, and it's

almost a kind question, really. Not half so cruel as Mindy's tugging, working hand on his cock or the sight of Lydia's body through her clothes, like something he's always wanted but ever out of reach.

Only then she turns to Mindy and tells her to unzip his shorts and get it out, so really he doesn't know what to think.

At the very least he has to protest, but when he tries to she claps a sudden hand down over his mouth, as though he's the woman and she's the man and this is all some very different sort of scenario altogether.

"I'll hold him down," she says. "You do it."

However, when she speaks she doesn't address Mindy. She looks down at him, that same devilish delight in her eyes, and something inside him veers left when it should be going right. He should be telling her to stop, now. He should be throwing her off—he is, after all, far bigger and stronger than both of them put together—but somehow he doesn't seem to be doing anything like it.

Instead, his body thrums and thrums, and a sound comes out of his mouth. It's an embarrassing one too—a real low and deep down groan—but he can't stop it. Mindy has gotten his shorts open and he can feel air on his bare and humiliatingly stiff cock, but more importantly Lydia has still got her hand over his mouth. And after a moment she puts a knee against his shoulder, as though she suspects he's about to struggle and try bucking them off.

"That's good, baby," she says. "Just stay still and take it." He has absolutely no clue what they expect him to just stay still and take, but God, those words. His body trembles all over, minutely, just hearing them. Lydia—sweet little Lydia—behaving like this, being this fucking dirty, fucking making him…it's unreal.

Even though he sort of knew it would come to this, all along. He could see it in her—this need to tease and torment, this desire for games he can barely fathom—only now that they're being actualized he finds himself on uncertain ground. How far is she going to go exactly?

Take it implies something very specific, he knows it does. Like maybe they're going to do the kind of things that only girls usually get. Maybe they're going to lube their fingers and fuck his body in a way he's never thought of before, no, God, no, he's never thought of anything like that before, not ever.

And he's certainly never thought of other things, like maybe something bigger and thicker, sliding into him.

He thinks of those words again—take it—and bucks beneath their restraining hands, but then something hot and slick brushes the head of his cock and it's like a relief. It's like one, but maybe not quite all the way to being one.

Still, it feels good. And it feels even better when he manages to push himself against the bonds of Lydia's hand and sees Mindy with her skirt all the way up around her waist, the hair between her legs so fluffy and fine it's barely there, sinking down onto his cock as though it meant nothing at all to do something like that.

"Ohhhh God," she moans, and there's something thrilling about that. Something that makes him want to be smug, because she has her eyes closed and it obviously feels good to slide down on his cock like that. It must, because she starts rocking almost immediately, and when he glances up at Lydia she's biting her lip.

Then after a moment she tells her friend to hurry, and he understands in an arousing rush that she means to take her turn next. They're both going to use him for a quick, hot fuck, and something about that makes him almost delirious.

They don't like him enough to talk to him or share themselves with him or ask him how his day was. But they like him enough to pin him down and fuck him like some loose little slut.

"Oh fuck he feels so good," Mindy pants, and he can see her tits jiggling underneath her T-shirt as she bounces up and down on him, and her little porcelain doll face is creased with concentration, and sometimes, sometimes he can see flashes of her slick, red pussy as it parts and slides around his cock. All of which should have been more than enough to

get him off. He's tugged himself to far, far less—just the thought of Lydia running a rude hand over his covered cock has been enough, in the past, to make him come.

But right here, now, his orgasm is a distant, waiting thing. It coils, in anticipation of Lydia being where Mindy is right now. And even when Mindy moans that she's coming, she's coming, and Lydia says something that makes him flush, like I didn't think he'd be this good, *he doesn't let his orgasm off the leash.*

Not yet. First he wants Lydia. Even in these mortifying circumstances, with Mindy hopping off him as though he's suddenly become the latest ride at Disneyland, he wants Lydia. He can practically feel his body straining toward her as she takes Mindy's place, those creamy thighs straddling his hips, her eyes all over him.

He gets just the barest flash of her cunt, and then her hot little hand is on him. Stroking, briefly, before she aims the swollen head at that wet space he wants to be in most of all.

"Go on," Mindy says, and as she does so she threads a hand through his hair and tightens it, tightens it. Almost like pulling, but not quite. "Just slide it in slow."

For a moment he wonders what she means, but then it occurs to him why Lydia is hesitating. It's because he's big, much too big, and though her cheeks are flushed and her nipples are stiff and poking through her vest and she's obviously, unbearably turned on, she's hesitating.

And of course there's some sort of misplaced surge of pride about that, but mostly he just hates his stupid, oafish body. Hates it hates it hates it until she notches the thick head of his cock against her warm and waiting hole, and slides down on it one breathless inch at a time.

She's incredibly tight—more so than Mindy was—but it's not the feeling of her enveloping him that sends a spark of sensation all the way through his belly. It's the words she says that really get him, the words— oh God Ben—*because she uses his name as though he really exists and she sounds so desperate. So incredibly lust-choked.*

"I told you," Mindy says and then he has to close his eyes, briefly, because he's going to come. He's going to come just thinking about them discussing him like some kind of sex object, like something they could use and discard. He's going to come from feeling Lydia surrounding him, so slippery and delicious and, oh God, the sounds she makes…

She doesn't hold back, the way he always does. Mindy doesn't even have to put a hand over his mouth, because he can't get the words he wants to say out. Lydia just works herself on his cock, moaning and panting his name as she does, those glorious breasts of hers shifting beneath the material of that maddeningly thin vest.

"Feels amazing, right?" Mindy says, but Lydia doesn't answer. She's going to come, he knows she is. He can see her shivering, and she's staring at him with heavy-lidded, too-far-gone eyes, and when he arches up into her shallow, rocking movements, she gasps.

More than anything he wants to put his hands on her, but there's this weird feeling threading through him. It's been there since the start, but it's intensified as this whole thing has gone on—as though he's not allowed to touch. He's not allowed to move an inch, and if he does, they'll stop. They'll leave him like this, cock still hard, everything in him just hovering on the edge of orgasm.

Which is awful, it is, he knows it is, and yet somehow it's also… kind of darkly exciting. He can feel this dark excitement making a fist low down in his gut, and when she leans forward and wraps her hands around his wrists, it gets stronger.

And what's more, it's like she knows.

"You like that, huh?" she asks, and then she fucks down on him harder, fiercer, fingernails digging into his wrists. *"You like that, don't you, baby."*

It's the word, he thinks. The word *baby*, as though he's somehow a woman again—being taken, rather than taking someone else. It makes him surge up against her, and when he does she gasps out his name and her eyes stutter closed. For one brief, delicious second he can feel her cunt *clenching around his cock, and then he's spurting thickly inside her, great spasms of pleasure wracking his body and everything shot through with the sure and certain knowledge that this will never happen again.*

She'll never do it to him again now that she knows. He could have gotten away with it if he'd maybe just let her fuck him and use him up like this, and not said or done anything in response to it. But he can see when she looks into his glassy eyes and then down his shuddering body that it's not just a matter of him failing to protest. No, no, it's worse than that.

He enjoyed it. And now the girl he loves best in all the world knows. She knows.

———⁓⁓⁓———

I think I sit there for a hundred years or so. I have to, because my ass has rooted itself to the chair. My brain has ceased functioning. I can't even feel the cool air on my still only-covered-by-a-towel body, and though part of me is sensible that my hair is drying into a weird frizzy mess, and that I'm clutching this damned green book so hard my fingers are starting to bleed, there's nothing I can do about any of it.

This is *Cameron*. He actually wrote this thing in my hand. Of course, it could be that some troll from the X Dimension jumped inside his body at some point and started going for a career in erotica writing, but it seems unlikely, at best.

Though not as unlikely as Cameron Lindhurst actually picking up a pen and scribbling these words down. They're not even really scribbled, in truth. They're written calmly and smoothly with barely any crossing-outs, as though he had the time to think long and hard about a story like this before he ever put pen to paper.

You can tell he thought long and hard about it. And what's worse is…I'm pretty sure the girls are not really called Lydia and Mindy in his head. I mean, Lydia's identity is debatable—yes, I have almost-green eyes and, yes, I have dark hair but, no, I've never thought about making a guy feel bad about his predilection for domination—but it's pretty clear that Mindy is Kitty. The names even sound the same, for God's sake.

So maybe it's not me he likes at all. Hey—it could be the case. Maybe he just thinks of me as a friendly buffer in the ultimate battle for Kitty's heart, and soon I'm going to hear and see him banging her in the middle of the night too.

God, *God*.

"Allie?" Oh *fuck*.

Of course I knew I'd sat here too long. If they'd spent much more time out in the lake they would have all died of pneumonia. And yet still, my stupid brain wants to be all shocked that Cameron's suddenly at the door to his own bedroom, and I do even more ridiculous things like trying to pretend I don't have this book of writing in my hands. I totally don't.

Why are you looking at me like that, Cameron? I *don't*.

"Oh my God," he says, and then I have to watch in tormented silence as his eyes slide over the clearly moved copy of *Tehanu* on his desk, and the writing in my hands, and probably the fact that I'm just in a towel too. I mean, it's not the biggest problem with what's going on here, but the towel-wearing has got to look strange beside the other stuff.

"Cam—" I start, but I have absolutely no idea how I'm going to finish and he knows it. He cuts me off before I've gotten past the first word.

"What are you *doing* in here?" he asks, and oh he sounds pissed. You can really hear it in him too, because usually he's so calm and still. It's like a pool of motionless water suddenly taking out a small city.

"Well, the thing is…"

I do not know what the thing is.

"I can't believe you'd do something like this, Allie."

Oh God, he's disappointed in me. Oh no, I can't breathe.

"No, look—see, the thing is," I say, but I still don't know what the thing is. I stand up in the vain hope that doing so will help me find it, but it only makes it more obvious I'm holding his book full of writing.

His eyes flick down to it and I actually *see* the flush spread up and over his cheeks. Like, literally see it. I didn't even know such a thing could happen.

And then he looks back up to me and those glacial eyes of his are suddenly not very glacial any more. Instead they blaze hot, and his upper lip has gone all mean and thin the way it did the other night when Wade read that story out loud, and I just know something good isn't coming.

I've never seen Cameron like this before, and it's unnerving.

"How could you go through my stuff like this? I trusted you," he says, and then he gazes at the mess I've made again as though he can't process it. "This is just…this is just disgusting, it's—"

In my defense, I do not mean to butt in, here. In fact, up until the point where the words actually come out of my mouth, I didn't even know I wanted to say anything at all. They just rise up like some unstoppable tidal wave, and once they're out there I can't take them back.

"*You* went through *my* stuff!"

God I wish I could take them back. His head jerks up and he looks, quite frankly, stunned. He looks as though I slapped him, even though I totally didn't, I swear to God. I didn't mean to metaphorically slap you, Cameron, I promise. Oh Lord, this is dreadful.

"I don't know…" he starts, and I am completely aware he wants to finish the sentence with *what you're talking about*. It's obvious. His eyes even slide to one side, the way the eyes of all truly bad liars do.

I try to take a breath and think about how I can mitigate this.

"Look—you know what? Let's just forget about this. Let's just forget all about it. I'll forget what I saw and you can forget what you've seen here and we'll just go about our business, OK?"

Fuck knows how that's going to happen, but I figure it's worth a shot. Until he puts a sudden hand over his eyes and moans: "Oh God you *saw* that."

Then we can't pretend anything, unless there's a doctor around to perform two handy lobotomies.

"Cam—seriously. It's not a big deal! I hardly saw anything—"

He backs away from me—he actually backs away from me!

"Please—I can't talk about this, I can't."

He's almost out of the room, by this point. The urge to drag him back in and shut the door is strong—because God only knows where Kitty and Wade are—but I resist. I don't want to scare him so badly he becomes a vegetable.

Hey—I've seen it happen. People become vegetables all the time when I lay my hands on them.

"I think at this point we kinda have to, don't you?"

He lets the hand drop from his eyes and that fierceness is back, suddenly, in his expression. Gotta admit—it's intimidating. He's just so *big*. And then he says something that crushes my soul, on top of all the bigness.

"Maybe I should rephrase—it's not so much that I *can't* talk about it, it's that I *don't* want to talk about it with *you*."

It's weird, how much everything sinks inside me. I mean, if Wade had said something like that to me I'd be devastated, but that's understandable. I *love* Wade. It's not as though I love Cameron. I just had a different idea of him, that's all—one where he's gentle and calm and would never lash out like that.

But then he puts a hand to his face again—this time to squeeze at the bridge of his nose—and I can see how much pain he's in. It's not every day your friend discovers all of your secret possible crushes and hidden sexual proclivities.

Plus, he then says: "I'm sorry, I'm so sorry. I didn't mean that…the way it came out."

So, you know. I can't hold it against him. Especially when he then goes to the door and closes it, shutting us both inside. I don't mind admitting—a little frisson of excitement goes through me. Even though it hurt when he shut me down I kind of expected it, so this…this is like an illicit little treat, suddenly.

Is he actually going to have a chat with me? About something other than computers?

I watch him walk over to the bed and sit down, nerves written all over his face. Hands clenching and unclenching. It's like the bit in *Poirot* when he gathers everyone together in the room to root out the killer.

"Cam, seriously. It's fine. Whatever you want to say—it's fine," I say, because that's true. And also because I want him to keep talking. God, anything to just have him keep talking.

"Whatever you…uh…might have seen…" he starts, and I can practically feel him trying to squeeze it out of himself.

"It's just because I was, you know. Worked up. From…the other stuff that happened."

Hey, we all were, right? Wade's story was *hot*.

"Perfectly understandable," I say.

"And the picture I have of you…" He glances at the desk, where said incriminating photograph lies. "It's just because…you're my friend."

"Obviously," I say, because his answer sounds much more plausible to me than "I am secretly in love with you." Much. Much. He's clenching at the edge of the bed so hard his knuckles have turned white, but it's still a completely reasonable explanation.

"And as for the stories…" He pauses, then, and this time I can see him really struggling. As though possible love and illicit masturbation is no big deal, but this…this is like some kind of awful insurmountable obstacle the likes of which the world has never seen. It's like he's trying to climb Olympus Mons with a toothpick and some dental floss as his only tools. "Which one did you read?"

He asks the question in this horrible, faux-casual sort of way. Raises one eyebrow and won't meet my gaze. Seriously—how is someone this handsome *that* awkward?

"The first one," I say, then for some reason wish I'd gone with a different answer. I bet there's some nice romantic tale in there somewhere, about making love and buying people flowers and eating chocolates in bed or something.

But unfortunately for him, I read the one about two girls practically gang-raping a guy who resembles him in more ways than one. And so I have to watch his eyes kind of flutter closed in a way that almost makes me want to giggle. It's an obvious expression of mortification, but there's something about the way he almost rolls his eyes at the same time, and doesn't quite close them…it's very endearing.

"Oh that's wonderful," he says, while my mind flashes on every little detail of that particular story. The hand over his mouth, all the talk of *being used*, the feeling-like-a-woman stuff…

Cam is just so self-contained. It must be like someone's cut a hole in him and is letting all the stuffing spill out.

"I really, really didn't mean to pry," I say, but that's a lie. I did mean to pry. I watched him jerking off and it infected my brain with some kind of sex fever, and then I simply couldn't stop searching for further evidence of his…whatever this is.

However, I cannot use this as an explanation to him.

"It's fine," he says, and waves a casual hand. Everything is too casual. He's never casual. "Like you said—I did it to you, first."

"It's not the same," I say, because it isn't. Him going through my stuff is not a big deal. Me going through his stuff is like breaking into Fort Knox. "And besides, this isn't tit for tat. I didn't…that's not how I intended it. You just made me so curious!"

Ugh. Did I really just say that? And also: why did me saying something so dumb suddenly light up his face like that? As though he's *happy* about my curiosity.

"Seriously?" he says.

I immediately want to back out of my own natural snoopiness.

"Well…uh…yeah. I mean—you're not exactly the most forth-coming of people."

This is true. Once, I asked him if he liked cereal for breakfast and he replied he'd have to think about it. Evasion is practically his middle name. I'm surprised he even got as far as "whatever…uh… you might have seen."

I mean, the above actually implies there was something *to* see.

God, he'd make a great politician. I think his parents actually wanted him to be one, so that's not really a shocker.

"I'm sorry," he says, and then for some reason I feel really bad about having that politician thought. I don't even know why he's apologizing, in truth—after all, it's me who did the wrong thing.

"No, no—it's me. I shouldn't have come in here, and I shouldn't have read your stuff—it's up to you if you want to share, not me—"

He scrubs his hands over his face briefly.

"I *do* want to share. I just can't. Not this."

"Well, that's cool. No one says you have to," I say, which seems like a nice, calming thing to tell him. Only when he looks up at me there's an intensity in his gaze I haven't seen before. Not ever. He's usually so still, so to see him like this is…unsettling. Unsettling and something else, something I can't quite pinpoint.

My body is still on high alert from the story. Maybe that's it.

"You don't have any trouble," he says, and makes his hands into fists as he does so. The high alert ratchets up a notch. I think…and don't hold me to this…but I *think* I'm turned on. Because of the story, obviously. And maybe also because I'm still in just a towel and he's showing some kind of actual emotional reaction to something other than a website crashing.

"Of course I have trouble! What are you talking about? I have a bag of stuff down there I've never dared read to anyone," I say. Of course I then think of him reading that bit in "Hamin-Ra" where three men take advantage of my hero's inescapable and utter horniness to…uh…do stuff. To him.

Which just makes me flush even redder than I am already.

"It's different…" he starts, but I'm not letting him get away with that.

"Why is it different?"

"It just is. What you write about seems…normal."

Did he seriously just say those words? I think he did. And for the first time I'm starting to wonder if Cam's issues run a little deeper than *Oh I'm a bit reserved and I like computers a lot.*

"Don't say that," I say, and it comes out a bit stronger and darker than I intend. He straightens, as though I've admonished him somehow—though if there was anything I wanted him to feel bad about, it's this. He shouldn't think of something as not normal, he just shouldn't. Fair enough if he'd written a story about fucking himself on a horse's cock or something, but even then I've got to say…I don't think I'd be that bothered by it.

He spreads his hands, palms down. I've seen him make the gesture a thousand times before—a mea culpa move, a peacekeeping thing. And also, weirdly, very much like the kind of gesture a politician would make.

"I just meant—" he starts, but I cut him off.

"I've written about that kind of stuff. Are you saying I'm not normal?"

"*What?*" he says, and he looks appalled, just as I knew he would. "No, God, *no*. You're the reason I even think about stuff like—"

Of course he stops short before he gets far with a thought like *that*. But oh, not quite short enough, no, not quite short enough. My skin bristles and that same deep down jolt of pleasure goes through me—like the one I felt when I read the line *Just stay still and take it*.

"Stuff like…uh…you know…stuff like…um…" he says and it's adorable, it really is. I never thought I'd live to see the day I called Cam adorable, but watching him fumble toward an end to a sentence like that is just…delicious.

He clears his throat, and tries again.

"It's just how I feel about myself. It's not anything to do with you."

"Cam—it's not a big deal. *Loads* of guys fantasize about two women," I say, because really. *Really. This* is what he's beating himself up about?

And he is beating himself up about it, because when I actually stop dancing around the subject and lay it out for him, he goes bright, bright red.

"Not like that, they don't," he says, and I have a sudden image of a bunch of beer-swilling, loudmouthed dudes watching two simpering girls getting it on with some big manly man.

"Cam—"

"Look—I'd just really rather we didn't talk about this. I hardly want to think about it, so talking about it is, like, ten times worse."

"OK, but—seriously. *Loads* of guys think about things like—"

He almost stands up then, but seems to think better of it. He does, however, make some pretty big gestures. And his hands are massive too, so it's kind of like he's assaulting the air.

"But you know what—it's not just that, it's not, it's everything. There are literally hundreds of things I really don't want to be thinking about, ever."

Of course, I know he means sex stuff. But then he confirms it, so I can't even escape the idea on any level whatsoever.

"In fact, I think I preferred it back when I hardly thought about sex at all."

It's weird that around twenty-four hours ago, I would have pegged Cam as bordering on asexual. If he'd said something like that to me when I hugged him in the boat room, I might have nodded my head in agreement. He *seems* as though he hardly thinks about sex at all. He barely dated anyone in college, and it's obvious he's not with anyone at the moment.

But when he says something like that now, it's like a big sign painted across him in neon. *I'm lying, I'm lying.* He doesn't prefer it and even when he spends time not thinking about sex it's always there, humming beneath his surface. I can tell.

I was blind before, but now I see.

Chapter Six

I THINK WE'VE BEEN sitting in silence for about five minutes when Wade shouts up, "Are you guys coming down for something to eat or fucking what?" Or maybe it just feels like five minutes, because I've just spent this whole pause in the conversation trying to work out what to say. The best option seems to be:

Whatever you want to do is OK by me.

But it seems too much like a come-on. I *feel* too much like a come-on. I'm all ripe and ready and I don't even realize it until I stand up and go over to him—you know, maybe just to tow him downstairs for something to eat. But then he kind of jolts out of the reverie he's sunk into and he puts a hand out—he actually puts a hand out to stop me—and says: "No, no, don't come over here."

And I'm pulled up short.

"What? Why?" I ask, but even as I'm saying it I know I'm being stupid.

He kind of…winces.

"Because you're just in a towel," he says, then the wince becomes a frown of incredulity. "Why are you just in a towel again?"

I try to think of a good answer to that, I do, I really do. But all I can process is: *he likes the fact that you're just in a towel, oh holy shit he really likes it. It's making him think forbidden sex thoughts!*

My cunt clenches once, around nothing. I'm too on edge, that's the thing. I should have masturbated last night or let Wade fuck me today or just snuck out of this room before Cameron came back and seen to myself in my own bed, but I didn't, and now I'm stuck. I'm stuck half-naked in a room with a big massive gorgeous amazing guy who apparently wants me.

I squeeze my thighs together, but it doesn't help.

"I was cold after the lake, so I took a shower," I say, like a total idiot. I should have focused on the reason he doesn't want me close in just a towel, and I know it—but then again, do I really want to push him further, right now? He looks…harassed, to say the least. "Come on. Let's go downstairs and have something to eat, OK?"

I hold out a hand to him, but it's a friendly hand. An innocent, nonsexual hand.

He doesn't take it, however. He just eyes it like it's about to explode.

"You know what—I'll meet you down there," he says and although it's completely irrational, I can't help it. I let the hand drop to my side with what can only be described as *Oh fuck, I've totally just blown our friendship apart with my snoopy snooping.*

And I think he reads some of this on my face too.

"No, no—look—you need to get changed, and I probably should get changed…everything's cool, OK? We'll meet downstairs."

It does not sound as though everything's cool. I can feel myself fidgeting, suddenly, even though I don't mean to. I mean—he shouldn't feel bad. *I'm* the one who fucked up; I'm the one who pushed him.

"Cam, I just want you to know I'm really sorry about all of this. I know it's probably, like, messed up our friendship or—"

He stands up then, real suddenly. So suddenly that I almost take a step back, and not just because of his impressive height. It's also because, well, uh, how should I put this…

"No, our friendship isn't messed up. I just didn't want to stand because now you can see I have a huge erection."

He makes a little *voila* gesture, which drains some of the tension in the room. Some, but not all. Because now we're kind of half-laughing and I guess it's funny, but it's something else too. It's drawing attention to the real and obvious fact that we've just kind of talked about sex for ten minutes, and before that I spent a lot of time reading a dirty story he wrote.

"Listen…Allie…" he starts, and for one wild second I imagine him asking me for something. He could. I mean, I wouldn't say no. His cock looks absolutely amazing through the barely-there material of his sweatpants, all thick and solid and pushing right up against the things confining it, and I can just picture him groaning and pumping his hips as I take him in my mouth.

But unfortunately, I can't even conjure up the imaginary words he'd use. *Will you suck me off* just sounds too crude. *Please go down on me* too polite. There's no middle ground with him—I can't find it.

"None of this means anything, you know?" he finishes, but all I can see behind my eyes is that big, thick cock and all I can think about is how it would feel, sliding into me.

"I…have had feelings for you. But I totally understand how you feel about Wade. Totally."

It doesn't sound as though he totally understands anything. Hell, I don't understand anything anymore either. I came here so sure—of my feelings, at least—and now everything is mixed together and upside down.

I look up at Cameron, and my stomach actually does this weird woo-woo thing. I mean, I always knew he was handsome—beautiful, even—but this is different. This is Tenar and Ged and secret stories and, dear God, I want to know more. I crave more, and not from Wade.

"We'll talk more later," he says, finally, and that's that.

———

But the problem is—he doesn't want to talk more later. In fact, by the time the next day rolls around and then the next, I'm fairly convinced he's actively avoiding me. We've all fallen into a comfortable routine by this point, of course we have, but his routine consists of running from 6:00 a.m. to a million o'clock, and then finding every room in the house where I am not.

It's like an elaborate game of hide-and-seek that I haven't been invited to play.

And I don't want to go looking for him, anyway, because that would just seem weird and desperate. I mean, he *might* have spent the last five years pining for me, but it's only a might. I don't know the whole story yet and, even if I did, I think I'd still feel pretty pathetic and horny.

I've never thought about cock so much in all my days. I find myself pacing outside his room at night, wanting to go in and just say hi, how are you, but with the subtext being, of course: *let me get you off.*

My brain isn't even subtle about it either. Suddenly I'm one of the girls in his story, pinning him to the bed. I imagine holding his hips down as I suck him off; I think about him struggling and squirming against all the things he thinks aren't normal.

Is it blowjobs he's bothered by? I can't imagine it is. It's probably something a little more perverse and sexually confusing, like a finger in his ass. Yeah—he mentioned that in the story. I bet he thinks about things like that, then writes three million lines of boring computer code as punishment.

Jesus, why is that hot? Not the computer code stuff—the other stuff. The punishing, disturbed, finger-in-his-ass stuff. All I'm doing is thinking about it while lying in bed, and my nipples are stiff. My clit feels huge and swollen, and my mind is already mentally reaching for the vibrator I should never have packed.

I bet it's bigger than he is. But then I remember how he looked— the way his cock had pushed so hard against the material—and I'm no longer sure. He'd seemed so *thick*, and when I wrestle the vibrator out of the secret compartment in my suitcase, it seems…insubstantial to say the least.

But it sure feels good when I slide it through the slippery folds of my sex.

I don't turn it on—artificial buzzing isn't the sensation I'm looking for—but I do let the tip just play over my clit, briefly. Just the way a real man might feel if he was over me, seeking entrance.

And then I push it down, down, down until it's just poised to slide in, every nerve in my body waiting for the orgasm I've denied myself for about five days too long. My nipples are chafing against the rough cotton of my nightie, and when I buck my hips the tip almost goes in. Almost, almost.

God I'm going to come so hard. I can feel it building already, and it keeps my fingers away from my clit. If I stroke myself I'll go off, and although I'm full of this frantic clawing feeling, inside, I want to draw this out. I want to picture Cameron fucking into me in some deliciously perverted way—maybe with something in his ass as he does it or his hands tied or, oh God yeah, a gag.

Only his silence in my head—it makes me realize how much I want to hear him. I bet he'd be so quiet in bed, so full of all the things he shouldn't say, and just imagining him moaning or telling me what he wants or what he's doing…it's enough to make me fuck myself hard against that slick plastic flesh between my legs.

I bet he'd tell me when he felt his orgasm approaching. A quick and dirty *God, yeah I'm close* or *I'm gonna come*. And though I've no idea why the thought is so electrically exciting, it is, it is. My clit is humming—just begging for me to stroke it in time to the frantic slippery thrusts I've worked up to.

And I would—I totally would—if Wade didn't choose that moment to stroll right into my bedroom like fuck yeah! That's OK! Come right in at seven o'clock in the morning and bug the shit out of me just as I'm about to get off to the thought of someone *who is not you.*

I'm not even embarrassed about my flushed cheeks and my obvious breathlessness. Mainly because I can't feel anything but extreme frustration. Is everything in this house designed to thwart me? I've got the horny seducer who refuses to follow through on one side, and the repressed politician on the other.

"You OK, Allie?" he asks, but he's grinning while trying to act casual so I know he's not really expressing concern. He totally grasps what I've just been doing and you know what? I don't give a fuck.

He's the one who keeps teasing and fucking with me. These are the consequences, asshole; now just let me get on with what I really need to get on with.

But instead he just saunters around my bedroom, glancing at things that are not me and my hidden sex toy. He has a ball in his hand, and I watch him toss it back and forth with all the disaffected-ness he can muster.

"I'm sleeping," I tell him, though it's pretty obvious I'm not. He must be able to see it clearly when he finally makes his way over to the bed and looks down at me, all swaddled in the comfy nest I've made, face flushed, eyes probably glazed.

I feel red hot under all of this, suddenly, but throwing off the covers is a bit out of the question.

"You sure?" he asks, and his voice has taken on that same soft, crooning sort of tone he had out by the lake. That he had in the kitchen. That he has all the time, now. Though the real problem with it is not how it makes me feel or how it sounds, no, no. It's the idea of him meaning it I can't shake.

It's like he honestly and sincerely desires me, and can't stop his voice from slipping into something seductive. And the way he looks too—so greedy, suddenly. His eyes are the exact same color as the steady point at the center of a flame, and when he leans in a little closer I've got to say—I find it hard to resist.

"You look a little…feverish."

God, he's like the hero of some ridiculous steamy novel. I almost roll my eyes, but it's really hard to with a fake cock still pressed deep in my pussy, and my fingers all wet and sticky with my own juices, and my body just ready for anything, anything.

"I'm fine," I say, but it doesn't seem like enough on its own, so I add: "Perfectly cool, if you really want to know. Almost glacial, in fact."

He puts one knee on the bed and all I can think is: *You're now three inches away from the exact place I'm touching myself.*

"Really? Because it looks like you might need someone to give you a hand. You know. Cooling off."

This time I *do* roll my eyes at him.

"Just go so I can finish doing myself, OK?"

There doesn't seem to be much point in denying it now. It's pretty obvious he knows, even though he tries to pretend otherwise for at least another thirty seconds.

"I'm shocked, Allie-Cat, real shocked that you would say such a thing. Makes you seem almost sexual."

I don't really want to think about what he means, but I kind of have to anyway. Was that the problem, back in college? Was it just me seeming all prudish or something like it, the way I used to view Cameron?

How completely fitting. It's almost some kind of justice.

"Well, you should know by now I'm not. I'm completely asexual, in fact," I say, and he cocks his head. Raises an eyebrow.

"Really?"

"Yeah. It's practically a nunnery down there. Think the whole lot just closed over some time last Tuesday."

"Thought as much," he says, but then he does something that in no way matches the conversation we're having. The conversation we're having is apparently about how sexless I've always seemed to him, whereas him kind of rubbing a hand down over his own body is all about me getting turned on.

Because, oh God, it just absolutely sends me. I'm not even going to pretend otherwise, because he runs it right over that hard body of his, and down over the thin but obviously expensive trousers he's wearing, to the growing bulge between his legs.

And I just watch the whole thing with my newly heated gaze, until it seems as though it might be OK, to keep right on touching myself.

"You seem so different, Allie," he says, just as he did back at the lake.

And I have to wonder if I seem different now because it's Cameron who's lighting me up. My desire for Wade was apparently muffled, closed off, kept down. But whatever this is—it's rampaging through me like a thunderstorm. It's busting out of me, even as I'm lying here beneath Wade's shadow.

"So…wanton," he says, and I want to laugh, I do—but I can't.

I'm too far gone. Before he's even finished talking and running his hand down over my almost bare shoulder, I'm rocking again against the thick cock between my legs. I've got a finger back on my clit and just the tiniest touch almost gets me there.

"I almost came in here a million times, you know? Every morning, every night. But after the lake I wasn't sure you wanted me to…" he says, then just leaves it trailing. As though he's waiting for me to reassure him on that score.

He should know that's not going to happen. I'm too stuffed full with the insanity of this, the suddenness of it, how badly I want him even so.

"But then I passed by today and I could just hear you. I could hear you. Sounded sooo good."

I want to demand to know why it didn't sound good five years ago, but of course I don't. Truth is—he's right. I didn't make anything to be heard five years ago. I didn't let him have even the smallest sexual sense of myself—not even in stories.

"Stick around. Pretty sure I'm going to make some more soon," I say, and he grins wolfishly at me.

There's something so easy about all of this, and I don't even know why.

"You wanna come, baby?" he asks, and this time I don't stop myself. I stroke firmly over my clit the way I've always wanted him to stroke me, and rock against the solid length inside me the way I've always wanted to rock against him.

And when I moan and turn my face away he says: "Fuck that's hot. What are you doing down there—playing with your clit?"

I moan again, louder this time, but I still hear the sound of a zipper going down over it. It *burrs* in my ear like a thousand angry bees, and all I can think is *God, all these years and this is how it's going to happen? Like this—this seedy thing?*

Only it doesn't feel seedy, exactly. It feels like I'm cramming as much food as I can into my mouth before it all evaporates, instead.

"I'm fucking myself," I tell him, and he sighs in response. Of course he does. He's always been a horny fucker.

"Oh yeah, tell me Allie," he says, so I do.

"I'm fucking myself on this big hard cock."

He groans—partly in shock, I think—and even though I'm still turned away from him, eyes closed, I can tell what he's doing. I can hear the slick sound of a hand shuttling up and down a cock.

"Show me," he says and I honestly think about doing it. I've waited long enough to see him doing something like this, and I can have it if I give him myself in return. I mean, that's the deal, isn't it?

I turn my face and look at him and it's just like a few nights ago—I can see the start of that rippling, rock hard belly, and he's shoved his trousers down around mid-thigh in the way I so wanted to do to Cameron. He's bare and exposed and he's shamelessly tugging on his frankly gorgeous cock, unfazed by my gaze all over him. By the breathlessness I immediately descend into, on seeing him work himself like this.

It's glorious, and yet—just like a few nights before—there's something remote about it. As though I'm watching him jerk off through a pane of glass, and said pane of glass takes me back five years to things I can't taste or touch or know.

"Go on," he gasps, but I just watch his hand flex along the length of his curved shaft—thinner, I think, than Cameron's, but almost impossibly long—and draw out little beads of precome every time he gets to the head.

It jerks a chain of arousal inside me, to see him this turned on. Because he obviously is—his cock is slick and red at the tip and I can see him pulling back with every stroke, as though going too fast or too hard will push him into orgasm—and the thought almost does the same for me.

"God yeah," he says. "Work yourself on it."

And I do, I do. I pump hard for just a second, just to chase that tingling, surging feeling that takes away the other, less pleasant ones, and then I can't help it. I call out his name and moan too loudly, body bucking into the first rolling wave of climax.

All I have to do is brush my fingertips over the slick tip of my clit and that's it, I'm coming and coming with Wade wavering in and out of my sight line, the thought of his cock and his body and him saying these things to me filling me up.

And then even sweeter, even dirtier, he groans loud and long: "Ohhhh baby, I'm coming, oh God that's so good."

Just before he does just that, all over my mouth and face. My orgasm gets tighter, stronger to feel him spurt hard against my cheek and over my lips. There's just something so naughty about it—not like the sweet encounters I'd always imagined finally happening between us—and when I taste him, I can't stop the finger I've got rubbing over my clit. I don't want to stop—it feels too good. I just want to come and come and come and keep on tasting him forever, and not have to think about any of this.

Though I do, when he leans down to kiss me. Right in the middle of the shuddering I seem to have sunk into, and with the still-hot stripes of his come all over my face. That's how we kiss—that's the first time I kiss Wade. With all of this between us and the suspicion he's tasting himself at the very top of my thoughts.

Strange, that I feel almost nothing at all.

Chapter Seven

I THINK KITTY CAN tell something's not quite right. But I'm no help on that score, because I've got no idea what the *not quite right* is. I mean, Wade fucked Kitty and then I found out Cameron is in love with me and also kind of weird sexually and then Wade came on my face.

But apart from that, everything's cool. Even when we're all sitting in the living room, talking in awkward fits and starts, everything's cool. Until Cameron goes to the bathroom and Wade seems to take that as his cue to desert us too, and then I'm just exposed to Kitty's deadly, deadly questions.

Which she asks, of course.

"What the fuck is going on?"

I consider, briefly, that she might hate me and think of me as a betrayer if I tell her what happened with Wade—she did get there first, after all. But then I realize that I'm being an insane person. Kitty once tried to make me fuck her boyfriend while she was fucking him, for God's sake.

"Something…went on between me and Wade," I say, but as soon as it's out I understand what I really wanted to tell her.

Something went on between me and Cameron.

"Yeah, uh, durrrr," she whispers, and I have to laugh. How is she just this awesome? "A blind person could see that much."

I have to say, I'm not so certain about that. I'm not even sure if a sighted person could see what's going on, because I've got two eyes and I don't know. And then she makes another little comment, all oblivious with one hand in her curls and her gaze on nothing at all, and I know even less.

"What I don't get is why he's pissed *now*. I thought he was desperate to fuck you—all he talked about mid-flagrante was how he couldn't wait to get you into bed. Seemed like he was angling for a threesome but I think it's more like leftover sexual tension between—"

"He's not desperate to get me into bed!" I say. And I shove the words out too—much louder than I'd intended.

But Kitty just looks at me, startled, as though she really isn't in the slightest bit bothered whether Wade wants to fuck me or fuck her or have a threesome or God only knows what. So then I'm just left stranded, with this stupid guilt-ridden sentence I blurted out for no reason at all.

She's not bothered. I don't know why I thought she would be.

"I mean…he never was desperate to get me into bed. I don't know why…I don't know why things have changed…" I say after a moment, while she eyes me curiously.

"It's all right if he does, you know," she says, and then I feel like a complete idiot. She's just not like that, Kitty. I wish to God *I* was just not like that. "You've waited bloody long enough."

I flush red then and try to look away from her. But it's hard, when her blue eyes are so guileless. So open and honest and full of a love I somehow let myself forget.

"Did you always know?" I ask, and that steady gaze doesn't let me down. She keeps to it even in the middle of words that could so easily be a lie.

"No," she says, and I know it's true. Not because of how she looks or sounds, but because she's Kitty. She would never fuck a guy she knew I loved, and I can see she knows now that I love him.

Or at least, that I *did* love him.

"But I do wish you'd told me." This time she looks down when she speaks, and I watch her focus on the wineglass in her hand, suddenly. I watch her turn the stem between her two little hands—both of them decorated with pink and yellow polka-dotted nail polish—and it occurs to me then, with a jolt. She doesn't care about Wade. She doesn't care about Cameron. She cares about *me*. About what *I* think. "I thought you told me everything."

"I do—I did—we're still—" I stammer out, but I don't get any further. Mainly because it's a lie. I *didn't* tell her everything. I don't tell her everything. We're not still best friends.

"It's OK," she says, and shrugs. But it's not OK. It makes a great big rush of feeling go through me, and I have the strongest urge to put a hand on her arm. To whisper to her the way I used to back in our dorm room, all those years ago.

I think back on it and it's as though I'm still right there, wrapped in a duvet as the cold knocks on our flimsy window, the hopefulness of love and desire still blooming in me. Still making me lean forward and murmur through the darkness about all the boys I long to have.

It's the word she used to use: *have*. As though boys were things that could be taken, the way girls could be. As though all of this—all of life—was just one big, grand game, and wouldn't you like to join in, Allie?

Yes. Yes, I would, Kitty.

"Something else happened," I say, and *then* I put my hand on her arm. I lean forward, as though I'm wrapped in a duvet and the cold's knocking on the window.

She leans right back at me, like nothing's changed at all.

"What?" she asks, and of course I think of words like *betrayal* and *trust* and *Cameron wouldn't want anyone to know*.

But then again, he hasn't wanted anyone to know for about a thousand years. I think his time for secrets—much like my own—is up.

"Cameron had a picture of me," I tell her, though it's clear that isn't enough once I've got it out. And I can hear them coming back, so I have to go for it. I have to—it's my one beautiful shining little gift, in all these years of utter nothingness. It's rich and glorious and Kitty deserves to have it shared with her, for all the things she shared with me. "And on the back he'd written *Tenar*. As though…as though he was Ged and I was…you know. And then I found something else of his too—a book filled with writing. He was lying—he does write all the time. Only it's dirty, filthy dirty, and he caught me reading it so I had to—"

But then I have to stop mid-sentence, because they're back. Wade tosses himself into the armchair next to Kitty and Cameron lets himself slide rigidly into place and there they are. Our two bookends.

I glance at Kitty, and her eyes are as big as moons. Her mouth is a moon too. She looks like she wants to laugh or cry or maybe die of incredulity, which should really mean something to me. At last, I had something worth telling! At last, I had a story that means something.

But instead, all I can think is this: *What was it, exactly, that I had to do?* And when I look at Cameron now, why is it that I want to do it so very, very badly? I don't even know what *it* is, but I want it. He just looks so still, sitting there, so contained—it's almost impossible to imagine all of this is going on inside him.

And judging by Kitty's expression when I glance back at her, it's doubly so for everyone who isn't me. Her eyes are even bigger now than when I last looked, and she's using them to goggle right at him. Any second, and he's going to notice.

"So, Kit!" I start, with such bright falseness she immediately jerks a look at me. Her upper lip is still curled in what can only be described as explosive incredulity. "You were going to provide tonight's entertainment, right?"

I hope to God she doesn't think I mean stripping. Actually, I just hope to God she gets what I'm trying to do here—steer things away from the topic of Cameron, and how he's a secret sexual maniac.

"Huh?" Kitty says. So that's a no, then.

"You were going to read a story," I nudge her, but she just stares at me blankly. Was the news about Cameron really that much of a shock to the gut? She looks like I electrocuted her, five minutes ago. Wade even comments on it.

"OK. What did you do to Kitty while we were gone?" He grins that all-tooth grin, and I try not to have flashbacks to the other morning. To the feel of him, all hot and slick all over my face. "If you went down on her, we're gonna have to hear about it."

God he's disgusting. Was he this disgusting before? And did I like it *this* much?

"Hey, just 'cause you got to have both of us doesn't mean we're, like, your little sex nymphets," Kitty says, and for the barest of moments I almost laugh with her. I really do. I guess I just don't process what she's said properly and besides, it's almost a tension breaker. It's good, in a way, to get everything out in the open. Wade slaps his thigh and roars about it, and Kitty hurls a cushion at him, and everything's cool.

Until my blood freezes and my insides turn to ash and I glance at Cameron in slow motion. Seriously—it's like the world winds down. And then all I can see are Cameron's eyes widening—just a barely-there flicker of expression, nothing more—before settling back to normal again, and maybe his shoulders go back a little too. Like he needs to pull himself up in his chair.

No big deal.

Only it is a big deal. Of course it is. I know it is because I've felt exactly what this is like—to love someone and then watch them go fuck a bunch of other people instead of you. How many times did I watch Wade do that exact thing to me? A thousand? A million? And now here I am doing exactly the same thing, only I *didn't*, I *haven't*, I'm not the same. I swear to God, I'm not.

I care about Cameron. I more than care. He's wonderful, and

he should know it every day. He should know how kind he is, how good. How fantastic his story was, and how I can't wait to read more. And how I can't stop looking at him right now, because his face is so perfectly lovely that my eyes just have to make up for lost time.

Kitty and Wade are still having the dumbest argument somewhere behind me, but I can't hear them. All I can hear is my heart pounding in my ears, and I keep staring and staring at Cameron as though I could just will him to look at me with my mind. I can make him, if I just keep staring.

And then after a while, sure enough—he can feel me. I know it. He's gazing straight ahead as though at nothing, but I can almost slide myself right into his shoes and feel my eyes on him. I can feel that little prickling sensation running down my right side, and how it is to never want someone to know how much you care. How much you're hurting.

Look at me, I think at him. *It's OK to. It's OK.*

But it takes him a long, long time. Far past the point at which I'm comfortable. I've never stuck with something this long and when he finally and slowly turns his head I feel wrung out. The effort of hanging myself out on a limb is almost too much, but by God I'm glad I did it.

Because when he turns and fixes those glacial eyes on me they're not glacial at all. It's like he's on fire inside instead, and understands that if he just keeps on staring he'll set me alight too. I know it. I know because I recognize the look immediately, as though I've seen someone stare at me in just that same manner.

And I suppose I have, in a way. I've seen Wade stare at me like that, in my head. I've cast him a thousand times as the One who stands in line for the Queen, waiting for her to choose but not wanting her to, burning but hating himself for doing so.

But I was wrong, I was wrong. It could never be Wade. It's always been Cameron.

"Hey, dinkus, you still with us?" Wade yells, though even the bellowing sound of his voice is barely enough to break me out of this realization stupor I've fallen into. He has to lob a cushion at me just to get me to turn around, but all I can think then is what a stupid fucking thing it is to throw. I mean, when did they become the missile of choice? They're so dainty. They have tapestried birds on them. There are tassels involved.

We should be hurling bricks, in all honesty.

"I'm still here," I say, but I lob the cushion-that's-really-a-brick-in-my-head back at him, as I do. Sue me—he's just interrupted the most profound moment of my life. I think I had minor embolism, I epiphanied so hard.

It's Cameron, I think. *It's Cameron. It's probably always been Cameron.*

And then I have to hold onto the arm of the couch for support.

"So do you or not?" he says, but I'm on a ship in the middle of the sea. I'm sinking. I don't know what he's talking about.

"Have a *story* to share?" he asks, real carefully, as though I'm slow.

Of course I go to shake my head, but Kitty whacks my arm.

"Yeah, you do," she says. "You know—the ones you were just telling me about."

At first I don't know what she means—she doesn't think I'm going to tell all about this whole Cameron thing in the guise of a story, does she? But then it comes to me—a great wave of *Oh my God, no.*

She wants me to find and read one of *Cameron's* stories. It's obvious. Even without her winking and nudging her head in his direction, it's obvious. Despite the fact that it's also insane and stupid and there's just no way I'm going to do that.

"Oh yeah, those ones," I say, and then I give her all the *Stop right there* expression I can muster. "No, no—those ones are no good. But

I've got these other ones. I could read those." It seems like a perfect plan as I'm saying it, but once it's out I realize what I've just offered. Now, somehow, I've got to go upstairs, find a story of my own that doesn't suck, and read it aloud for the entertainment of my peers.

Did I say I loved Kitty, earlier on? I actually hate her. I hate her even more as I root through my still-unpacked bags, looking for something I could feasibly read aloud. I won't lie: there are a lot of stories about fucking Wade. And even more stories about fucking someone who looks like Wade.

But then…then I get to "Hamin-Ra."

Half of it's still crumpled from the force of Cameron's fist. By the looks of things he got up to page forty-four—after my hero has just been tormented for the first time by the Queen. And, oh God, she tormented him *good*. No wonder it drove him nuts—I can barely look at the words on the page, and know now why I didn't reread to see what so excited him.

It's filthy. Worse than filthy, probably. After page forty-four it only gets worse and worse—some of it in frantic long-hand, some of it typed—and then I flick to the part where…I flick to the bit where…

God, I wonder what he would have thought of this. I can't even imagine, in truth. All I can see behind my eyes when I picture him reading it is him looking at me like he wants to kill me, the way he had downstairs only worse, ten times worse. As though I really am the Queen and he just wants to punish me with sex until I die.

Even though that's insane. He doesn't want to punish me with sex until I die, for God's sake. He just wants to…maybe he wants to…oh, I don't know.

But there is a way I can find out.

Kitty trapped me, but that doesn't mean I have to stay trapped. Maybe it's not even a trap at all, but a new and different path spread out before me, one where I'm not closed off or afraid or ready to just give up everything I am so easily.

I think about Cameron turning his face to me, those eyes of his like a storm over the ocean suddenly. Not like something sunk to the bottom of it anymore. And all I have to do is just take this story downstairs and read aloud, to see that look again. I know it's true.

And so I do.

The first one is rough, real rough. Not enough to hurt exactly, but certainly not enough to give him what he wants. When the guy's done he feels sore, and used, and his pulled taut body is yanked even tighter than it was before.

He's still hard, and that's probably the worst thing of all about this. That he's always mortifyingly hard no matter what, and they know it. They know how service to the Queen gets him—so riled he can hardly see straight or speak or do anything but go about his duties mindlessly, with his cock sticking out in front of him—and they take advantage of it, shamelessly.

Last time it was being on his knees, with their pricks in his mouth. This time it's worse, it's worse and it's better all at the same time, because at least now he's getting the contact he needs but even so…

Lord, it's hard to take. Even with everything he's experienced here in service to her Majesty, he's never had anyone be…there. And when the first guy had slid an oiled finger all the way in—all the way to the hilt—it had forced him to buck against it. He'd let out a gasp, even though they'd told him to be quiet.

And then the other two had tightened their grips around his arms.

He wonders, half in a fog and half out of it, if they know he could break their hold with barely a flick of his wrists. That he could buck the big guy behind him off, as though said big guy weighed nothing. They probably do, because he's pretty huge himself and much more thickly muscled than them, but there's something blissful in the charade.

Like a warm veil, drawn over his eyes. Which he closes, as the second guy says something crude like, "You're not supposed to come inside him. The Queen will know if you come inside him."

He imagines her cool green gaze on him, on something dirty like a trail of jism running down his thighs, and shivers inwardly.

But Lord—it's a pleasurable shiver. It's like that time she told him, "Corin, Corin, how I want to use every little part of you up," and his stomach had clenched and his cock had lurched and he'd thought, blindly: I could come just hearing her talk like that.

And he could, he seriously could. The tip of his cock is wet, just thinking about it and then feeling someone behind him, stroking over his already used and leaking hole.

"Oh yeeeaah he feels so good. So hot and tight," the guy says, as he slides a finger in.

But Corin understands. These three—they're just as desperate as he is. Just as teased, just as tormented, and none of them permitted a woman. They've had the Queen's sylph-like assistant sucking them and touching them, just the way he has—and none of them ever allowed to come. It's just too much, sometimes, and oh Lord it feels like it now.

It feels like it when the blunt head of this one's cock nudges against him, seeking entrance. He tries to breathe into it, just as he had the first time—but it's not necessary. His body's too eager for it and the way is made slick by the other guy's come and oh, oh.

It's too much. It's not enough.

"Ohhhh man, oh so fucking sweet," the guy says, then does something humiliating like slap his ass. He starts pumping almost immediately too, shoving Corin hard against the table they've thrown him over, no thought to the aching and leaking cock that's still straining between his legs.

But that's fine, because Corin feels pretty sure he's going to come soon anyway. The guy's cock is thick and hard and every thrust is butting it up against that place inside him, that sweet place, and when he turns his head just a little bit he can see the last guy—the one who hasn't had his turn yet—stroking over his own prodigious erection.

"You wanna suck it a little?" he asks, and there's something weird

about that. Something weird and uncomfortable about being asked, as though force is now the only thing he understands.

But then the guy gets a fistful of his hair and it's better, it's better. He's stroking the tip of his precome-slicked cock over Corin's lips, and that's just fine.

"Come on, man, open up," he says, and underneath the table Corin's cock kicks. Pleasure jerks through his belly, low and too much.

"Fuck yeah," the guy pounding away behind him grunts.

"Make him suck it—he goes tight when you make him."

He thinks the guy with the cock at his lips doesn't quite gather what the other one is talking about, but that's OK. He gets it. He understands totally. When he parts his lips and lets a hot, hard cock sink into his mouth, it sends such a dirty gush of sensation through him that his body clenches, and the guy behind gets a better ride.

All there is to it, really.

"Ohhh God, yeah like that, oh suck it, you little bitch—you like that? You like his cock in your mouth and my cock in your ass?"

He doesn't answer—of course he doesn't, he can't—but it's OK. He doesn't have to. The guy behind clutches at his hips, suddenly, then moans all long and guttural, before gasping that he's coming, he's coming.

And then there's just that hot wet rush inside him, and the guy jerking and jerking almost right over his prostate, it seems.

Still not quite enough though.

"Hurry up and do his ass," he spits to the guy with a cock still in his mouth, and is it weird if Corin finds himself thinking the same?

Hurry, hurry, he thinks, because he's slick and raw and right on the edge, and a couple more thrusts of something heavy and hard against that little bundle of nerves inside him will send him right over. It's bound to.

Especially when he feels how big the third guy is. Bigger than he'd seemed in his mouth. Bigger than the other two and ohhhh he just slides in like a knife through honey. It's glorious. It's like nothing else he's ever felt, and now it's clear that the other two don't need to hold him down.

He's scrabbling at the table and panting for more before the guy's even started thrusting.

"You want it," the guy says, but Corin doesn't deny it. He always wants it. He wants it in the middle of the day and the middle of the night, he wants it when he's currying the horses and when he's sewing rents in his slacks. He wants it even when he doesn't want to want it, which is most of the time.

"Yes, God yes fuck my ass. Just fuck me, fill me up, come on," he says, and then he jerks back against the guy's cock because now that he's free he can.

The guy grunts in surprise but he doesn't stop, he keeps right on fucking into him while the other two hoot about how much Corin needs a man to fuck him. Which he supposes is true, even if they don't know that the man he wants to fuck him is actually a woman.

Your Majesty, he thinks, and moans into the rough wood beneath him. God, she'd take him so hard, she'd fuck him just like this, and when she let her hand slide beneath his body to wrap around his cock, she wouldn't do it the way this guy is doing it. Regretful, ashamed, like maybe she'd become sensible of doing something wrong.

No, she'd do it with a hint of triumph in her slick stroke. She'd be aware of how perfectly she'd broken him, and she'd use it against him even as she came apart over his sweat-streaked body.

And it's this thought that pushes him those final few inches. He feels his cock jerk in the rough grip around it, and the thick cock in his ass swells just as the guy grunts that he's coming, and then ohhhhh, bliss.

Hot waves of pleasure surge through his body, forcing every muscle to contract as they go. His teeth clench tight shut which keeps most of the noise in, but some escapes—his final protracted groan as he spurts onto the ground, and then the little stuttering gasps afterward.

Gasps of relief, he thinks, because even though this was the worst and most seedy thing possible, it's given him a respite. A respite from having to dream about her, and never have her.

He feels them slapping him on the back and knows what they mean—yeah, we get it. It's hard for us too, you know. But they don't really understand. It's only hard for them in a peripheral sort of way, needing a woman, any woman sort of way.

Not like this. It will never be like this for them.

Because every day he wakes up sure that the agony has gone, and every day it hasn't.

※

It's only when I'm done reading that I realize something bizarre. Corin hasn't just *become* Cameron in my head. This story I wrote, over five years ago? It sounds like I wrote it *about* Cameron. It's like a weird echo of the things he said to me in the bedroom, and the things I read about in his little tale.

With a heaping dose of man love, that is. God, there's a helluva lot of man love in this thing. I don't think I fully appreciated how it would all sound until I got halfway through, and now my face is burning and burning and I daren't look up from the page to see their reactions.

Judging by the silence, their reactions range from flabbergasted to outraged.

"That was…" Wade starts, but Kitty cuts in. Kitty cuts in like a goddamn tornado.

"Holy shit—did you seriously write that, Allie? Did you—you know what? I have no words. Just bravo. Bravo," she babbles, and then she applauds furiously.

Of course she does. I glance at her and she's beaming like I just won the Nobel Prize for literature, over a story that would probably get me stoned in at least ten countries, then critically reviled in about seven hundred others.

Did I mention? She's a peach.

"You're stupid," I tell her, and give her a shove, but she just throws her arms around me in response. Squeezes me so hard my ears pop.

"You're a goddess," she says. "I knew you had it in you."

I don't know what *it* is, exactly. The ability to write dirty, filthy sex? Well, whatever it gets close to it sure seems to have pleased Wade. Funny, because somehow I'd imagined he'd be awkward and uncomfortable about it but no, no. His grin has reached epic proportions, and he's sprawled back in the armchair to Kitty's right with his legs apart. As though to say *Yeah, I want you all to know I have an erection. I have absolutely no problems with weird forced man love whatsoever.*

I think I go even redder than I was before, though it doesn't seem possible.

"*Why* did you waste all those years writing about walls that eat people?" he asks. "*This* is your true calling, clearly."

I've got to admit, I bask in that a little bit. Who wouldn't? The most he used to say about my stories was *That part where her head came off was cool*, so it's not really a shocker that I'm gratified.

But it is a shocker that I can't look at Cameron. I just can't, and I don't even know why. It should be Wade I'm embarrassed to look at. It should be Wade I don't want to face. But instead all I can think about is Cameron's steady gaze. How close the story seemed to things he's told me and things I uncovered. Will he think I'm taunting him somehow? I felt as though I was taunting him, even though that's ridiculous.

And then I *do* raise my eyes to him, and maybe it's not so ridiculous after all. He looks…he looks as though I just set fire to his sleeve, and now he can't move as the blaze slowly consumes him. His gaze has progressed from possibly wanting to kill me to actually wanting to kill me, even though I'm certain I've done nothing wrong.

I haven't, have I?

"Don't you think it's a great story, Cam?" Kitty says, because she's as sharp as a tack. She's as cute as a button, my Kitty. Obviously she can see what I can see all over his face, and unlike me she's not afraid to address it.

She wants him to give himself up. At gunpoint, if necessary.

"Marvelous," he says, and he enunciates every last syllable as though each one tastes like poison. As though he has to gag and choke it down.

Clearly he doesn't care if there's a gun in his face or not. Kitty's silvery little knowing tones do nothing to draw him out, and then once she realizes he's not going to stop staring at me like he wishes *he* had a gun, she tries to lighten the mood by giggling with Wade over various elements of my apparent masterpiece.

I hear him say something like *Well, if I knew a Queen as hot as the ruler of Hamin-Ra, I'd let three guys alleviate some of my tension too. And by alleviate my tension I of course mean ream my ass until I cry.* And then Kitty squeals and kind of jumps on him, and there's lots of reaming of asses talk going on. Lots of it. Probably way too much for my sanity, if I'm honest.

But it's OK because my sanity is already being destroyed by Cameron's furious gaze. So much so that when Kitty demands we all play a game, I think she's said *There's a ghost coming out of the wall* and almost jump right out of my skin. Though in truth I'm just not sure how else to explain my reaction. Seriously—I nearly throw the pages of "Hamin-Ra" across the room.

Kitty says: "Oooh, jumpy, huh?"

Then bumps my shoulder with her hip. I'm not even sure how she gets to my shoulder with her hip, in truth, but somehow she manages it. And then she stands in the middle of the room—oh Lord how I remember her announcements, made in just the place she's in now—and tells me I should be jumpy, because now we're going to play extreme sardines.

Oh God, no, not extreme sardines. Especially not when we're all like this. Wade stands and I can *see* his erection making a tent of his pants, for God's sake. I can *see* it. And then he says: "Yeah, but this is all just totally an excuse for us to get naked, right?"

To which Kitty replies: "Hee hee hee."

Lord, I don't want to be the one to find him in a cupboard somewhere and then demand an item of his clothing—because those are the stupid rules of extreme sardines. Kitty thought it up, of course. Maybe she just got bored of extreme Boggle, I don't know. Either way, the sardines have to give up their pants or their tops or in the case of Cameron catching me, once, in the downstairs linen closet—one shoe. He always went with something innocuous like a shoe, whereas getting caught by Kitty meant you were a dead man.

One time she demanded my bra, even though I still had my top and trousers on. I felt naked long before we got down to the other stuff that time, I tell you.

And I've got a feeling I'm going to feel very naked long before we get to other stuff here too. For a start, she nominates herself as the hunter. Then she turns off all the lights, so that we're all just sitting there in front of the flickering, demonic fire, while she informs us she's going to go by torchlight alone in her quest for flesh.

She actually uses that term. *Quest for flesh.*

Cameron still looks pissed. I'm not surprised—I'd be pissed too, if someone did something that made me extremely angry for no apparent reason and then another person threatened to steal my shoes. But even so, I don't expect him to interject. Not even when it's clear this is going to be some sort of "get everybody to have sex with each other" game.

"I don't think I'm going to be able to participate," he says, though he doesn't mention why. Of course he doesn't. The reason is probably "I fear I might murder Allie in the dark if we do."

But Kitty just flashes the torch she's produced from God knows where in his face, and waits until he feels good and interrogated.

Then she tells him: "Don't you try to get out of fun, Cameron Lindhurst. We'll tie you down and *make* you have fun."

I can hardly see him through the flickering darkness, but I know he flashes a look at me after she's spoken. I know it. I can *feel* it, rubbing against my skin like something ever so slightly prickly. It gives me an idea of what his anger is about, but only a nebulous one—maybe…maybe he thinks I told Kitty something? Maybe he thinks the story I read out was some sort of coded signal to her, about him?

It's possible. Oh God, what if he really does murder me in the dark?

"You've got thirty seconds," Kitty says. And then we all make a run for it.

Chapter Eight

AT FIRST I'M SURE Cameron isn't going to play. But then I really start thinking about the rules of extreme sardines and realize—hell, why *wouldn't* he want to play? Hiding is the thing he's best at! He's six foot five but somehow he's always the last one to get clocked, so he can just find himself a nice, safe corner and wait the night out.

Maybe with a good book and a cup of cocoa, to while away the hours.

But unluckily for him, I'm on his trail. He's pushed it too far now—inventing imaginary reasons to be pissed at me! I can't have that. What if the reasons aren't imaginary at all?

So I follow him down the corridor of stepping stones—so eerie and gleaming in the darkness—to the door that doesn't exist. The one underneath the stairs, the one he doesn't think Kitty knows about, which in all honesty she probably doesn't. And she's the hunter, so why should he care whether I know about it or not?

Because I do know. I found it back when the boat room turned out to be a stupid place to hide, and I thought I was so clever pressing against the place where there should have been a door to a cupboard. Only to find that there was an actual door to a cupboard.

Then throwing up my hands on realizing Cameron had already come to the same conclusion, about ten games of sardines ago. It had made me imagine him creeping about in the dead of night, exploring the house without us and rootling out its little nooks and crannies, and the same idea comes to me now as I press the door he's closed behind himself.

The shape of it springs out of the wood, too small for a real door and almost creepy. In fact, it's all the way creepy and always was, and when you stand in there beneath the slanted ceiling, it smells like every weird thing you've always imagined. It smells like forbidden rooms and creatures hiding in the walls.

And the side of me that still thrills at the idea of such things gives a little shudder, before I plunge into the darkness behind the door that isn't there.

"No, don't, Allie," he says, and weirdly the first thing I feel isn't hurt. It's surprise—that he knows it's me so quickly. Everything is black as tar and impossible to see through. How can he tell I'm not Kitty?

"Allie, don't," he says again, but I close the door behind myself anyway, and shut us into utter darkness.

I can feel cool air against my back, immediately, as though a draught seeps in from the direction of the stairs, for no reason at all. Always makes me think there's something back there, in that ever-slanting-down corner, but I don't let myself think about it. I focus on Cameron in front of me, all solid and obvious even when I can't see him.

I can hear his harsh breathing. I can smell his expensive man-perfume scent. I can feel him bristling, like a cat with its hackles up.

"Don't what?" I ask. It comes out as a whisper I don't intend.

"Talk," he says, and I kind of hate him for that. So much so I simply have to call him on it.

"So you're just going to be this asshole, then?"

I think I *feel* him flinch. The air definitely stirs around me.

"I'm not trying to be an asshole," he says.

"Yeah, but you're definitely succeeding at being one."

"Please don't say that. You just don't get—"

"I don't get what? Look—none of what happened was a big deal. And it would be less of one if you'd just stop for five seconds and have a conversation with me. You know a conversation—that thing where you open your mouth and sounds come out, then I open mine and sounds come out?"

"Allie …"

"What? What's so bad? Is it really so horrible of me to want to know what's going on with you?"

He snaps then. I feel it happen before he gives voice to it—a shift in the temperature of this little room. A rush of air coming at me, as though his big body rammed right against everything it could.

"No, it's really horrible of you to use it against me in front of everyone."

I have to say that's not what I was expecting—even after kind of thinking it earlier on. And if he could see my face I'm sure it would show.

"I … what? *What?*"

"You wanted a laugh, and I guess you got one."

"You think…laugh…*what?*"

He does something loud and air shuffling. Claps his hands together, maybe. I feel something almost brush the front of my jersey.

"Come on, Allie! You knew the kinds of things that turn me on so you thought you'd get me riled up and have a laugh at my expense. What do you think I am, stupid?"

At this point I really, really want to say: *Yeah, I think you're stupid.* But instead I go with the most mind-boggling part of his little declaration there.

"Did the story I just read out really turn you on?"

Of course, I knew it was a possibility. Or at least, I thought he might react to it somehow, and then talk to me about it. But him reacting with *that kind of thing really turns me on* is just a little beyond what I was expecting. As is the other stuff about laughing.

I mean, seriously. He thinks I find this *funny*? Does funny mean horny, in his language?

"What?" he says, irritated—I think—that he's been caught out somehow. "No, no."

"You bi, Cam?" I ask, and I swear to God I do it in all seriousness. But he just gets even more irritated and hand-wavy about it.

"Yeah, keep it coming, Allie. Keep tearing one off me—it's real funny. It's a great joke, I'm gonna start laughing any second—"

"Cam!"

I shout it much, much louder than I intend. And I do something worse too—I reach out through the darkness and grab his arms. They're easy enough to find because he's waving them about like nothing else, and he lets me too. He lets me get a hold of him.

"Cam, *knock it off*. Hey—I'm not trying to make fun of you. I don't even know why you'd think something like that. Have I really been so cruel to you, so unfeeling, that you'd think I'd read a story to torment and then *laugh* at you?"

Silence.

"Cam—is that what you think? Why would you—"

"No—*no* it's just Wade did it first and then I thought—"

He shuts himself off before the rest of *that* little sentence can come out. But oh ho ho it's too late for that, Cameron. Far, far too late.

"Wade did *what* first?" I ask, and though I try to sound normal my voice comes out low and strange.

"Nothing," he says. "Nothing."

So it's obviously *something*. And it's like the *something* is just boiling away inside him, because although he's straining at my grip it's not as though he's really trying to get away.

I can almost *hear* him wanting to say it.

"Cam, remember back when you could tell me just about anything? Let's go back to that, for a second."

"I could never tell you anything about myself," he murmurs, which smarts, I have to say.

"Then at least try now. Because you know if Wade has done anything to hurt you, I'll kill him. You know that, right?"

"Oh, you won't do anything," he says, and tries to shake me off, just a little bit. I think he's turned his face to one side, like he's looking for an escape route—but of course I can't be sure. "You're totally in love with him—you've fucked him already, for fuck's sake!"

I don't think I've ever heard Cameron swear before. It sounds wrong in his mouth, as though he had to bite down on hard on something to get it out. He seems sensible of this fact too, because once he's got the words out he breathes too hard and tilts away from me, a weird sort of judder making its way down through his body to the hands I've still got around his wrists.

Is it odd if his suddenly blazing jealousy—as offensive as I should probably find it—just makes me want to slide my hands down and clasp his?

"I'm sorry," he says, after a moment. Flatly, bleakly. "I'm so sorry, Allie. That was completely unnecessary and uncalled for and I've really got no excuse. Just none."

"It's OK—hey. It's OK."

I make a mistake then. I run my hands up over his arms, right over his heavy biceps beneath the stupid Pringles-style jumper he's got on, and I really shouldn't have. Not because it makes him shiver—which it absolutely does—but because it makes *me* shiver. It makes me realize how illicit it feels somehow, to touch him in any sort of intimate way. Even when I'm just trying to get him to calm down or some stupid shit like that, there's a sexual undercurrent now that I can't easily deny.

He feels good. He feels strong. He's making me wet in the middle of a fucking argument.

"It's not OK. It's not—you *should* be with him, you know? He can give you things that I'm…not even capable of."

"You mean, like, talking about your feelings? Because I gotta agree—you are *terrible* at that."

"No, Allie. No...*Jesus*, it's not even easier in the dark." I think I actually hear him swallow. "I mean...I can't give you all the...sex stuff he gives away so freely. I can't just...I don't know how to—"

"Who says I want that stuff?" I whisper, but he just laughs, bitterly.

"Your stories say you want that stuff."

"So do yours," I tell him, and this time I *don't* whisper. It comes out fierce, fierce, and for the first time in my life I actually tug someone down to bring them closer to me. As though I'm going to kiss him any second and, oh God, I want to. I do.

"It's not the same," he says, but I can think of many ways in which it is. Not least of which is the thing pressing between us, suddenly— the one that's brushing against my belly even though we've hardly done anything at all. I haven't kissed him; he hasn't touched me.

But he's definitely hard, anyway.

"Really? Then how come the story I just read out turned you on?" I can feel his breath on my face, all hot and too quick. It's making me buzz higher than all this oddly frantic talk is. "You like the thought of a cock in your ass, Cam?"

"Don't say that," he whispers, though really I think he means the opposite. He sounds so hoarse and tremulous suddenly, and I understand why.

I feel hoarse and tremulous too, saying something as dirty as that to someone like him.

"Or maybe you want me to do it to you instead, huh? You want me to fuck your ass?"

He lets out a little short, awkward breath, then definitely presses himself against me. Just a little, just enough for me to know it's his cock doing the pressing.

"Tell me what you want," I murmur, into someplace good and warm like the side of his throat. He's leaning down into me now, so it makes it kind of easy—even if he won't answer me. He won't give me anything.

"You want me to touch you?" I say, and finally he shifts against me. His mouth opens against the side of my face, hot and soundless.

Then finally, finally he manages to get out words—even if they're not the words I expect.

"Don't ask," he says. "Don't ask me."

And then a spike of arousal jolts through me, hard and unyielding. Somehow, somehow I know instinctively what he means. I know because he's told me in a thousand ways—with the stories he likes and the looks he's given me and all the meaning between the actual real words he's used.

And sure enough, when I don't ask—when I just *do*, instead—he moans loudly. I don't wait for his permission, the way I would usually. I don't let him lead the way—*I* lead the way. I run the heel of my palm right down over the solid ridge of his cock, and when he tries to back off a little I squeeze the wrist I've still got clasped in my other hand.

I squeeze it, and hold him in place.

"No," I tell him, as though I've suddenly become someone much more powerful and sexually sure, in my head. "No."

Then suddenly he's breathing hard and bucking toward me, as though I said something encouraging instead of that one harsh little word. Funny, how it so often means something bad, a refusal, a barrier in the way of everything good and yet here it feels…it feels like that word he used to describe Wade.

Free.

I think of all the things I've wanted to do to him since reading his story and finding my picture, and I just get to pick the one I like best. I get to choose, and I do: "Keep still," I tell him, then I push the words right out of myself. "I'm going to go down on you now."

He makes the dirtiest little sound, at that—caught somewhere between a forced-out breath and a moan—and for the first time I really wish I could see his face. I can feel his lips are parted, all hot and wet and almost kissing me in little fits and starts, but it's his eyes I want. They must be pretty lust blown by now if his mouth is open and his cock is this hard, but I can't know for sure.

I want to know for sure.

But more than that I want to suck and lick and stroke his big, gorgeous cock—because it is. When I finally manage to fumble open the buttons on his jeans—him squirming and bucking into my touch, all the while—he feels immense.

Smooth as silk and so thick I can barely get my grip around it, and oh when I stroke down to the tip there's far more of him than there should be.

"Sorry," he blurts out and I have no idea why. None at all. It's lucky he fills me in, really, because I'm so mesmerized by the smooth, solid feel of him I can't do anything but sigh with arousal. "I know I'm insanely big."

God, he's even apologizing about *that*?

"Stop saying sorry," I tell him, and then I squeeze that glorious cock just once. Hard.

He grunts as though it goes through him like a punch to the gut, but he still keeps on trying to explain.

"Women say they like it but they don't. Mostly they scream and run a mile."

"Really?" I say, but I don't mean it as a question. I'm not actually making idle conversation. I'm just saying meaningless things while I stroke up and down the fat length of him, tingling all over with each new discovery.

He's not cut, for starters—that's a surprise. I'm sure I heard somewhere that most American guys are, but when I work him just right I can feel the soft skin sliding over the slick head of his cock and, God, God he feels amazing. All I have to do is swipe my thumb over the slit at the tip and he leaks precome, copiously, everything getting slippery the more I stroke until finally he's just talking absently through a haze of moans and sighs of pleasure.

"Really," he says, and jerks into my touch as he does so.

"My last girlfriend—I had to go down on her for hours before I could get inside her."

I think *I* moan then.

"But it's OK. It's fine. I love…doing it."

I definitely moan after hearing him say that.

"I love it more than getting anything for myself, you know? Because anything for myself just feels like…like I'm being…I don't know."

Dirty, I think for him, though I'm not sure if that's true. There definitely seems to be some shame-based nonsense to his behavior, but he speaks so little I can't tell.

All I know for sure is when I put a palm flat against his belly and push him back a little—just to make room, just so I get on my knees and finally have him in my mouth—his cock jumps in my grasp. More fluid leaks from the tip and runs in a thin stream down over my working fist.

He likes being pushed; he really likes being pushed. He likes being pinned, and he likes it double when I sink suddenly to my knees, one hand suddenly on his upper thigh, holding him fast, the other on his cock as I sink my mouth down over the tip.

In truth, I can barely take more than that. He's so thick and fat, and when I suck hard it doesn't take much to tighten my mouth around him. It takes so little, in fact, that he's moaning and trying to thrust before I've done a single thing.

Any second and he's going to come, I think, but he doesn't. He doesn't. He just stands there, shivering, with his big cock barely sliding in and out of my mouth, the salt-hot flavor of him immediately on my tongue.

I work him quickly, sucking hard then licking over the little slit at the tip. Over the ridge on the underside—the one that makes him almost buck right into my mouth. But he doesn't come. He doesn't even do it when I make my hand nice and slick and rub over the shaft as I lap around the head, though he does make a sound when I make one.

When I gasp with the sudden pleasure of it—God, this is *Cameron* I'm sucking off, oh Lord he's so slick and hot and hard—he gasps too, like an echo of me. As though it turns him on to hear me, which I suppose it does. He did say that thing about preferring giving over receiving—probably because he's a god sent from the heavens to stun us mortal women into submission—but I didn't really register it until now.

Until I break away from his swollen cock just long enough to tell him how wet he's making me, how hot, how I don't care what other girls think—I can't *wait* to feel this big thing inside me. Arousal makes my tongue loose and I really go for it. I even slip a hand inside my knickers to chase it, to make my words dirtier, hotter.

"Oh God, I just want to rub your cock over my clit—do you know how swollen it is? How hard? I can't even touch it—it feels too good. I'm gonna come any second just thinking about you fucking into me, hard, hard—"

"Jesus Christ," he gasps, then even better: "Are you touching yourself, Allie?"

He sounds incredulous, even though it seems pretty clear to me. I can hear the folds of my slick pussy, parting around my busy fingers.

"Yes," I tell him, but my voice is wavery now. I'm pretty close—too close to do anything decently—so I just stroke over him roughly, flicking my tongue over the tip until his thighs start trembling and his hands go suddenly to my hair.

Of course I assume he's going to force my mouth over his cock. But since it's Cameron we're talking about here, he does just the opposite. He tries to push me away, instead, and when I won't go he gasps out a little frantic: "Ohhh no, baby, no—I'm really close."

It takes me a second to realize what he means, and when it comes I'm struck for the first time by the similarities between this, and my encounter with Wade. No real sex, just stroking and touching ourselves and then finally Wade covering my face with his come.

But apparently, Cameron doesn't want to. Or at least, he's giving me a choice—again. *I can do whatever I want*, I think, and then after a long moment filled with shivering thrills I push his hands away from my hair.

I *order* him to keep them at his side.

"No," he says. "No."

But I ignore him. I slide my mouth down around him and suck, strong and steady, while his fists remain somewhere around his hips. And then when he chokes out a sound, I rub him in time to the slippery wet rhythm I've worked up.

It takes about ten seconds. Maybe longer, but I find it hard to be sure because I'm suddenly delirious with the grunting, guttural noises he makes and the sound of that cultured voice telling me he's coming.

It gets me there too. Just hearing him and feeling him swell in my mouth, then all the hot, thick spurts of come over my tongue. The whole thing goes on for a long, long time and I work myself through it, stroking my clit until it's almost painful. Until I'm shuddering and boneless and just waiting for him to tell me how sorry he is.

Only he doesn't. Instead, I feel him sort of…relax against me. Just a little bit, just enough for me to realize how heavy he is and how much I need to prop him up against something other than me.

And then, after a moment, he says: "God. Never thought I'd feel your mouth on me…there before I got to feel it pressed against my lips."

I like how he says *there*. It's so him, it really is.

"You want me to kiss you, Cam?" I say, and I guess I'm teasing a bit. I certainly expect him to say no, because…well. I don't exactly taste like cake and puppies, right at this current moment in time.

But he just fumbles through the darkness for me, and I feel his big hands go underneath my arms. And then he's almost lifting me, I'm almost off my feet, right before his lips graze mine and, oh God, why is this more intimate than the thing I've just done, oh Lord, I'm going to kiss *Cameron*—

And then he pulls back, just as I knew he would. I mean, Wade might have liked the idea of getting all in the mess he made of my face, but this is Cameron we're talking about. He probably needs me to douche my mouth before he even considers it.

Though really, it's not such a big deal. We can kiss another time, after all! It's not like we're going to wait another five years, right?

"Hold on," he says, and then I have to squint and blink because I think he's just struck a match. I've no idea where he's got one from but I can definitely smell sulphur, and then after a moment of temporary blindness I can make out the little dancing flame.

In fact, I can make out Cameron too.

I can see the lines and curves of his face, made ghostly by the almost completely enclosing darkness. I can make out the exact tenor of his gaze, so much softer and more liquid than it was but no less passionate. And when he says, "If we're going to kiss, I want to be able to see it's you," I confess, I turn to water and wash away.

I'm still there on this ocean of him when he leans down through the flickering gloom to touch his lips to mine—softly, so softly. I can make out that lush upper lip distinctly, and even though I'm sure he's not going to press in deeper for fear of what he might taste, he does.

He moves his lips over mine and then for one brief, thrilling second I feel his tongue stroke into my mouth. Just a hint of it, but oh so lovely all the same. It sparks some satiated nerve endings back into life and I squirm against him without shame, sure that things are going to progress to more.

But then the light sputters out and I feel him go still against me, as though the match was the only thing keeping him in this one delicious moment. His breath ghosts over my face through the darkness, and I can almost hear stopping sorts of words welling up inside him: *We should... We need to... We can do this again later...*

You know the kinds of things.

Only he takes that one moment in utter darkness and utter stillness to say to me, quite distinctly: "I can't wait to taste you the way you've just tasted me."

Chapter Nine

I THINK OF THOSE words a million times: I can't wait I can't wait I can't wait. He makes me think of them when he's just standing there in the kitchen, cooking eggs on the big double-top stove, in a jumper that barely fits him and which seems as though it could just slide right off one shoulder at any second.

When he turns around I can see his chest hair, poking out of the top of the slight V-neck. It's almost obscene, with those three words rattling around my head as a backdrop. And then he flicks his gaze up to mine as he pushes a mess of scrambled eggs onto four plates, and I don't know what to say or do or think.

He's so…he's so…my Corin.

"You want more eggs, Allie?" he asks, as though those are the thoughts I'm trying to transmit to him through my wildly staring eyes. I'm all about a need for breakfast foods, rather than an insane lust for his glorious, gigantic body.

I wonder if he knows now that I lust for his glorious, gigantic body. He must, surely? I'd whispered to him in a fever the night before, about how I couldn't wait for that too. And then we'd spent an hour shrieking down dark corridors with Kitty hot on our heels, everything like some strange fever dream that's only tangentially based on reality.

Looking back on it now I think of Byron and Shelley and Keats, only we're the budget version. The bizarre, erotic version, with every one of my thoughts turning back to his hands underneath

my arms and his mouth on mine and the hint of a promise in
his words.

When, I think, *when?* But no *when* comes. He had gone to bed
in the middle of the game, leaving me susceptible to Wade's wander-
ing hands, in the dark. Half my clothes gone already because, by
God, Kitty's a ruthless player, all of me wondering if I was brave
enough to just throw caution to the wind and find my way through
the shadows to his room.

I think that may be what he wanted me to do. To just creep
there and lock myself in with him, then explore all the things Byron
and Shelley and Keats probably did, anyway. Their real books
How We Had A Giant Orgy: Volumes I, II, III were buried beneath
the floorboards in that big house in wherever-it-was, never to be
seen again.

My real book is right now, trying to read the hidden messages
behind Cameron's veiled gaze.

"I'm fine," I say, because I am. But I'm maybe not so AC/DC
when I realize a tense sort of silence has descended over the kitchen.
Both Wade and Kitty have forkfuls of food poised in front of their
mouths, as though they went to eat then forgot how midway.

Or more likely: they saw something much more interesting than
eggs, and started paying avid attention to that, instead. I mean, I can
practically feel their avid attention crawling all over me. It's dense
and sticky, and it's also a lot like being accosted by Wade in the dark,
in just my underwear.

Come on, he had said. *Show me where that little secret room is,
under the stairs.*

And of course I had wondered if he'd heard us. If he'd known
I'd go to that place, and followed me there, and heard me doing
something with someone who is not him.

Good, I think, suddenly and surprisingly vicious in my own
head. *Good.*

"Something you want to tell us?" Kitty says, and she has this absolutely wicked look on her face. So wicked, in fact, that it matches the *good* my mind spat out only moments earlier.

"No," I say, but I can feel the heat spreading across my face. The only thing that halts its advance is how prickly Cameron looks, suddenly, like he's been caught doing something he shouldn't and needs to rein himself in.

It makes me want to grab said reins and cut them. Or maybe yank on them. I can't decide which and, even if I could, I'm far more concerned with how much this might make him pull away. Do I get ten less kisses for every humiliation he has to endure? Will he refuse to talk to me for another week if I let Kitty or Wade embarrass him over a blowjob in a cupboard?

I can tell he hates it, you know—the idea of being a joke. Of being exposed, somehow.

"Great breakfast, Cam," I say, and when he looks up this time his gaze isn't stuffed full of hidden sensuous meaning or longing or anything else so delicious.

But it is full of gratitude, at the subject change I just initiated—and somehow that's even sweeter.

Yeah, it's even sweeter by a million miles.

I think it's the sense of trust or the hint of his smile or the feel of his fists at his side that gives me a long stretch of freedom. Whereas before I felt nervous about going to him and demanding he talk to me, it's easy now.

Or at least, it's *easier*. My heart's still beating a little high and fast when I finally catch up to him, by the lake. And though I know he slowed down to a barely-jog in order to let me catch up, I can't really pull off casual as I pick my way through the long grass and the sudden flood of wildflowers to the place where he is.

He watches me coming in fits and starts. Picks up a pebble or two and skims them across the glossy surface of the water, as he waits.

God he looks like a Gap model, when he sends the pebbles out. Like one of those outdoorsy sorts of pictures with a cagoule-clad hunk in them, doing outdoorsy sorts of things. Arm whipping out, eyes scanning the horizon, all the copper highlights in his hair suddenly flashing bright and beautiful in the early morning light.

"Hey," he says, and the way he does so is just completely at odds with the way he looks. His words *bristle*. They have thorns all over them and they're so unsure, as they creep out of his mouth.

The contrast is unsettling for a moment. Mind-bending. Why didn't it so impress itself upon me before? All I can remember thinking is how funny it was, to be so handsome and so awkward, at the same time.

"You wanna toss one?" he asks, and all I can think is *No, you idiot. I want to kiss you. Don't try to hand me a pebble. I want to kiss you.*

"Sure," I say, then just as I take it from him and he turns to throw another, he goes for it. Just like that. Right into awkward conversation. No awkward pause.

"Did you tell them?"

So maybe he doesn't trust me, after all, worse luck. He thinks I'm a blabbermouth instead.

"No," I say, and intend to leave at that. I do. But then other stuff blurts out with it. "Though they've probably figured it out. It's not as though you were really quiet and discreet."

In truth, I'm sure he thinks of himself as the very soul of quiet discretion. In truth, I do too. But I say it anyway and once it's out he blushes, of course, and does that little eye flicker thing. The one I found so charming in his bedroom, and the one I can't get out of my head. It's like he thinks he's a disaster in some way, and can't disentangle himself from that feeling.

I want to rob him of it, before he struggles himself into an even deeper mess.

"I don't know whether I'm happy about that or not," he says, then seems to consider. "Though it would have been nice to have you as my secret, for a little while."

"Then spring it on Wade, right out of the blue," I suggest, and am honestly not sure how I dare. I mean, it implies all kinds of things about myself that I almost never believe in—that I'm worthy of jealousy and deception and intrigue.

Only then he says: "God, yeah." And gets very close to grinning, as he does so.

Though it only makes me want to dig deeper, to see this pleasure written all over his face. To see him reveling in the demise of someone I'd always thought of as his friend.

"Why do you hate him so much?" I ask.

He doesn't answer for a long while. And when he finally does, he looks…conflicted.

"I don't," he says, which is an absolute lie and we both know it. "I don't…*hate* him. I have…mixed feelings about him."

Another pause, and this time when he speaks it's flatter. More honest, I think—or at least, he believes it is.

"He's not worthy of every second you spent pining for him."

It crackles in my blood, to hear him say something like that. It really does. But I think he's being hard on himself, in all honesty—painting his animosity toward Wade as simple jealousy. As a fault of his own, and not of Wade's.

And this idea goes through me especially hard, when I remember a little glimmer of what he'd said the night before.

"So…nothing to do with the thing you said he did to you," I say, and though I'm certain it means nothing when I set out to bring it up, he flinches.

His shoulders go back, the way I've seen them do a thousand

times. *Thorns around his words*, I think, but he answers more honestly than I expect.

"I wondered if you'd get back to that."

"I'm like an elephant. A shameful secret–remembering elephant."

"It's not that shameful."

"Really? It sounded shameful."

"Everything I say sounds shameful."

Oh God, yeah. That one sentence sums him up so perfectly it's like cracking open his psyche and getting a peek inside. Which is no mean feat, I have to say, because he's sewn himself up so tight you can barely see the seams.

"Sounds like heaven to me," I say, and he flashes such a look at me then! I think I burn alive. I think he melts me on the spot.

Christ I need to fuck him.

"Haven't you guessed yet, what he did?" he asks, instead of saying all the lovely dirty things I can see, simmering behind his cool gaze.

Of course I try to think and go over everything we were talking about. *The story*, I think, *he was mad about the story, and me reading it out, and the idea I might have used it as a taunt or a tease, just the way I'd kind of known he might do. As though I knew him so well already, and just didn't have any faith in my own "interpreting Cameron" abilities.*

But in all honesty, I think my abilities have improved since then.

"The story Wade read out, that first night," I start, slow, slow. Man, it feels like an age ago now, though in reality it's only been a couple of weeks. A couple of weeks of packing away Professor Warren's things—his shirts smelled of pipe tobacco, oh they did, they did—and re-plastering the study and avoiding all the things we all long to say but can't, God we just can't.

"Yeah," Cam says, and boy howdy does he sound bitter.

"Was it yours?" I ask, because that's the most logical conclusion. Wade found a story of Cameron's, and read it aloud. I mean, it didn't sound like Cameron's style—or at least, the style I discovered in his green book of magical sex stories—but I'm not expert enough on things like that to know for sure.

And what Cam says next only confirms my blundering ineptitude in the field of style matching.

"No," he says.

Which is a relief. Or it is, until he follows it with: "It really happened to me."

And then he keeps talking.

"I confided in Wade, and he took it, and put it in a story." I think maybe that tight seam just bust.

"He's so…smooth. He makes it easy to tell him things but then, by God, you wish you hadn't."

Oh, how familiar that sounds. How silent I used to keep myself, for fear of that *wishing I hadn't*. It was like torture, it was like madness, but I knew—or thought I did—that he should never know the way I felt about him. Back then he would have laughed if he'd known, I'm sure, and now…well. Now it's a different kind of agony, as he does his best to tangle me in the mess of himself.

I've never felt so chased as I did last night, running down endless corridors away from him. I've never felt so crazy, knowing I was running away from something I once wanted so bad.

"You watched a girl," I say, and mean it to come out matter-of-factly. But somehow it comes out full of wonder instead.

"Yes."

He tosses another pebble, true and strong.

"She didn't know," I say.

"Yes," he tells me. "But she knows now."

It's obvious he doesn't want to say that. It shows on his face, and in the color that spreads up over his neck, and in the way he whips the last pebble he has, so hard it simply shoots right through the glassy surface and into the depths beneath.

But he goes with it anyway, as though he can't help himself. Like maybe I've got hold of a thread inside him, and I'm pulling and pulling.

"Jesus," I say, but only because it's shocking. Not because I'm appalled, or anything—quite the contrary.

"I never meant—" he starts, but I cut him off.

"Did he get it right?"

"What?"

"Did he get it right? Did you really want me that much?"

He breathes out through his nose, just once. Harsh, like an out-of-breath pant.

"Some things were…a little strong," he ventures.

I think of the view he got of my pussy. *My pussy*, for God's sake! Good Lord, he's a maze of secrets.

"But you spied on me?"

I feel like I'm accusing him. Like he's on trial. But I can't help the words slipping out. They just need to be aired, to find fresh pastures, they're jostling for attention in the heated mess my brain has become.

"Don't say spied," he says. He's squirming, and that's even more delicious and intriguing than this whole new revelation.

Or maybe not quite.

"And then you masturbated."

"Oh…fuck. No. Yes. Sort of," he says, all in a rush. Then after a moment he sets his shoulders, and continues in a more orderly fashion. "It wasn't exactly the way he described—I don't even really like to…do…that. On my own. With no one else around."

Is it weird that even a fact like the one he's just uttered sends a flush of heat through me? What does he mean *I don't even really like to*? Like—never? He never likes to masturbate? My God, how horny *is* he?

"So why did you?" I ask, even though there are a million other things I want to ask more. *Do it for me*, I think. *Jerk off right in front of me, so I can see the glorious sight you denied me all those years ago.*

"I think you could make me do just about anything," he replies, right in the middle of my already hot thoughts. I'm suddenly boiling with the idea of him with his hand on his cock, watching me make myself come—God knows where.

God knows when.

And then he goes and says something like that too. It's like a match, striking—I don't mind admitting. It's like my insides are suddenly alight, even in the cold mist of early morning.

"Good," I say, and I say it fiercely. "Because I want to make you do anything. Right. Now."

∼∼∼

It's weird, climbing the stairs together. Like we're going to our deaths, or something—only in reverse. I suppose it's because I've never done anything like this before, never come in after a date and led the guy I'm with upstairs. Tentatively taken our clothes off, you know.

All the kinds of stuff that happens on TV, but never in real life. In real life my dates are like miniature battles with my own inability to make conversation, and once they're done and I'm sweaty and raw and bloodied from the fight, the guy will occasionally smash his mouth onto mine.

Somehow, I don't think Cameron's going to smash his mouth onto mine. I see him looking behind us instead, listening for the sound of the radio blaring in the study. The sound of Wade, being nowhere near us.

And then once we're in his room, he shuts the door so carefully. Like he's not sure if he should or not. Like he's not sure if this is really going to happen, and is door shutting acceptable? Will I think he's presumptuous?

I want to tell him he's not presumptuous enough. He's so big—he could just rip my clothes right off me. He could do anything he fucking liked, though maybe that's the point. Why should he need to prove he can, when he's so clearly and easily capable of it?

"What do we do now?" he goes with.

I swear, he couldn't have asked a better question if he'd lived to be a thousand. It sounds so much like the words I would say that for a moment I'm sure there's an echo. And I'm also sure that he makes me utterly giddy.

"Wanna get on the bed and roll around?" I ask, and oh he gets very close to grinning. Very close.

"Just like that, huh?" he says, but he's a bit behind. I'm already clambering onto the big blue four poster, and for once I'm not in the least bit concerned about how my skirt is rucking up to show my enormous ass, or whether it's cool or not that I'm wearing non-matching underwear.

It's hard to do any of that normal stuff, when he looks like his seams are bursting. When he does something awesome like going to yank off his sweatshirt, before pausing mid-material wrestle.

"Do you…want me to take my clothes off? Or is that…too fast?"

I think about his cock in my mouth, the night before.

"We're a little past too fast, don't you reckon?"

He swallows visibly. Lets his gaze wander over my breasts, my almost spread legs, my face—before reining it back in.

"I don't know. I've never gone too fast in my entire life. Usually I'm still at dinner and dancing at this point."

I can't help asking. He still has his elbow stuck in his sweatshirt.

"You take girls out to dinner and dancing? Do you visit the drive-thru afterward?" He flinches then, but I think I've hit the nail on the head. He's not just like a politician. He's like a politician from the 1950s. "Are you courtly? Do you give them courtly kisses on the wrist?"

Of course, as I say this I reach forward and put a hand between his legs. So I feel it takes some of the mocking sting out of it, you know? And if it doesn't, well. He can have my other hand pushing up underneath his sweatshirt, just for good measure.

"Fuck," he says, and I'm again reminded of how lewd it is, to hear Cam swear. To see his face sagging as I stroke him, nice and slow—in a way I'd never usually dare to. I can feel almost everything through the loose material of his sweatpants, and all of it weighs heavy and solid in my hand. The swollen outline of his tight-as-anything balls, the curve of his cock, and then just to be extra rude—I push two fingers down, down between his legs, and right over that strip of skin there.

Of course, he jerks. In fact, I think he starts jerking on an almost continuous loop. And he makes a little noise too, so that I just have to look up at him.

I'm not disappointed, when I do. He has one hand in his hair, and he's watching what I'm doing avidly. Mouth open, cheeks flushed, chest rising and falling—the works.

"Sensitive, there?" I ask, then stroke again. Just once, nice and firm.

He moans in reply.

"You're so *easy*," I tell him, and his eyelids sink lower over his eyes. His hips are rocking, just a touch.

Only then he says: "I didn't used to be."

"No?" I ask, as I roll the heel of my palm over his balls.

I like the little hitching sound he makes, the best. The one that's almost a little *ah*, but not quite. His lips move around it, and his chest rises to push the necessary air to his vocal chords, but no real sound comes out.

It makes a flood of warmth go through me. It makes me squirm against the bed until my panties feel soaked and my clit feels as stiff as his prick looks, and I'm just waiting for more. I need more.

"I mean, I'm not. When I'm not around you. I barely even thought about sex, until I met you."

"And then after you met me?"

"I started…masturbating too often."

"How often?"

"I don't know. Twice a day?"

"That doesn't sound like a lot."

He presses his lips together tight, then grinds the words out.

"OK. Maybe…maybe more like three or four times a day."

"Is that what you've been doing here?"

This time, his frustration gets the better of him.

"Stop *asking*. Don't ask. Just *tell* me."

Of course, my immediate instinct is to ask another fucking question. Something along the lines of—*Is that what you like? You like to be forced, rather than make the decision yourself?* But really, there's little point. And besides, I know the answer by now. I know it so well that instead of another question, some entirely different words come to my lips.

"Spread your legs," I order him, and he does it. Just like that. He spreads his legs and I stroke further, harder, more. I get right between his legs—almost to the groove between the cheeks of his ass—and he moans unashamedly.

It's the latter word, I think, that gets me. *Unashamedly*.

For a second he's not a politician from the 1950s, or someone who lies about how often he masturbates. He's just a horny little fucker, trying to get more contact on various parts of his body.

By the time I get my hand all the way up inside his shirt to the tight little peaks of his nipples, he's trembling. His tongue keeps coming out to wet his lips, and he's breathing almost completely through his nose.

I pinch one small nub, and then fight the urge to ask a question.

"Tell me how it feels," I say, instead, and oh the response is almost immediate. No hesitating, no blundering. Just a rush of words that go up and down the harder I pinch.

"It's amazing when you do it hard."

I trap his nipple between thumb and forefinger, in response. Tug at it, until he makes a sound like a whine.

"Yes, yes—just like that," he says, and when I do it again his cock kicks against the material of his sweats.

"Tell me what else you want," I say, because by God I'm getting the hang of this no questions thing. It's easy, once you know how.

"Uh…uh…" he fumbles. He strokes his hand through his hair again, then squeezes a clump at the back into his fist. His eyes flicker back and forth, searching and searching for something.

"Tell me," I say, fiercer this time. I squeeze the root of his cock as I do so, hard enough to hurt, and the ensuing grunt is exactly the same sound Wade made when he came all over my face.

But Cam doesn't go over.

"Uh…I want to…" he starts again. Then when I mouth the shape of him through the sweats, he finishes with a flourish: "I want to return the favor. I need to return the favor. Right now. Before I come in my pants."

A fresh rush of liquid floods my slit. I feel it happen, though I know it's not for the words "return the favor." I know exactly what he means, but it's the *come in my pants* that gets me.

All I can imagine, for a moment, is him jerking and groaning as he spurts against the material. As he soaks it, and makes himself all messy, and then afterward maybe he could look all shamefaced and awkward and *ohhhh God*.

What's wrong with me? Where has this kink come from? It's got to be the worst kink in the world. Most women don't fantasize about a guy creaming his pants. They fantasize about the *opposite* of that, of stallions going on forever and ever, shoving at them and fucking into them and—

"Can I go down on you? You must be so worked up by now. Unless, you know, this doesn't turn you on—which it might not. No one says you have to be turned on because you gave someone... oral sex. Or touched them, through their—"

"Cam—I'm really turned on, trust me. I've soaked my panties. I need to come so badly, I think I've started hallucinating."

He makes a little desperate sound then. A *greedy* sound, I think.

"Then tell me to," he says and, oh Lord, I'm lost. He's clearly mad, but that's fine. I don't give a shit—I'll tell him to do whatever he wants me to, and you know what? I'll *love* it.

"Lick my pussy, Cam," I say.

And then he just goes for it. He just goes for it, the way I had imagined him doing only a few minutes earlier. His arms tangle with my legs, briefly, and for a moment I'm overwhelmed by his size. He gets a knee on the bed and just looms over me, frankly, but I won't say it isn't exciting.

It's incredibly exciting, and especially when he actually pushes his hands up my skirt and finds the elastic of my knickers.

He's not clumsy about it, that's the thing. He's rushed and blustery, and the moment he gets a hold of my knickers he yanks too hard, but it isn't *clumsy*. It's raw and good and I think I actually moan when he practically rips my underwear off.

God, I must look a sight down there. I don't think I've ever been this wet in my life, and the moment my knickers are gone I can feel the slippery liquid running between the cheeks of my arse. I can feel it sliding over my agonizingly sensitive clit, whenever I move my legs.

And I can see how greedy his gaze is, when he finally gets my legs apart and sees my cunt all spread open for him.

"Oh, Jesus," he moans, then lower, hoarser: "Look how swollen your clit is."

I blurt words out in response. Him being dirty like that *makes* me.

"Then get to it," I say, and oh man there's something so arousing about him just *doing it*. He simply stoops down—big hands spanning my thighs—and tastes me, he actually tastes me.

As though I'm a particularly interesting vintage that he needs to just dabble his tongue in.

Though he doesn't dabble for long. I see his tongue—long and red and oddly pointed—flicker between the folds of my sex, and then his eyes roll closed and his entire body sinks down over me and suddenly I can't see anything at all, except for the top of his head.

But Jesus, can I *feel* it. Oh, it's like I've never had someone's mouth on me before. And he doesn't just put his mouth on me either—he doesn't just lick or suck or do that weird swirly thing my last boyfriend seemed to think was so awesome. He buries his face right into me, knee deep, and when I let out a little cry of absurd protest he goes for more. As though I'm going to stop him any second and he needs to take all he can while it's on offer.

I swear, I never understood the term "eating out" until now. Licking pussy isn't anything like eating out. There's no chewing involved, and only the barest minimum of swallowing.

Or at least, that's what I thought until Cameron Lindhurst decided to go down on me.

I think my back arches so violently that a vertebrae pops. Something makes a sound, at the very least. And when he spreads me open, oh God, when he licks over the flesh he's made all smooth and taut with the pressure of his two scissoring fingers…I come close to a sob.

And I get closer still the moment he sinks those said same fingers right into me, all the way to the hilt.

It's his knuckles, you see. They're immense and…I don't know. Brutal, somehow. And every time he slides his fingers back and forth, I can feel those big, bolt-like things dragging over some place inside me that didn't previously exist.

I'm babbling his name before he's even gotten around to licking my clit. Though I have to stop, after a moment, because the sounds I'm making are drowning out the sounds he's making and oh, he's definitely making them.

A great rumbling purr works its way up his body and out of his mouth, and it hums against my swollen flesh so exquisitely I could cry. And then just as I'm recovering from that, teetering on the brink of a glorious orgasm, he licks some tender place just to the right of my swollen clit and, dear God, I'm shaking.

I'm shaking all over in great spasms, as though arousal now makes me have some kind of fit. Though in my defense, I *have* been denied too long. I think I was starting to forget what another person's hands on me felt like, and I've *definitely* forgotten what a tongue feels like.

Though I don't think I'll ever forget *this* tongue. He licks all around my clit in tender little strokes, so careful that I'm left completely unsure as to how he's doing it. How is it possible to touch everything *but* my swollen bud? It feels immense, it feels like it's throbbing, oh God, I just need him to touch it.

I roll my body in an effort to get closer, get more contact, but he edges away at the last second—like some goddamn tease. I don't even know where he's getting the nerve from, to be honest.

But then I realize. It's not *nerve*. It's him urging me to tell him, to force him, to get a handful of his hair and yank.

Of course he gasps against my heated flesh, when I do.

And the gasp folds down into a moan, the moment he hears me do what he so obviously craves.

"Lick my clit," I tell him, then louder and more desperate: "Fuck me with your fingers and lick my clit, hard and fast."

It sounds filthy, even to my ears. But he's pretty far from the politician now. He's so far away from it that he sits up for a moment, panting and slick-mouthed, his fingers still in me and everything about him saying that he just wants to *watch*.

He wants to see what it looks like, when he fingers me. And he wants to flutter a hand close to his clearly raging erection too.

God, it looks gargantuan, by this point. I can almost see it throbbing through his sweatpants, and it just makes me wonder why he's not doing what he so obviously needs to do.

Only then I remember what he said—what he's said several times to me, in fact, as though trying to impress a really important idea into my lust-addled mind. About how he doesn't really like to touch himself, how he doesn't really *need* to, and Lord just the thought makes my tongue loose.

"Touch yourself," I tell him, and his foggy gaze flicks up to mine. He still has two fingers in me, sliding back and forth, slow and easy. And yet *this* is the thing that startles him.

As though I wasn't going to take the hint.

"Ahhhh," he says. Probably because he's forgotten how to make real words. Instead he defaults back to the mediating politician, trying to come up with a safe middle ground without really refusing me. "I really think…"

"You really think what?" I ask, and as I do I work myself on those big, thick fingers. Just a little undulation of my hips— nothing serious.

"I really think I'd rather do this," he says, sure of himself now. Closed off I think too.

"And if I'd rather you slide your hand over your cock?"

His eyes flutter almost-closed—it's that embarrassed expression again, only this time it has a hint of dread about it.

"Don't," he says, and it's so heartfelt, so full of a weary sort of pleading, that I'm pulled up short. I mean, I'm not going to force him if he feels so wretched about it, you know? I could never do that to Cam. I could never, I could never, or at least I'm sure I couldn't until he says: "Don't make me."

My breath catches in my throat. And it's not because he

twists his fingers in a very specific and very pleasurable sort of way as he says those words, either. It's because the embarrassed, torn sort of look leaves his face, and a strange, flat kind of expression replaces it.

I want to call it *deadpan*, but it isn't exactly. It's more like… more like all the will rushes out of him, all of his sense of self, and instead there's this vast void that he's just waiting for me to fill up.

And then, of course, there's the fact that he said *Don't make me*. I mean, if you really don't want someone to do something, you don't leave those two little words on the end there—as though the person *could* actually force you, if they wanted to.

Or if he wanted them to.

I reach toward him slowly. It has to be slowly, because he's crooked a finger and is rubbing very insistently over what I'm now certain is my G-spot. I've got no clue how someone like Cameron knows where it is—when I think of him in bed with someone it's still under the sheets and with the lights off, despite the stories—but he definitely does.

And it's making it very hard for me to think straight, or test my many theories about him out.

"Touch yourself," I say again, and this time I clasp a vice-like hand around his wrist, as I do.

He goes rigid automatically, and for a second I'm sure I've done the wrong thing. He didn't want me to push him further. He really did want me to stop, and not make him.

Only then he makes that little breathless sound again, and it turns into a strangled sort of moan. His fingers jump inside me, suddenly frantic and fumbling, and when he starts shoving down his sweatpants with his free hand I get very close to coming.

A great swell of sensation goes through me, thick and oppressive, and then I can see his swollen erection. I can see the slickness at the tip, all of it spilling over to run down the length of his shaft.

"How?" he says, so breathless it kicks another arrow of pleasure down into me. "How do you want me to?"

My mind reels. Are there really so many ways to go about this? *Just fuck yourself*, I want to say, but somehow I doubt either of us could take it. He'd probably come just hearing me say the words, and then I'd come from watching it happen. I can almost see it with my mind's eyes—lovely thick streamers of his spunk, marking my spread and swollen cunt.

"Just grab yourself and stroke," I tell him, but only because that's all I can manage. He has his thumb on me now, sliding ever so slightly between my labia and my clit. Not quite touching, oh God no, not quite touching, but really—does it matter?

"I'm gonna come," I say, then add what I need to: "Quickly, baby. Do it."

His eyes roll upward, this time, as he lets out a choked, "Oh, Jesus Christ." And then finally his hand goes around his cock, while he's busy not looking.

Not that he needs to. I'm doing enough staring for both of us. I watch him stroke, and it's a sight to see—if a little slow and ineffectual. He's not grasping himself tight enough—anyone would know that—and he's sort of slackening off when he gets to the head too. As though he knows he'll go off if he lets his palm graze that slippery red tip.

But that's OK, because then he blurts out: "Say something else."

And after a moment, he manages to get out the magic words— the ones that have so obviously crystallized inside him.

"Force me."

They crystallize inside me too. I tighten my hand around his wrist—the one that ends in his pumping hand—and I urge it back and forth—faster, harder. I order him to make his grip narrow and brutal, then bloom bright with pleasure when he starts moaning on almost continuously.

"I'm close," he tells me, and as he does he runs his thumb right over the tip of my clit, just brushing it. Almost as though he didn't mean to at all, and it was just the aftereffect of the feeling running through him currently.

He's jerking and shuddering with it, and the hand he has on himself is making the lewdest sound. So wet and sloppy and like he's somehow found a gallon of baby oil to douse himself in, even though there's nothing. There's nothing and, oh God, oh God, when he pressed down on my clit like that—when he worries it beneath his thumb and groans that he needs to do it—I stutter under the pressure.

"Ohhhh God I'm coming, oh God, right there," I tell him, while he gasps almost identical words. He forces them out and then the first spurt hits my inner thigh. Another gets all the way to my pussy, to the place he's rubbing and stroking through the most glorious orgasm I've ever experienced.

It goes on forever—and by the looks of things, so does his. For one long moment he really gives in to it, massaging his cock through his protracted climax, coating me in thick strands of his come.

And I watch it all—I watch his cock as it leaps and jerks in his fist. I watch his face, when it slackens and goes blank with pleasure. He's so beautiful, in that moment, so not himself. Lost in a maze of sensation he didn't want to experience, and unashamed about wanting to coax every last drop of it out.

Though it's easy enough to tell, when sense comes back to him. His hand drops from his cock almost immediately, and his eyes take on this busy, where the fuck did I put my sack and washcloth look.

That's Cam, I guess. Not even able to enjoy the afterglow.

"Come on," I say. "Just lie down with me for a second."

And I confess, I do it more out of frustration with him than anything else. I just want him to relax, to give in, to stop being so uptight about everything, but it's only when he goes very still again, that I realize something both shocking and delicious.

He doesn't just want me to have power over him sexually. He wants me to have power over everything.

Chapter Ten

"Why do you like it?" I ask, before I know I'm going to. He's lying on his back, almost sprawled—but it took him a good ten minutes to do so. At first he had put his back up against the headboard and hugged his knees to his chest, as though doing so really counted as "lying down."

Then gradually I had coaxed him into a slouch, and then a leaning-on-one-elbow kind of thing, and finally this. Sprawling. Of course he had pulled his sweatpants back up and so he's still fully clothed—which had definitely made me want to test out my new-found authority, I have to say.

But hey—baby steps. Baby steps.

"Like what?"

I'm surprised he asks. I mean, there's only one answer to that, isn't there? And judging by the way he's stroking his thumb over his brow—almost shading his eyes in the process—I think he knows what the answer is going to be.

"Being forced," I say, but to his credit he doesn't flinch. And he doesn't look away either.

"Is it really that big a deal? I mean—I wouldn't call it a…ah… fetish, or anything."

"You think there's something wrong with having a fetish?"

"That's not what I said."

"It kind of is."

He does look away this time. Pinches the bridge of his nose between thumb and forefinger, and makes a little unhappy sound.

So it's surprising to me, when he answers anyway.

"It's easier," he says, then with more conviction: "It makes things easier."

I have to ask. My better judgment is telling me no, but then again my better judgment just received a glorious, world-beating orgasm from him and all of his hang-ups.

We're going to this place. I need to know.

"What was it that made fucking so hard for you, in the first place?"

"It's not hard for me," he says, but he's lying.

"Come on, Cam. Who am I going to tell?"

He glances at me then, and there are whole vast worlds in his eyes. Great and terrible things he's probably imagined, a thousand times.

"Wade and Kitty."

I take his face in my hands then. I have to. It's a necessity.

"Hey. Hey—you can trust me, OK," I say, and then I realize how easily I can turn it on its head. How I can make an order into something sweeter—a soft pull on him, as though my fingertips are on that mythical-beast-ending thread inside him and all I have to do is tug a little to get him to unwind.

"You can tell me anything. Tell me anything."

"It's not that easy," he says. "There's not one thing that makes someone the way they are. I just *am* this way."

"Ashamed," I fill in, for him, but he won't say yes or no. I suppose he doesn't have to really.

"Sex isn't something to be ashamed of."

"Really? Do you wanna maybe stop by my mom and dad's house, and share that with them?"

I find a little curl of hair close to his ear, and wrap it around my finger.

"They live in a huge red brick in Connecticut. You can't miss it."

He's trying to make light of it, I can tell. On Cam, it's almost terrifying, and it makes me want to change the subject. I have to change the subject—and in fact, I'm sure I've done it very neatly when I say: "What was it they wanted you to be again? Was it a politician?"

Only then I realize that I'm just talking around in circles, drawing back to the same thing over and over again.

"Is the president a politician?" he asks, and I have to giggle. I giggle even though I feel dreadful inside, suddenly.

"They wanted you to be president?" I say, still half-laughing.

But only half.

"My mom used to say—people vote with their eyes. I think it was her way of telling me I was handsome, in between all of the *Don't slouch, be polite, be perfect.*"

"You are perfect," I blurt out, and after I've done it I realize I've never actually told anyone anything like that before. It's the first time I've ever said to someone—freely and quite easily—that I think they're incredible.

I don't even blush over it either.

"It won't go away just because you say something like that to me, you know," he says, but I can see him bending.

He bends even further when I kiss him softly.

"You are perfect. You're perfect to me," I tell him, and by God I mean it. I actually mean it. I look at his gorgeous eyes and his full mouth and his amazing half-curled hair and I want to say more than the word *perfect*—I want to make up a new word that encompasses everything he is.

"Do you have any idea how long I've waited to hear you say something like that? Scratch that—I *never* thought you would say anything like that to me. It's like you've started speaking an alien language."

"Aishalem," I tell him, and secretly I know that's the word. The word beyond perfect. The one that's just for him.

"You know why I had that picture of you?" he asks, in the spaces between the smile I seem to have opened up on his face. "Because you were all the things I'd always wanted, and everything I couldn't have."

"I've gotta tell you, it's a pretty big deal when someone as handsome and amazing as you says something like that to someone like me," I say, but he just laughs—properly, this time. No faint smiles. No half-measures.

"You've got it the wrong way around, Allie," he says.

"You've got it completely the wrong way around."

———

It occurs to me much later, while I'm sitting under the window in the boat room, writing. In fact, I'm writing so much that my finger is starting to ache and I've made a mess of papers around me—all fragments of stories I was sure I'd never work on again—and then it comes to me.

This little kernel of realization. This little nudge into the brave new world I've found myself heading toward.

We need a safe word.

Oh God, we need a safe word. That's what people do, isn't it, when they plunge into things like this? He wants to be forced, and I've got to admit that I want to force him, but the fact remains—what if I take it too far?

I'm not even sure what too far *is*. He seemed to find masturbation a stretch, but since he'll barely talk about his stuffy, fucked-up family and his obvious issues, I'm guessing he's not going to go into detail about what he does or does not like in bed.

I've got to feel him out. Test his boundaries. Get him to give me a safe word.

Of course when I catch him later in the kitchen and just come right out and ask, he looks at me like I'm mad. Like he hadn't even considered, and if I'd had a mind to it I could have made him strangle himself to death with a pair of my own tights.

But I swear to God—it's not going to come to that.

"We have to have a safe word," I say, and his expression freezes in place. Mouth slightly open, as though he just tasted something bad. Gaze sliding off to something that is not me.

For a long, painful second I'm sure he's going to tell me how ridiculous I'm being—that he hadn't even thought of having sex with me again and even if he had, he's certainly not going to do anything that requires a safe word.

Only then he says: "Tehanu."

Quite matter-of-factly. As though he'd considered and weighed all of this out long before, and now is the time to just be practical about it. Or at least, I think he's being practical about it until he adds, without looking at me: "You can do anything you want to me. Anything at all—just don't let it show."

And then he walks right out of the kitchen, as though we had chatted about the weather for five minutes and now he's just going to check if it's still raining.

I think my heart is pounding in my cunt. My head spins with all the possible interpretations of the word *anything*, and then worse than that: the words *don't let it show*. I mean, for God's sake. Don't let *what* show? Does he think I'm going to bruise him somewhere?

Does he *want* me to bruise him somewhere?

I'll be honest—I hadn't even thought about pain. I had thought of simple sex shame—that he was troubled about getting from some basic A to B. Not that he wants me to spank him or hit him or, God, maybe he wants me to do it with something?

You know, like a flogger or a whip or…Lord, we're getting into some strange areas. It's bad enough that he's obviously got all these deep-seated shame issues about sex due to his perfect-crazy mother and his probably uptight starchy dad. But add in some actual *punish-ment* for whatever lewd things he's feeling…

I don't know. I don't know.

I *do* know that I'm turned on. Hugely. Wade even notices it, when he comes into the kitchen and finds me leaned against the fridge, grateful for the cold and with my nipples sticking out like fingertips.

He leans in and I feel that old twinge, that sweet little ache at the thought of all things Wade. Before it sinks down below the surface of me again, and all I can see is the smug look on his face, like he's got me.

I mean, of *course* it's him who's making my nipples hard. Of course it is. Who else would it be? He's handsome and hard-bodied and when he leans in he smells of the piney smell at the back of the wardrobe he's been clearing out. It's weird—I always thought he wasn't the kind of guy to get stuck in, you know. He was always more the sort of person to drift on a sea of laidback-ness. But his hands are rough with little bits of plaster and I've seen him going about the house with his little measuring device, judging the square footage and the value of this thing that will now be ours.

He's become business-y, hands-on Wade—which is good. But he's also become predatory, I-want-to-fuck-you Wade.

Which is bad. I never thought it would be, but it is. It's bad.

"How come you're still not finding your way to my room at night?" he asks, and I do my best to maneuver my way out from between the arms he's put either side of my body. It's sort of like limbo-ing, only without the catchy music and the sense of fun.

"You say it like it's an obligation," I tell him, which sounds too mean even to my ears. And though it looks like he doesn't falter, on the surface of things, I see him kind of jerk a little. I see that golden face of his snap to surprise, then right back out again.

Which is just him all over, when I really think about it. Don't let anything go too deep, don't let anything mean too much, just keep things calm and casual and no big deal.

"Oh, hey, no," he says, then makes a little noise. A little funny *brrrpppt* sort of noise that I would have laughed at before right now. "You? Obliged to do stuff with me? No way. You're obliged to look that good in a tight T-shirt—but then, that's always been the case."

I wonder if he knows he's given me the perfect opening. Probably not. He probably doesn't even know I *need* an opening.

"Really? Funny that you never found the time to tell me things like that back in college."

It comes out in direct contrast to the way I'd always imagined saying words like those. In my head I had blurted it a thousand times, been embarrassed and sweaty palmed about it then borne the weight of his anger. I've no idea why he usually decides to be angry, in my head, but there it is all the same.

And here it isn't.

I just say it, blandly, mildly, and he can only find the wherewithal to shrug. While my mind goes to the picture I discovered, Cam's confessions, how much my heart had pounded and wrestled with me throughout all of it.

My heart isn't pounding now. It hasn't even fallen down inside me, the way it sometimes used to whenever I thought of Wade. Instead he says: "I want you now. Isn't that the main thing?"

While I feel nothing, nothing at all.

"Keep wanting," I tell him, and then I just walk away. I walk away.

We swap. It takes some doing, but that's the good thing about Cameron. He always gives in, in the end. In truth he doesn't even give in. I just tell him that this is the way things are going to be, and he obeys with his face all red and his mouth all tight and the green book practically super-glued to his hands.

Even after I order him to swap my stories for his, I have to wrench it from him. And then I sprawl on his bed, as comfortable as anything in my little sleep shorts and vest—something I've never been with any other guy—and I flick through the pages greedily.

"Is this all you've ever written?" I ask, as I take in snippets of the stories: "Pepper," "The Girl Who Wouldn't," "Comfortable Distance." To me they all have the ring of words long developed, of stories built on the confidence of other pieces of writing, but I can't be sure unless he says.

And he does.

"No."

I glance at him side-on, and find him still standing by the end of the bed. Half-leaning on one of the gloriously ornate posts, with my own mass of papers still in his two hands. None of it gone through, none of it touched.

Instead he just stares and stares at various parts of me—the too-rounded hump of my ass, when I spread out on my belly. The smooth line of my cleavage, when I prop myself up on my elbows.

"So where are the rest?" I ask, and he shrugs. Kind of like Wade did in the kitchen, only with more meaning behind it. I can read Cameron's shrugs, and, by God, they say a lot. This one tells me that he has a gigantic cupboard/filing cabinet/wardrobe full of them at home.

"You ever thought about sending them somewhere?" This time, he does more than shrug.

"I can barely let you read them, never mind some guy behind a desk with a big important brain and loads of important things to say."

It sounds so much like something I would say that I'm startled briefly. But then I recover and kick a leg out at him for being such a numbnuts—just playfully, you know. No real connection.

Though I suppose it shouldn't be a surprise that he doesn't dodge. He just lets my foot nudge against the solid meat of his upper thigh, and when I do it a second time—a little harder—his expression visibly changes.

"You don't just like being forced, huh?" I say, so low and dark that the room seems to hum with it. He seems to hum. He's looking at my body again, but it's with more intensity this time—as though his eyes have grown hands and they're pawing all over me.

"You want me to hurt you?" I ask, and he sort of…shivers a little. So I add: "I won't do anything drastic."

"So no cutting, then?" he says, and though it sounds as if he's joking, my heart still flutters inside me.

"I don't think I could bring myself to really hurt you." He smiles faintly at that.

"But maybe just a little. Maybe…some punishment. For the things I've done."

"Things?" I ask.

"Come on. You know."

"No, I don't," I tell him, though I'm lying, I'm lying. "Tell me."

"Spying on you," he says, after a moment, and I note how careful he is about it. No allusions to anything sexual. No dirtying his mouth with the bad words.

"Say it again, but filthier," I tell him, and when I do I push hard against his thigh. I dig my heel in, but he just presses right back at me.

"I spied on you while you…" he tries. I can see him searching for the right word, the word that he has to use instead of a euphemism. "Touched yourself."

"Hmmm," I say. "I guess that was pretty bad."

But it's not true, it's not true. When I think of the word *bad* I don't think of Cameron at all. I think of Wade, instead, reading out that story as though he'd written it, instead of just stealing it from his friend's life.

"So…" he says, then he just leaves the end of his sentence hanging there. Waiting for me to fill it in, most probably—waiting for me to order or demand or all of the things I'm completely not used to doing.

And, oh God, it's Cameron, it's Cameron—I can't hurt him. I don't want to bite him or flog him or spank him. I just want him to feel pleasure and know that it's OK.

"So read out this story to me," I say, and then I pass him his green book.

My arm stays in that position—reaching out to him with his words in my hand—for so long that the muscles start to protest. Clearly he was expecting something a little more…visceral. Something he wouldn't have to think about at all, while his body and his senses took a pounding.

But somehow, a spanking just doesn't seem torturous enough.

"You know I can't do that," he says, and I think of all the times he fumbled through stories about nothing. Stories about robotic people with no feelings and no desires. I think about how uncomfortable he seemed just hearing someone else read out a story that could have been his.

And I won't deny it. I go watery and weak inside. My cunt clenches around nothing, and when I squeeze my thighs together such sensations floods through me. I'm wet already, and getting wetter.

"Really?" I say, but I think it's the eyebrow that does it. I raise my eyebrow and he kind of flinches, expression suddenly tense and smoldering. "Because I could make you read it out in front of Kitty and Wade, if you'd prefer."

It's almost comical, the way he shakes his head. It's just a little movement, as though he realizes mid-gesture that he shouldn't be saying no.

"OK," he says. "OK."

But I can tell he doesn't want to. When he takes the book from me his hands are shaking, and that little tremor gets worse the moment he sees the story I picked.

I didn't even need to read it to know it was the right one. Its title is "Further" and the first line is *The moment she makes him come on my face, I know nothing will ever be enough.*

Oh, he is a bad, bad boy inside, and I want more than anything to make him badder.

"Go on," I say, and then I push my heel into his thigh again. Only this time, he gusts out a bunch of words for me to delight in, all tumbled one after the other in a great mess of everything he doesn't want to admit.

"Yes, do that, do that while I do this."

He needs something to ground him, I think. Hell—I need something to ground me. Cameron Lindhurst is going to read me a bedtime story about a guy coming on his face, and I have to somehow lie here, just listening.

Makes me wonder how long I'm going to be able to resist him. He's already hard, of course, but it's only when he pushes out the first words that I really start to notice how good his cock looks, out-lined against those thin pajama bottoms.

"The moment she makes him come on my face, I know nothing will ever be enough. It tastes like him—arrogant and jeering as he kneels over me, his cock sliding slackly over my lips. And it tastes like my own debasement, so rich and thick I want to drown in it," he says, jerking to a halt on some words. Spilling all over others.

And I don't know whether it's his hesitancy, or his clotted tone, or the words themselves, but either or all ways I moan freely. After all, what use is there for restraint in a moment like this? He cuts me loose with every tense second of his shame-filled resistance, and I can't deny that I revel in it. I murmur his name, to hear him say: "Of course, she knows. She is smiling as she sits cross-legged at the end of the bed, and her eyes never leave mine. She wants what I want, I think—she wants *further*—and my cock swells to think of it. My cock is like a fist between my legs, and I don't flinch or stir when the man she's chosen for me wraps his hand around my length.

"He's going to make me come now, I think. But I don't let the idea penetrate to those deeper recesses of my mind—the ones that always tell me no, don't, stop. I hover on the edges of them instead, as a rough and heavy hand slides down over my swollen dick."

God, he thinks about *men* doing stuff to him. He thinks about some woman—some woman who is most likely me—forcing him to accept a man's hand on his body. On his cock. All over his cock, stroking and pumping and, oh Lord, I think I might pass out.

But I hold myself together. I keep my expression aloof.

Or at least, I do until he says: "I can feel I'm going to come almost immediately, because it's not the right thing. It's not a woman's hand, soft and smooth and feminine. It's a man's. He's too big and squeezes the base off my shaft too tightly, and just when I think I can't take anymore he slides his palm over the slick head of my cock, and rubs there softly."

And then I just can't stand it. I scramble across the bed as he forces himself through another paragraph, each arrangement of words getting firmer and more sure the longer he goes on. By the time he's talking about this strange man sucking the swollen head of his dick, his voice is as clear and liquid metal as ever.

Though it wobbles a little, when I echo the man in his story.

It doesn't take much. He doesn't try to stop me. I just yank his pajama bottoms down and his thick cock springs free, already hard and leaking at the tip. I swipe my tongue over the slit, for starters, and he bucks his hips.

But he keeps on reading. It's like hearing my favorite song playing over the top of what I'm now doing, all the fucks and cocks and comes running through me as I suck him deep. I want to choke on him, to feel him lose it in my mouth, and a sharp realization comes with those desires.

I'm not confined to telling him what to do. I can also tell him to do things to me.

"Fuck my face," I tell him, and he hesitates. Of course he does.

But when I put some steel in my voice I feel his hand go to the back of my head. I feel his fingers comb through my hair.

And then his hips rock forward and his cock slides over my tongue—not quite rough but certainly exciting.

"Can I stop, now?" he asks, and at first I think he means the thing he's just started. His hand is tight in my hair and I can feel him bristling with the urge to thrust, but that doesn't mean anything. He's always saying stop when he wants to go. He's always running when he wants to stay.

Only then I realize—he means the story. He wants to stop reading the story. And though it's glorious to hear and I'm slick between my legs because of it, I tell him yes. I don't want stories anymore—I want the real thing. I want sucking and fucking and every dirty thing imaginable, and I guess I'm still thinking that when the bedroom door suddenly swings open.

I must be, because I don't throw a sack over both of us and pretend we're not doing what we're obviously doing. My face doesn't heat and I don't let Cameron go when he immediately tries to make me.

I just keep very still, and right in the middle of this stillness I let my tongue curl out to catch the very tip of his cock, in one long, lovely lick.

"No, don't," he says, and his hands push at mine—the ones I've bunched into the material, at his hips. Of course the thing of it is—Cameron could easily force me away if he wanted to. He's as big as a brick wall and twice as solid. His hands seemed to span the entirety of my head, when he finally dared to hold me and fuck my face.

But he doesn't make much of an effort, here. He just kind of scrabbles at my clenched fingers, while Kitty stands in the doorway, watching.

To her credit, she doesn't even try to go with some casual, breezy sort of thing. No *Hey, what are you guys doing in here?* No bubbly innocence. She just eyes us both like a person with a camera, bursting in to catch the dirty duo in flagrante delicto.

Only she hasn't got a camera, and after a moment she stops simply standing there. She comes right in, and closes the door behind her.

"I told you. You never share things with me anymore," she says, finally, and my body definitely jolts. I mean, there's just such a double implication of the word *share*, isn't there? It could suggest how nice it would be, to have a friendly little chat about the person you're fucking, with your best friend.

And it could suggest something that makes Cameron very, very uncomfortable indeed.

"You *are* a big one, aren't you?" she says, and it's not just Cameron who shivers with arousal, this time. Slickness floods my already slippery slit, just to hear her talk in that naughty, teasing tone.

Of course I've heard her use it before. Through the darkness in our dormitory, as some guy panted between her legs and I pretended not to hear. But I can't pretend right here and now. I can see every detail of her clearly: the way her little mouth has curled up into a smile on one side. The hand she has on her chest—like some oldie-timey lady getting ready to swoon.

Though everything about her is pretty far from swooning, I know. It's Cameron who looks like he's about to fall over, and for the second time he tells me "No." As though he suspects some sort of plan behind all of this, some little scheme me and Kitty cooked up while he was busy being normal and decent.

Which seems crazy, until I think of his story again. The one he knows I read.

"What's he saying no to?" Kitty asks, but oh she looks as though she understands, all right. Her mouth is now the very definition of the word *tease*, and she takes a step closer for every single one he tries to take back.

"He's not saying no," I tell her—though I swear, I try to stop myself. I try to feel jealous or weird about all of this, I do. It's just that it won't come, and before I can get a proper grip on myself more words spill out: "He has a safe word for that."

Cameron snaps his gaze down to me, teeth clearly gritted, suddenly. And I guess it looks like anger, on him—his fingers press tight into mine and his body locks, like he's about to do something bad.

Only the thing of it is—he doesn't say the word. He doesn't say the word that will stop this. And though Kitty squeals and dances a little closer, his erection doesn't flag.

"A *safe* word," she marvels, as though she's never heard the term before—even though I know full well she has. "So, like, he could say no, while meaning yes?"

I think he tries to keep his expression simmering somewhere around anger, but if so he utterly fails. The moment she says *no meaning yes*, his eyes flicker wide and his body jerks toward me, that grip he's got on my hands turning to water.

Somehow, I've got the feeling that she's going to be much, much better than me, at this.

"Like, say, if I were to run my hand down over his ass in a way he wanted to pretend he didn't like…"

I can't even imagine what it is she does. It makes him put a fist into his mouth, at the very least—though from where I'm sitting it hardly looks like anything. She just runs a hand down behind him somewhere and then he's clenching all over, even something as stupid as a pretend protest completely lost to him.

"Is that nice?" she asks, with just a hint of giggle in her voice. "I think he likes it, Allie!"

And it's true, he does. A fat bead of precome wells up in the slit at the tip of his cock, and when it overflows and spills down the solid shaft she makes another giddy sort of noise. I can't stop myself thinking, deliriously, that he had her so right—that it was her in his story, alongside me. It was her, all mean and innocent at the same time, and now she's going to twist everything upside down and inside out.

"Oh that's so nice of you, Cam," she says, and I feel my cheeks heat for him. I know what she's going to point out.

"Giving us something to lick up, like that. You want to lick it up, Allie?"

Our eyes lock, in that one burning moment. And then she asks, and it's as though she's communicating something to me. Something underneath the words, about the level of my consent.

"Or shall we both do it?"

Cam sags against my hands, his body practically fizzing. When he puts one heavy hand on my shoulder, it feels as though he wants to squeeze me down to nothing. Like he could just force this all away from him if he really tried.

Not that he seems to want to.

"I'll hold him," I tell her, and he groans my name. His eyes are closed, but I can almost feel him focusing on me. "And you suck him off."

Kitty sighs, then—all bliss. I watch her sink to her knees by the bed, slowly, slowly—not like the jagged actions of the girl in the story, but no less arousing for it—and then she leans toward him. Mouth open, hands by her sides.

It's like I'm one part of the body, and she's the other. Like we're two people strung tight together by the same purpose.

When she murmurs that he's so thick, and long, and stiff, I'm the one who feels it.

And then she licks a wet stripe over the head of Cam's cock, and I'm sure I can feel that too. The sensation of being stroked like that, and of stroking—it zings through me, hot and strong, and though I try to get away from it, doing so proves impossible.

It's like the stories and Cam's strange will and Kitty's teasing mouth have hold of my sense and my vocal chords, and both combine together to say all kinds of wicked things.

"Yeah, suck him good," I tell her, but it's Cam who reacts.

"Ohhhh God I'm really close," he blurts out, as she laps at the gleaming swollen head of his cock. But I've got to remember that I'm in control here—even more so than Kitty, really, because I know the safe word and she doesn't—and I have to call the shots.

I have to show him that it's me doing this, all me.

"Stop," I say, and yank her back so suddenly that two sets of blue eyes flash wide at me. Their expressions mirror each other so closely that it's comical, for a second—like two kids having their favorite toy snatched away.

But then I explain, and two pairs of bright, startled eyes become something heated, and wanting.

"We don't want him to go off too quickly, do we?"

I think she likes that idea almost as much as I do, because her grin broadens and suddenly I can see all of her neat little white teeth. She runs that pink pointed tongue over both rows of them, mouth so close to his cock she could kiss it, if she had a mind to.

But she doesn't. She plays along with me, instead.

"That would be such. A shame."

"Exactly."

"I mean, you've hardly even gotten to taste it," she says, still big-eyed. Still full of musing innocence, in her tone. Though I've got to say, she's pretty far from musing innocence in her words. "Here... want to try?"

She strokes him lightly, tugging him ever closer to my waiting mouth. Of course I put on a show of nonchalance, and barely let her graze my lips with the slick red tip, but I can't deny that inside I'm boiling.

It's the *noises* Cameron's making. Those little stunted *ahs* are long gone, and in their place is the kind of filthy guttural groaning that only porn stars make. His hips roll toward the clasp of something that isn't there, over and over, and when I lap at the slickness coating the head of his cock he breathes out in a tense rush.

But more than that, he finds his voice.

"More," he gasps out, then after a tense and desperate moment: "Suck my cock."

It's like hearing Jesus curse somebody out.

"You want me to make you come in my mouth?" I ask him, and he visibly balks at the more graphic version of his demand. So I make it firmer, surer—not a question. "I think we should just kiss around the head of your cock, and see what happens."

"Oooh, yeah," Kitty says, because she's amazing. She's amazing, and it takes nothing at all for her to simply lean in and curl her tongue around that sweet spot on the underside of his prick, while I lick over that juicy slit.

It takes nothing for me, either. I'm so wound tight, so slick and swollen between my legs that anything would seem like a good suggestion right now. I want to strip and have them both lick my stiff clit, or maybe ride this fat cock while Kitty sits astride his face or God, God—I can taste her lipgloss on him.

I can almost feel her mouth on mine around the thick stretch of his cock, and when she murmurs into his slick flesh, when she says something dirty and good like *Mmmm, yeah, you want to taste his come, Allie?* I think *I* almost go over.

I've got no idea how Cameron's holding on. It seems insane that he's gotten this far, with two girls pushing him and sucking on him and, oh man, oh man, I think she's stroking between the cheeks of his ass.

In fact, she's definitely stroking between the cheeks of his ass, and when she does something completely beyond the pale he lurches forward quite suddenly, his cock sliding along my cheek as though it had been aiming for somewhere warm and wet but will settle for this soft contact.

For the feel of my skin, as his cock jerks upward almost painfully, and a hot stripe of liquid paints my face.

"Fuuuccck," Kitty groans, as though it's almost as arousing for her as it is for me. Though I suppose it could well be—she has a handful of him, and when she strokes him suddenly, rapidly, her little fist pumping like nothing else, he gives it up for her too.

He lets her take a spurt of his come in her hot little mouth, before she aims his still swelling prick back at me.

I taste him, then. Salt-sweet and copious, great vicious jets of it flooding over my tongue. It's electric, impossible and, oh Lord, it's even better than that when he calls out my name.

"Allie, God, Allie," he moans, though it's the sound of his voice breaking in the middle that really does me in. Well—that, and the words he says next. "You make me come so hard, baby."

As though I'm the only one in the room. As though I'm the mastermind behind it all, the purveyor of his every carnal delight, even though it hadn't seemed like it at the time. Wasn't it Kitty?

She's the one, isn't she?

I look at her—mouth still slick with his spend, eyes as bright and sharp as a newly minted tack—and I can't imagine how I could ever equal her, how anyone could write that dirty story about the two girls with me in mind.

It has to be her, I think, but then I glance back up at him and he's just staring down at me, waiting. Waiting for me to say *You can lie down now* or maybe *Tell me how that felt.*

I don't go with either, however. Instead, I hold his gaze and say the kind of thing I know Kitty will be thinking. I know she will, but that's OK. Because it's me. It's me. I'm thinking it too and I have done all along.

"Well," I say to him. "What are you waiting for? We deserve a kiss for that, don't you think?"

Chapter Eleven

I don't know whether I meant to let things go this way or not. But they have done anyway. I wanted to explore all the facets of Cameron Lindhurst and…well. Kitty's like the Christopher fucking Columbus of sex.

She even says as much to me, as we're sitting in Professor Warren's old bedroom, dividing his button collection into awesome, weird and not-sure-it's-a-button.

He's so fucking raw and uncharted, she says. *Like new, unexplored territory.*

Which I suppose I could take badly. I could see it as a claim on the terra firma I've marked with my flag, and I would. I really would, if she didn't then say things like:

But you get to go there first, OK? You just tell me if you want me to back off—he obviously wouldn't mind. He looks at you like…like I don't know. Like you're some giant diamond he found at the bottom of a cesspool of idiots.

Of course, it makes me wonder what exactly the cesspool of idiots is, in this equation. Pembroke? Humanity in general? Wade?

I just can't tell, and I don't want to ask. I'm too busy just trying to let all of this settle for a while, to give Cameron some space without the pressure of sudden threesomes. I mean, he's definitely the kind of guy who needs space. He always chooses the armchair on its own, and he likes long runs by himself, and after he'd kissed us both—in a number of sweet places—he had fallen asleep with his body so far from Kitty's it looked as though he'd erected some mystical force field.

As though he just wanted to forget or pretend or I don't know. I can't figure him out. It's three days later and I still can't make head nor tail of the Thing We Did, not even when he comes to my bedroom door quite suddenly, at 11:30 p.m.

I mean, he just stands there. And then after a long, weird moment in which he glances between me and Kitty—her curled up by the pillows with a fistful of playing cards, me sprawled across the width of the bed with a story of hers in my hand—he goes with: "I just thought I'd come and say…good night."

Of course, I think of all the times I've heard him hesitate before getting a particular word out, and what him doing so usually means. He's got another word in his head, instead—one that isn't good night.

And his hands are sweaty too. I watch him wipe them on his pajama bottoms—this time they're striped blue and white, instead of all one color the way they were the night before—and then he seems to gather himself. Folds his arms across his chest, you know—that sort of thing.

"Good night then, Cam," Kitty says, and she gets just the right hint of cheek into her voice. The way she did so perfectly when we all decided to go mad and act out one of Cameron's wildest fantasies.

Because it was, wasn't it? I mean, I didn't really let myself think about it too much, at the time—and I'm certainly trying not to think about it now. But what it boils down to at its core is a desire of his, made flesh.

"Uh, OK," he says.

Weird how two such nothing words—uh and OK—make my stomach dip. They do more than that, in fact. My nipples automatically stiffen beneath my T-shirt, and my clit twinges. Just once. Just enough to let me know why I haven't masturbated over these past few days.

Because I've been waiting for this. I have. And even more incredibly—so has Cameron.

He makes to leave—awkwardly, too slowly—and my heart prac-tically races with the realization. *He* has come to *us*.

He doesn't want distance at all! He wants to get down with this, the dirty little bastard!

And then I look at Kitty, and she's almost bursting with laughter. Her lips are squeezed tight together and her body's shaking, while tears of sheer amusement start making their way down her cheeks.

I have to whack at her to get her to knock it off. He'll never recover if he thinks she's laughing at his bizarre attempts to initiate further threesomes.

"Cam!" I call out, just as Kitty whacks me in return. "Cam—come back here!"

And he does. But he looks decidedly less hesitant and unsure by the time he finds my doorway again.

"Are you guys fucking with me?" he asks, suddenly bullish. Bruised too, I think—in a way I definitely don't want him to be. I mean, we might have done a few sexual things that definitely count as "fucking with someone," but that's different.

One is a game I want him to enjoy. The other is rooted in emo-tions I didn't even know he felt on a regular basis.

"No, honey," Kitty murmurs, as she wriggles back into the pillows behind her. "We're not fucking with you—though I think my esteemed colleague and I might like to."

It's cute, her saying something like that. And she pulls it off—everything about her living up to her name. So kittenish and sexy and ready for all kinds of fun.

But I want some sincerity to be there too. I want him to know that I might thrill at the thought of acting on our wildest desires, but I also remember the picture he kept of me. The words he said to me through the darkness, about how much he wanted to see me when he finally got to kiss my lips.

"Come here to me, baby," I say, and for a moment it rings dumbly

in my ears. It isn't enough, it's too cornball, I should have said more—
Just let me hold you or *I want you so much* or something, something.

But as soon as I've spoken all the tension leaves his face, and
his eyes take on that delicious, smoky, hooded look. As though all
of the rigid sense that holds his mind together just pours right out
of him.

"Have you been waiting for us to come to you?" I ask, as he
closes the door behind himself.

And to my delight, he responds, "I kind of suspect I might
have been."

Of course it's nothing definitive. But I don't expect definitive
from him. I expect words said in between other words, and lots of
hedging and use of vagaries. And you know what? This vagueness
no longer hurts or leaves me baffled. This vagueness just makes it
sweeter when he actually walks over to the bed, leans down, and
finds my mouth with his.

He kisses me deeply too. Hungrily. As though he's spent the
last three days on some kind of tremulous precipice, unable to push
himself over. It makes me wonder if he's masturbated, or if he's
stored up all that delicious sexual energy for me to savor, now.

It's not that farfetched an idea. I've done the same thing. I've
done it so that I can feel my clit right now, as solid as anything—every
part of me so aroused that I'm willing to go as far as he might want.

It makes me a different person, being this turned on. It makes
me moan when Kitty laughs and says *I never realized you guys were so
horny*, in a voice that tells tales about her own feelings on the matter.

Her own feelings make her reach forward and yank on Cameron's
arm, until he sprawls forward on the bed as though he's made of
nothing at all. So solid, in reality, and so light as air when it comes
to something like this! It's a beguiling contrast, and it's made more
so by the stifled sound he makes when he pushes face first into the
bed sheets.

"God, he's so *pliable*," Kitty says, and then she takes my hand and places it on his back—so clear and clever that I can read what she means me to do without asking. *Hold him there*, I think, and I shiver.

"You really want this, huh, big guy?" she says, and I realize— much as Cam seems to—that this is the last time she's going to give him an out. He can back away right now, if he wants to.

Though somehow I know he never will. He didn't say *Do whatever you want to me except XYZ*. He said *Do whatever you want to me.* He said *Don't ask.*

And really, we don't need to. I mean, she knows all about his stories now. I didn't mean to tell her everything but somehow I ended up doing it anyway, and now she's got this little ace in the hole. She's got what I have: a sure and thrilling knowledge of everything he doesn't know he always wanted.

But still, I don't expect her to use it so quickly. And so ruthlessly too.

"You know, Allie's told me all about your...little foibles."

Oh God. Here we go.

"There's one in particular that caught my attention."

I mentally run through all the ones that caught mine: being attacked by two women; being forced to walk around the room like a dog complete with collar; sucking a man's cock; the sheer volume of biting scenes—as though he's secretly one of those crazed vampire fetishists. And then there was...

"But I think we'll have to get you a little more naked to make it happen."

I jerk, when she does it. Real quick—like ripping off a plaster. I'm not even sure how she manages it, to be honest, because Cam is so heavy and his legs are so long. But somehow she gets a hold of the waistband of his pajamas, and just rips those suckers right off of him.

All in one smooth move. Bam. Naked from the waist down. Perfectly curved ass exposed to the elements, just waiting for her to do things from the story about the girl with the dirtiest collection of sex toys I've never heard of.

"Go on," she says to me—smile as wicked as ever I've seen it—and I try to pretend I don't know what she means. I absolutely cannot see Cameron's description floating behind my eyes: of smooth skin covered in red bracelet bite makes, and then…and then…

"Or do you want me to?"

Cameron *mmpfs* out a moan, then does something I think I'll still be aroused over in a hundred years' time. He kind of squirms— as though he's attempting to get away. Only he makes a really poor job of it, because from where I'm sitting it looks as if he's actually trying to get up on all fours.

Like a bitch in heat, I think—just as he'd described it in his story. And, oh God, how my sex swells to consider it. Liquid floods my already drenched slit, and I'm sure I'm about to lose control of him. I can't hold him down when he's like this—all urgent and breathless—and I certainly can't after he's blurted out that he doesn't want Kitty to do it.

"Allie," he says. "Allie, God, Allie."

I glance at Kitty, only to find her grinning with all of her teeth. Like some miniature Machiavelli, so certain and sure in her powers that she can just sit back and watch me fumble toward him.

And when I get my teeth around the glorious curve of his flesh, I hear her applause in the background.

Cam grinds back into me hard, and I can't hold him. He's up on all fours now, for definite, but it's not those things I think about. I consider how soft his right cheek is, instead, how easily it gives under the press of my teeth.

And then I think about how much I want to soothe the pain I've just caused, with a long slow lick over the red brand he's now got.

He moans for that too. A sharp sound for the bite, and then a softer one for the soothing lick that follows. It's powerful, glorious, and made no less so by Kitty's words, humming through my body as I lick and suck and get closer to that groove between.

"Go on, go on," she says, and I don't have to look to tell that she's stroking herself. "Lick his pretty little arsehole."

It makes me want to give commands of my own, dirty ones that I didn't know I wanted. And when they come out in between tender little licks of his flawless ass, our moans tangle together. Cam's sharp and breathless—as though he can't quite believe how good something so simple feels—and Kitty's high and tight.

As though she knows all too well.

And finally mine, all mixed up with the things I want to say.

"Watch her," I tell Cam. "Watch her touching herself."

He turns his head automatically to see Kitty with her hand inside her shorts, the material shifting with every little move she makes—until she decides the view would be better with them off, of course.

I pause in the middle of marking Cameron's ass and watch her wriggle out of them too quickly, everything about her suddenly as breathless as Cam seems. As though she just can't wait to have all eyes on her juicy cunt, while she rubs and worries at her obviously stiff clit.

I can see it from here, standing out proudly between the neat little lips of her sex. She has almost no hair down there—of course she doesn't—but I'm pretty sure the view would be as delicious either way.

Or at least, I *think* it's delicious for Cam. For me it's just a reminder that my own clit is being sorely neglected, and for a moment I think about slipping my hand under the waistband of my pajamas. A couple of strokes would do it—I'm pretty sure.

But then I think about Cameron's mouth on me—or even better, the feel of his solid cock finally, finally stroking into my pussy—and I hold back. I need to hold back. I need to keep everything on an even keel, while my two partners in crime moan and writhe and talk about coming.

"Lick him, lick him," Kitty pants, but I don't need her to tell me anymore.

I want to taste him there, right over the tightly clenched knot of his arse, and when I do he makes a sound like something bursting. His fingers scrabble and grasp at the sheets, and I think about odd and random things.

Like the word *rimming*—so filthy and forbidden. Or at least, it's filthy and forbidden to him. I feel nothing but pure carnal delight when I finally manage to work my tongue into that too-tight ring of muscle, whereas he…well, he has some very interesting things to say about it.

"God, don't, that's disgusting," he says to me, loud and clear. And I suppose if I didn't know him so well, I'd stop at that. I'd feel ashamed for licking and lapping between his arse-cheeks, until he feels just as slippery as anything there, and twice as hot. But I *do* know him, now—I really do.

I know him so well that I wait for him to say the words I'm sure are coming, hot on the heels of that great big bucket full of mortification.

And they do. They do.

"Oh Jesus, I think I'm going to come," he blurts out, at which point my body sings. Oh God it just *sings*. Just hearing him say something like that, about something like this—it's enough to get me searingly close to orgasm.

Though I'll admit I'm pulled back, somewhat, by the sound of someone knocking on the door. Like the ghost of Professor Warren, come back to tell us all off for participating in dirty, rimming-based threesomes.

We all freeze in position. Of course, I suspect that Kitty and Cameron aren't thinking of the dead haunting our ménage—Wade is the much more plausible assumption, my brain tells me, in between lust spasms—but even so. They don't just carry on with their almost-orgasms and their copious frantic moans of ultimate pleasure.

They turn and look at me, instead, as though I'm the arbiter of this door-knockery. And then just to make it clearer, Kitty hisses: "What do we do now?"

I want to laugh. Of course I do. But then the door-knocker would hear me. And it's definitely going to be Wade, because, well… everyone else who currently lives in this house is right in this room, having sex.

But with this understanding comes the only possible end to the equation *Cameron + Kitty + Allie*. Any way you look at it, it's going to equal: one seriously pissed off Wade.

"What the fuck are you guys doing in there?"

Oh yeah. He's pretty pissed off, all right. So pissed off that I think we all actually look worried for a moment. As though Wade's going to come in here and start hurling things, or something—which he totally isn't. And even if he was, Cameron—of all people—is the one to defuse the tension:

"Just tell him we're all in here…eating ice cream."

Kitty giggles and I can't help following suit. He just says it so deadpan, so calmly, and with his bare ass sticking up in the air too. It makes me wonder what he'd do if the equation was Kitty + Allie + Wade, and I've got to say—I don't think he'd be a hammering-on-the-door, throwing-a-tantrum-in-the-hallway asshole about it.

I think it's much more likely that he'd just take it with the same brooding, almost-bruised calm he takes everything, until I fall head over heels in love with him and try to eat his face off. Or eat his ass out.

Whichever.

"Seriously, man, this is *not* cool," Wade says, and it makes me wonder why he doesn't just open the door. The Wade I know is all about sauntering into a room, as breezy as anything.

This Wade is…I don't know. Unraveling at the seams? Mad with jealousy?

He certainly sounds like it.

"So come in then," Kitty says, and I have to say I have no compunction to refuse her. I don't even think Cameron does. He just stays exactly where he is, naked from the waist down and with his ass still practically in my face—which seems singularly unlike him, on the face of things.

But underneath, oh underneath. Underneath, I understand perfectly well. What better way to stick it to someone, than having them find you being serviced by two women? And he *is* being serviced. A fool could tell it. He's got my bite marks all over his pale skin, and Kitty has one hand between her legs and one hand on his great curved back.

"Hey, Wade, how you doing?" he says and, oh God, I love him I love I just love him. In the middle of all of his shame-based issues, there's this incredible streak of humor—as liquid metal as his glorious voice.

And I want to *eat* it.

"Fuck," Wade says, and boy oh boy it comes out as hard as a bullet. His face is the color of Cameron's—red as a fresh new apple—but for different reasons. Anger, I think—but there's something else there too. A little hint of embarrassment, maybe, in amongst all the rest of it.

"How long have you guys been having this party without me, seriously?"

Trust him to call it a *party*. And also: is it wrong if I get the sudden and mysterious urge to tell him *since college*? It doesn't seem that farfetched, after all. In truth, I'm not even sure *why* we haven't been doing this since college.

"I've been trying to get this going for *weeks*," he adds, after a second. Hands on his hips. Blue eyes *almost* showing an amused awareness of exactly what he's saying. God, he's such a manipulative prick!

"Get what going?" Kitty asks, but she should know. And she does, after a moment of musing. "A foursome?"

Wade puts a hand out, palm down—the universally accepted gesture for *Let's calm things down a little here.* Not that I think he actually wants to calm anything down. And Kitty's mischievous grin tells me that nothing's going in that direction anyway.

"Well, maybe not a foursome exactly," he says, only then he grins back at her, all wolfishness again. "But you know. Not that far away from one either."

And then Kitty crooks a finger at him and I can't help it. A great flood of weariness goes through me, while my mind throws up the words *Oh. Just like that, huh?* Because you know—Wade *always* gets things just like that. I was actually enjoying seeing him squirm and stamp his foot, because I'm so filled with the memories of him getting the opposite of that, it's painful. It feels like I'm bursting with those images—of girls rolling over for him and guys slapping him on the back and professors saying, hey, don't worry about it.

You're Wade Robinson. You don't have to worry about anything.

And now here's Kitty, crooking her finger and beckoning him over as though yeah, he should just get this too. Me and Cameron have blundered and fumbled our way toward one tiny little bit of fun, but no big deal. Throw it at Wade, the moment he walks into the room.

Only then…then…oh Lord, my lovely little Kitty. I think I almost punch the air, when she presses a hand to his chest. He's almost on her, the assumption so obviously all over him I can see it from here:

He thinks he's going to fuck her now. But I've got to say—I don't think he is.

"Ah ah ah," she says, and there's such steely control in her voice.

How does she *do* that? She's so tiny—the hand she's still got on Cameron's back looks ridiculously small. And yet she holds him in place as though all the world is at her command, as though *she* is the Queen of Hamin-Ra.

Lord, I don't think I could ever be. I certainly couldn't say what she next does to Wade.

"If you want to join in, you've got to start where we left off."

At first, I don't get what she's saying. But Cameron *definitely* does. Oh yeah, Cameron gets it all right—he goes tight all over, suddenly, and when I stroke a soothing hand down over his ass he flinches.

As though maybe someone else entirely did the honors, while I wasn't looking.

"No," he says, as flat and cool as the surface of a lake.

But I can't help noticing that he doesn't use the word *Tehanu*. And he gets no closer to blurting it out when Kitty clarifies, for a narrow-eyed Wade.

"I mean, that's only fair, right?" she asks—only you know. She's not really asking. "We were seeing to Cameron, when you walked in. So if you want to interrupt, you should at least offer him some payment, for the privilege."

I think I worry right through my lower lip. My heart pounds in time with every single *no* Cameron utters, and by God there are a lot of them. They get louder and louder in volume too, but still, *still* he doesn't use *the* word. He doesn't try to get up or walk out and I've got to say—even *I'm* willing him to do any or all of the above, by now.

I don't want him to be hurt. I don't want anything to hurt him—not ever.

"You can't be serious," Wade says, in that buttery voice of his— the one he uses to oil his way out of any tricky situation.

"I mean, I know what you guys were doing."

I had wondered. What exactly does rimming sound like, through a door?

"And there's just *no way* I'm going to do that."

Thank God, I think, though I'm pretty sure my brain speaks too soon. Because a minute after the words drift behind my eyes, Kitty sinks back onto the bed. All neat pointed toes and *Playboy* pin-up posing.

"Well," she says. "I guess Rudolph won't be playing any reindeer games tonight."

Lord in heaven, I think she's made out of pure bonkbuster. It's like Jackie Collins wrote her. It's like Jackie Collins wrote her as the person I want to marry most, in all the world. I'm sniggering without even meaning to, for God's sake. Wade is looking at me like he wants to kill me, and I'm *still* sniggering.

"Hey, Cameron," she says, while her devil's eyes stay on Wade. "You want to fuck me, now? Oooh, no—I bet I know what you want. I bet you want to line me and Allie up on the bed, and then take turns. First you can slide that big, delicious cock of yours in her tight little cunt—and oh, you know she'll be so tight and sweet— and then you can try mine."

I don't mind admitting it: pleasure gushes through me. And I think it goes through Wade too, because his mouth comes open and his gaze flicks down to Cameron, just as Kitty adds: "It'll be like pin the tail on the donkey. Only with orgasms."

She is very, very bad. And getting badder by the second.

"And if I do that," Wade says, after what is possibly the longest pause in history. "If I do…*something* to him—" Oh God he knows. He definitely knows she means *rimming*. "—you'll let me have that?"

He glances at me then. Something like despair on his face, I think.

"Will you let me fuck you, Allie?"

I picture what Kitty described: me and her, lined up on the bed. Waiting to be filled, waiting to be fucked, both of us moaning and begging, most probably. And the thing of it is—all I can see is

Cameron. So I suppose it's doubly cruel of me to say, finally: "Lick him there, and I just might."

I expect him to ask for something more, in return. I mean, me and Kitty are going to get a show. It seems only fair that he gets one too.

Only he doesn't so much as demand we snog each other, while he actually puts his face in a place I've only been once before. I've never even licked someone's arsehole, prior to this moment, so it seems like an almost impossible ask of a man like Wade.

But after he's palmed his face a few times, and maybe taken a few deep breaths, and also ripped off his shirt like the Incredible Hulk, so that me and Kitty are fully aware of how manly he is before he does this…he manages to stroke one hand down Cameron's extremely solid flank.

Of course, Cameron bucks like a rough-ridden stallion and tries to get away. But I've got to say—he doesn't try that hard. He gets about as far as a hand on my thigh, gripping tight, too tight to bear, and then he burns a stare right at me until I can't look away.

I want to watch what Wade does. I do. It's just that it's impossible with Cameron in front of me, his expression so muddled by tension and anger and heated, unquestionable greed that I think it melts me on the spot. He wants this, I think, he wants it in some feral, retaliatory sort of way, and I won't deny that I take some pleasure in it too.

This low, mean sort of smile spreads across his face—slow, like burning syrup—and it's so delicious I want to taste it. I want to taste it while Wade licks long and wet over the rudest place on his entire body, and I do.

I just lean right down and kiss his mouth, expecting something soft, I think. Something tentative. But in truth I think he passed soft and tentative about three hours ago, because what I get is a lot like having my mouth eaten off.

He bites me—he actually bites me—and I can hear every moan and sigh passing through his body and into me. Though it only occurs to me that he's doing to me what Wade's doing to him when he licks into my mouth—dirtily, wetly—and finally drags me down until I'm almost beneath him.

And then he fucks me with his tongue, the way Wade is fucking him. I know he does, because I can hear Kitty moaning that Wade is such a dirty bastard.

"Go on, go on—lick him right there," she says, as Cameron all but grunts into my mouth. I think about how aroused he was before, how close to coming, but then suddenly I don't have to imagine anymore.

He pushes forward when Wade does something particularly dirty, and I feel his thick, slick cock slide against my thigh. Of course he backs off almost immediately, but that just means I get to see his face again. So flushed, and lust-slack, and *mine*. All mine.

"Does that feel good, baby?" I ask, and this time he doesn't need anything else. He doesn't need me to demand. He just answers, breathlessly, that it feels incredible.

While his hands pull and tug at my pajamas.

"I want you," he tells me. "I want you."

And I swear, I don't think I've ever heard anything finer. I help him get me out of my clothes, all in a frantic rush, the strength of whatever Wade's doing making him sloppy. Hell—it's making me sloppy. I can hear the slick sounds of Wade's mouth as he gets greedier and greedier about it, Kitty egging him all the while, and it's making me so wet that Cameron shudders when he finally gets a hand between my legs.

He strokes through my silky slit, easy as a knife going through hot butter, and when he gets to my grasping hole he just slides all the way in. Two thick fingers, as simple as anything.

I don't even recognize the sound that comes out of me. I certainly don't recognize the words: *fuck, yeah, fuck me now, fill my cunt, fuck, Jesus, I want it, I want it.* And then I feel him pushing blindly against the side of my face with his, like an animal seeking comfort, and I can't stand it. I can't.

"Oh yeaaahhh put your finger in his ass," Kitty says, and I can't stand that. I don't want to look—it's too much. All I can hear are dirty words and the slippery sounds of Kitty rubbing her clit or maybe Wade finger-fucking Cameron the way he's finger-fucking me, and then something else. Something else that I can't quite pinpoint—a rustling sound, and the bed creaking.

Then Kitty says, loud and clear: "Go on and do it."

Of course I've got no idea what she means. She could be talking about pinching her nipples with clothes pegs, for all I know—she's kinky enough for just about anything.

But Wade isn't, apparently, because after a second he lets out a little frustrated breath, and tells her no.

"No—I want your cunt," he tells her, and I can't think what she offered him instead. Her mouth? Her ass? Something I don't really want to process, right now?

But then I have to process it, because I feel Cameron panting against my mouth, eyes as wide and round as moons, and when I twist I can just about see Kitty's hands on Wade's cock, as she sheaths it in a condom she probably got from *my* bedside drawer.

Then slicks him with lube she *definitely* got from my bedside drawer.

Of course I have to ask Cameron if he's OK. I don't give a shit about Wade—I care about Cameron and, by God, Wade is doing something absolutely filthy to him right now. I know he is—I know it before he says a word to me, though they spill out of him when I hold his face and ask.

"He's…" Cameron starts, then squeezes his eyes tight shut before he can get out the rest. "He's scissoring his fingers inside me."

I think it's the dirtiest sentence I've ever heard another person utter. Never mind Cameron, who started trembling about five minutes earlier and has now reached critical mass. I can feel his cock against my thigh, so slick and swollen it's like getting stroked by a baseball bat coated in engine oil.

Though I've no idea why a baseball bat would be coated in engine oil. And it's beside the point anyway. It's beside so many, many points. The primary one being: Wade is going to fuck him. Wade is going to put his cock inside Cameron and fuck him, and even more thrilling/insane/terrifying—Cameron doesn't look like he wants to choke out his safe word, in answer to Kitty's absolutely disgusting persuasions.

"Mmm, yeah, make that little arsehole nice and slick. You want to fuck it, huh? Go on, go on—God you're making me so wet," she says, while I try to keep Cameron focused on me. If he focuses on me, he can say no. He can tell me what he really wants, how he really feels—but apparently how he really feels is this: "Oh Jesus, yeah, right there."

I'll be perfectly honest. It's not me who makes him come out with that. And then Wade jerks his hand in the exact same way, again, and oh it's definitely not me who's pushing Cameron past the point of no return.

I think Wade is hitting his prostate, and when I manage to curl and look up at Wade's face—all red with determination and something like bitter anger—I know for sure. He's tormenting Cameron, absolutely tormenting him, and in that moment I so want to tell him to stop.

I want to make Cameron say his safe word, for God's sake— which just seems crazy. Though it's crazier that Wade is almost certainly pushing his cock into Cameron's body, right now. I know he is, because Cameron chokes out a sob and Kitty moans that she's going to come all over her own hand, and Wade can't seem to say anything at all.

He just falls to jerking against Cameron, sloppily, until Cameron can't seem to take it anymore. But that's OK, because neither can I. There's a guy getting fucked on top of me, and he's got his curled fingers right up against my G-spot and, oh Lord, that's heavenly, it's unbearable. "Cam," I gasp, while he shoves and manhandles me up the bed.

Of course, I only figure out why he's doing it when I feel his tongue lashing over my clit. And then after I can't figure out anything anymore. He's got his hands on my ass and he's pressing his face hard against my spread pussy, and all I can think of is how it must feel to have a prick sliding against the nerve-rich opening of such a tight little place, how it must feel to be opened and separated.

But all that does is make me realize something incredible: Wade is fucking Cameron, before he's fucked me. I've never had Wade anywhere between my legs, but he's right there between Cameron's. And he seems to be enjoying it too, after a moment of panting and thrusting and hot wet slapping sounds.

His breathing gets shaky and his thrusts get jagged, and then I hear Kitty say in an almost relaxed sort of voice: "You gonna come, baby? You gonna fill him with your load? Yeah, that's it. Spurt in his ass."

Because she knows, apparently, what gets Wade going more than anything. I don't know when she learned this information, but judging by Wade's hoarse moans it's a solid source. They ring out loud and clear, these moans, and I'm reminded of how much I would have paid to hear them, once upon a time.

But now all I can feel are the sounds Cameron is making, right into the swollen folds of my pussy. His frantic gasps as he licks and laps at my clit, followed by long, luxurious moans that burr through me, too heavily.

He's going to come, I think—he's going to come just from the feel of a big, fat cock in his ass—but I'm not sure I believe it until it actually happens. His mouth mashes messily against my stiff little bud, and then a second later I feel something slippery and hot splashing against some part of my leg.

I can't mistake it for anything but the thing it is. It comes in rhythmic pulses, so intense and glorious that I can't help myself. I call out his name as great surges of pleasure roll through me, cunt clenching around his still-working fingers, body shaking under the pressure of it all.

"Ohhh I'm coming," I think I manage to gasp out, but it's much easier to just go with the word I want to say most of all.

"Cameron," I say. "Cameron."

And yes, I know how this would seem if I was writing a story about it. *Subtext*, Professor Warren would say, and I'm sure he'd be right. Wade just fucked Cameron while Cameron fucked me, and there's probably supposed to be a lot of metaphorical bullshit in there about how that really means I still want to fuck Wade, or that I need a barrier between me and Wade before I can do it, or fuck—I don't know.

But the truth is: this isn't a story. It's not a tale I'm telling. It's real and there's only Cameron's name on my tongue, Cameron's arms around me, Cameron shuddering through every big breath as he presses his face to my thigh, my hip, my belly.

Then he looks up at me, long and slow, and I'm so grateful I can't help myself. I think it before I even know it's a part of me, that I want to feel it, that it's as real as the story I'm not telling.

I love you, my mind shouts out, and though it should be terrifying it isn't. It's only terrifying to discover that I don't have the courage to say it—just like back in college, and all that time I wasted over someone as nothing as Wade.

Chapter Twelve

I'VE OPENED A LITTLE crack in him, I think. So it doesn't seem like too much of a hardship to just slip under his skin a bit. To just ask him a couple of questions that have been burning in me for the better part of the last twenty hours.

Questions like: "Was it too much?"

He's lying on his stomach—in my bed now, not his—with the latest chapter of "Hamin-Ra" in his hands. The one in which the Queen declares to Corin that she loves him above all things. You know—just to underscore the point to him in great big bold lettering. Just to ease myself into the idea of telling him, in a way I could never tell Wade.

It's you I love, I think at him, but it's no more effective than it was last time. It won't come out of me and he can't seem to read between the lines. Mainly because he's an impenetrable fortress when he wants to be, and the sign above the giant fortress-y door says *I'm never going to believe you because you just spent the last five years loving the wrong guy.*

And then you let him fuck me.

God, I really hope that's just me inventing thoughts to go inside his labyrinthine and mysterious mind.

"Was what too much?" he asks, because he's labyrinthine and mysterious, I guess. He's leading me down the corridor that takes me back to the beginning again, instead of the one that takes me to the heart.

"The stuff we did, Cam. The stuff. You know."

I say "you know" because I can't bring myself to go with "and then Wade shoved his dick up your ass." I mean, that has to be causing him some conflict, right? How come he doesn't look conflicted?

Wade sure does, and he was practically a sexual mountain climber before all of this. If you'd put the pair of them side by side and asked me which one would be comfortable fucking a man, I'd never have gone with Cameron. Never never never.

And yet he *looks* comfortable. He looks content. He looks like someone who's probably realized he's gay and is now just putting the final touches on his plan for a civil partnership with Wade Robinson.

"Ah," he says, and I practically sag with relief. Until he finishes with: "You mean the re-plastering of the downstairs hallway. Well. It certainly seemed a *little* excessive."

I flick his shoulder.

"Come on, Cam. Yesterday you had someone's cock in your ass."

It sounds even ruder when I say it out loud. But he doesn't blush, or shrug me off—the way he had when I first tried to make him talk about sex or his feelings or just anything at all. It's like...I don't know. Like something's let go, inside him.

"Wade's cock," he says, and there's something so devilish and triumphant about the grin he shoots me that I have to say. I just have to.

"If you tell me you've been holding a torch for him too, I'm going to kill myself. Then kill you."

He laughs, then, half-burying his face in the pages he's still holding. It's a good sound to hear, I have to say.

"No! *No.* Absolutely no torches are being held for Wade." He looks up at me, as the laugh dies down. Eyes slowly moving from amused to something soft focus and sweet. "Just you. Just you, and anything you want to make me do."

I put a hand in his hair, for that. Stroke through the thick strands until his eyes drift closed, and he presses into my touch.

"I didn't make you do that," I say, but he keeps on rubbing against me—like a cat in heat, I think.

"No...but you make it easy."

"Easy to do what?"

"All of the things I never knew I always wanted." He pauses then, while I catch my breath. By the time he starts talking again, I think my pounding, love-addled heart is back to normal speed. "You make me feel normal."

"You *are* normal," I say, but for the barest second he doesn't look convinced. And though he then goes on to pull me down into his arms, that idea is troubling. So troubling that I can't quite shake it—not even when he starts telling me how much he loves the chapter I've just written.

He even goes into the reasons why. Because it's *dirty*, he says, with the kind of relish I never thought I'd see from him.

"Tell me how," I say, and he bites at my hand. So playful, suddenly, so not the guy I thought he was.

"Because she gags him."

He snaps at my upper arm, this time, and I wonder what he's angling for exactly.

"You like that part, huh?"

"There are a lot of parts I like in this particular story," he tells me, and this time he succeeds in sinking his teeth into my flesh. Close to my shoulder, hard enough to sting—but oh, then he licks over the mark he's made and all I can think of is how he'd looked, with the bite marks all over his smooth, upturned ass.

"Like the bit when Corin gets forced by those three guys?" I ask, suddenly breathless. He'd seemed so bullish after I'd read it out, that I have to know how he feels about it now.

And he doesn't disappoint.

"Let's say—it's certainly gotten more interesting now I know where my prostate is."

I laugh, shocked, and tell him, "I think I've warped you." But he doesn't let up.

"Your words have warped me. There are whole days when I can't think about anything but the way your stories used to make me feel. The way they make me feel now."

God he's glorious when he talks like that. It makes me imagine stupid stuff, like flowers unfurling and birds flying and, Lord Almighty, how ridiculous is it to be thinking of someone so massive and masculine like that?

Very ridiculous.

I run my hands all over that massive masculinity, instead. He's pretty much naked—just a towel still half-around his waist, from the shower he took before he woke me—and I uncover various parts of him.

The heavy, rounded shape of his shoulders, in particular, before moving down to his solid chest. He twists as I run my hands over things, but he doesn't try to stop me. I don't think he'd ever try to stop me now, which is so freeing I can't even say.

I just get to tug at his tight, sensitive nipples until he breathes hard and unsteady, then maybe slide down to the thick outline of his hipbone, beneath his honeyed skin. There are marks there for me to uncover—strange, shadowy marks that I don't understand, at first.

But then I realize and have to take an extra sharp breath. The marks are the bruises Wade left behind, when he fucked the man I want to fuck, right now.

"Sometimes," he says, as I stroke over each finger imprint.

"I imagine how I'd tell my father about how I really am, inside. Not upstanding, not reserved, not worthy of the Lindhurst name. But I can't *ever* imagine telling him how I got those bruises. I can barely believe how I got those bruises."

"They're beautiful," I tell him, because that's the first and truest thing that comes to mind. They make me want to kiss them, and I do. I kiss them while he's still gazing down at me, half in that world he grew up in, half out of it.

More than half out it, I think. After all, he moans when I lick over each shadowy mark. And when I stroke my hand down over his side, he turns as though there's something more he wants me to do.

Like maybe get a nice handful of his ass, and squeeze. Though I have to say—I don't expect him to blurt out some words, when I do it. And I certainly don't expect the words to be so lust-choked either.

"Ohhh God, I wanted it to be you."

I glance up at him, but his eyes are tight closed. The way they were the night before, when Wade first…did that.

"Wanted what to be me?" I ask, because I've genuinely got no idea. I swear to God, I don't.

"What he did to me. I wanted it to be you."

My mind draws a blank again. Probably because I'm an idiot, but also because…well…I don't have a cock. I *can't* do what Wade did to him. I mean, maybe I could if I had something, but it's possible that he just means—

"Like this?" I ask, and then I run my finger between the cheeks of his ass. Just like I did the night before, only with a touch more suggestive pressure.

"Uhhhh yes," he says, both syllables so drawn out that all I hear is one long burr.

But that's not the best part. No, the best part is how he looks, suddenly—completely abandoned, mouth open and pressed against the pillow, eyes closed. And when I reach over him to get the little bottle of lube that's still on top of my bedside drawer, he gets worse.

His tongue flickers out, to wet his lower lip. His big body twists beneath my hands, then goes stiff when I spill a streamer of liquid between the cheeks of his ass.

"Are you really gonna do it?" he asks, to which there's only one real answer.

"Don't ask," I say, and then, oh then I slide my finger down through that hot groove, to the tiny tight circle of his arsehole.

I do it slow, slow—or at least, I intend to. But he's so shockingly relaxed that I just slide right in without really meaning to, all the way to the webbing between my fingers.

And it feels so different than the way I'd expected it to, even though I had no idea I'd been expecting anything at all.

It's slick and smooth, really smooth, and when he clenches around the intrusion it's not half as tight as I had thought it would be. But it's definitely hot, and he squirms and moans as much as I'd imagined, and when I rub and stroke he tells me in no uncertain terms: "Yes. Yeah—right there."

And then I can feel it—a little bump inside him, so small it's almost nonexistent. But, oh God, it makes him jerk and gasp when I press against it, and I can feel his cock brushing against my breasts, as stiff as anything.

I glance down and I can see it, swollen and stiff and so big, so mind-bendingly big. It almost feels wrong to want it inside me suddenly, because I'm sure it's going to half-kill me. I'm sure, and yet I'm slick anyway, thinking about it sinking all the way into my body. I want him to grab my hips the way Wade grabbed his, and shove into me with just that right amount of good, good pressure.

Like the pressure I'm applying now, over his prostate. The pressure that's making him shiver all over like a man who's just been plunged into a vat of icy water. And then he tells me *God, God, ohhhh you're making me do it*, and it becomes an absolute necessity to do what I'm craving.

"Fuck me," I order him, and for a moment he does nothing. He doesn't obey or even give me a sign that he's heard me. But when I rub myself against him—that ever-wet cock sliding wet trails over my tits—he seems to come around.

He focuses on me, laser-like suddenly, and this intensity only gets stronger when I tell him what I'd really like, more than anything:

"Fuck me while I fuck you."

He moans, then, hands suddenly greedy on my body. When he yanks me up the bed it's almost like the night before—like he's suddenly realized he's capable of manhandling someone, and needs to exercise that privilege right now.

But I also note that he doesn't do anything to disturb the slick finger I've still got in his ass. It's a struggle to get a condom, to get me beneath him, to maneuver our bodies into something like a sexual position with this seedy penetration going on at the same time, but he manages it.

He's really quite dexterous, when he wants to be. And he seems to know it too, because he bursts out a little laugh halfway through proceedings. As though he understands how clever and careful he's just been, and all in aid of something so filthy and ridiculous.

"You like that, huh?" I ask, but he just strokes a hand over my upturned face. Grins at me with all of his teeth, the way Wade would—only without any trace of smugness. He's happy, I think, and that sings through me like nothing else.

"Here, let me," I say, but I think that was a mistake. Getting the condom on him is like trying to squeeze a melon into an opening the size of a golf ball, with no lube and no end in sight. And I have to do it one-handed too, because my other hand is still seeing to him and, oh Lord, are we never actually going to have sex?

I'm pretty sure we're not, until he decides to help me out. And then I just have to watch the dark space between our bodies, as he works the thing on. Slowly, really agonizingly slowly and with all of these glorious frustrated sounds coming out of him, at the same time.

They get louder too, when I wriggle my finger inside him. He even gasps out a *No, don't do that for me*, just before he runs his big, fat cock down over my belly and then finally, oh finally between my legs.

There are several problems along the way, however. One is that I'm spreading my thighs as far as they'll go, but he still feels too massive to get them around him. And the other is a much easier to fix but far less likely to actually be resolved any time soon sort of problem—he doesn't seem to want to stop stroking my clit with the swollen head of his cock.

And I'll be honest—I don't really want him to stop, either. It feels absolutely incredible, so soft and hard at the same time and ohhh, just the right amount of slippery contact. Just a good, sweet slide over my stiff bud, until I'm shuddering and probably rubbing and fucking into him too hard and, oh man, oh man–

"Stop, stop—you're gonna make me come!"

I have to say it. I don't want to go over just yet and I can feel him triggering it, can feel it welling up from someplace low down in my belly. Any second and I'm there, and the slow, easy smile he's giving me isn't helping.

He kisses me with that same slow easiness, and I don't mind letting him know how good this all feels. I clutch at his shoulder and gasp into his mouth, and all the while I'm thinking about what he said to me under the stairs.

About how girls say they like a big cock, but really run a mile when one comes along.

Is that why he's doing this? Is that why he's waiting and waiting and, oh Jesus, can't he tell how ready I am? I'm so ready I think I could take a freight train. I'm so wet I can hear his cock sliding back and forth through my slit, and the thought is exciting enough to prompt me into doing some very dirty things to him.

I swear, I only meant to fuck him with one tiny little finger. I'm not sure how I end up pushing two in, until his face goes slack and his body judders from head to toe and he says to me, all in a rush: "I think I'm going to have to take you now."

God I love how he uses the word *take*. There are many, many things I hate about his old-fashioned politician vibe, but using a word right out of the porno Cary Grant never made is not one of them. Talk about *having me*, I think at him. Talk about what a *loose woman* I am, a fallen woman—I'll do my hair like Bettie Page and we can run away to the fifties together.

And just in case it wasn't clear enough by now: I have absolutely no idea what I'm thinking anymore. I'm delirious, lost on a tide of syrupy-sweet pleasure, and I show it when he finally, finally sinks into me.

He does it slow, so slow, while I make a sound like something dying. He just feels so solid, going in, so like something scratching a low down deep itch inside me, and then once he's there he rolls his hips all easy and languorous.

"God, Cam," I moan, then louder when he really goes for it. He can't seem to help it—which is even better, I've got to say. His eyes are half-closed and his body is jerking almost constantly, as though I'm pulling tight on some unseen strings without really knowing how I'm doing it.

Though I suppose I actually do know, in truth. I'm doing exactly what I said I wanted to—fucking him while he fucks me—and it's clearly too much for him. All efforts at suppressing the sounds he wants to make are gone, and he's grunting and gasping almost constantly. And when I shove my fingers into him hard, he lurches forward as though I struck him.

"I'm going to come," he tells me, so flat and matter-of-fact and yet somehow even more unbearably arousing than if he'd babbled it. It's like his whole sense of self is just accepting all of this now, like he's able to take it on board and let it out—no big deal.

And I love him for it.

Of course I love him more when he licks two fingers and slides them between our bodies—working hard to get into a good position for it, but getting there just the same—to worry and rub at my clit, but that's a given. I'm so swollen and so on edge that even the slightest glancing contact pushes me close, and then I feel him clench around my fingers.

I can actually feel it.

He's coming, I think, and the realization strikes through me, hard. My clit swells beneath his slippery touch and that's it, that's all it takes—my body bows and my cunt grips at his cock hard and I shout out his name just like I did the night before.

Only sweeter here, now. Oh God it's so much sweeter.

"Cam!" I say, and he pants and groans my name right back at me, cock jerking in my spasming pussy, body one solid, rigid mass between my legs. And he's so big too—so big I can almost feel it when he swells inside me and spurts, the thought like fire burning over my own orgasm.

It goes on for too long. I have to stop him—I have to dig my nails into his arm and force him to let me go, though when I do he doesn't seem to mind. He presses a hot, breathless kiss to the side of my face, instead, that amused sound he made for me earlier still thrumming through him.

Only then he says: "Sorry."

Just like always. As though we're right back to that place where sex is something to be ashamed of and he's always got to apologize for everything and, God, I could just kill him sometimes. Doesn't he know how great that was? Doesn't he understand, by now?

He can't possibly because he says it again, and I swear I'm just about to punch him when he finishes with: "Usually I can go a lot longer."

In so amused a tone that I can't fail to take only one idea away from it: If that was quick for him, what in God's name would slow be like?

—⁂—

When I come around from this doze I seem to have sunk into, he's reading again. One hand behind his head, as naked as a lord, pages clutched almost as tightly in his hands as they had been when he put on that little show for me.

The one I feel compelled to ask about, right now.

"Which bit did you do it to?"

He still jerks as though I'm catching him up to something. Even though we're in bed together, and the room smells like filthy, dirty sex.

"Do what to?" he asks, but I think he knows. I can tell by the way he turns away from me, as though, yeah, being caught masturbating is worse than having someone's finger in your ass. I mean seriously—where are his priorities?

"Which bit did you jerk off to?" I ask, and this time he answers more sensibly.

"When the Queen has Corin tied up, then does all of that…stuff in front of him."

I'd be disappointed that he still has to occasionally use one word in the place of another, but I can't be. It's part of his charm, I think. It's part of who he is, and I adore who he is.

"You like that part, huh?"

"Very much so."

"Because she torments him?"

It seems like a logical conclusion to come to. His masochistic streak isn't exactly well concealed anymore, and even if it was there's other stuff in that chapter. Stuff about being forced and subverting someone's will and all kinds of things that he seems to have a fetish for.

But as ever, he surprises me. He turns just when I think he's going to shy away, and gets his mouth real close to my ear. His breath gusts hot against the side of my face, and I feel a low ache start up between my legs. A good ache, that both reminds me of how thick and solid he'd felt, sliding in and out of me, and of how much I want him to again, right now.

And then he tells me, he tells me, so low and deep I can hardly bear it: "Because it's then that you know she loves him."

Chapter Thirteen

I HAVE TO SAY, I feel bad. I never thought I'd feel bad about something I did to Wade—ever since this whole thing started I've been sure I'd wind up hurting Cameron, somehow—but it's happened all the same.

He seems…unsettled. He won't eat breakfast with us. I was getting used to making massive omelets and now there's a whole big chunk of the thing we make in Professor Warren's huge frying pan left over, every day.

He seems prickly when I corner him too. As though the more relaxed Cameron gets, the less relaxed he is. Makes me want to blurt out something stupid to him, like—it's OK that you fucked a guy. Nobody's going to think you're gay.

Because by this point, I'm pretty sure that's what he's troubled about. He's having a crisis of sexuality, and is now just waiting for me to say some clumsy things to him about his issues—the way I did to Cameron, not so long ago.

I'm like the Love Doctor. Only hopeless and incompetent and unable to actually use that word to anyone in existence.

I'm the L–e Doctor.

"Hey, Wade," I say, and he jumps as though I ran into the room and hit him with a giant cock. Which I suppose is technically what me and Kitty actually did, two nights ago. *He didn't need any prompting*, she said to me yesterday, when I told her I felt bad. *I just handed him the condom and he went for it.*

And then she had spelled out the word *gay* in the air, with her fingers. I'm not even sure how she did it, in all honesty.

"Hey," he says. He's busy cataloguing what looks like a bunch of the Professor's old student files, and he doesn't stop being busy when I enter the room. The Box Room, we call this one—though I don't know why. It has no boxes in it—just filing cabinets and the remainder of someone's class project.

A store mannequin with feminist theory buzzwords written all over it.

"You OK?" I start out, then wince. Apparently, Cameron used up all of my tact, along with my ability to make someone feel better about themselves.

Though I suppose the fact that I'm not sure I *want* to make Wade feel better about himself has something to do with my sudden lack of interesting things to say.

"Sure," he tells me, but he doesn't turn around. And all I can think is *OK. This is the way things are going to go, I guess. I did that stuff, and now he thinks he's gay and we can never be friends again, for reasons as mysterious as where that one sock went between wearing and the laundry basket.*

Only then he surprises me. He surprises me all in a giant rush, while I do something weird like clutch my chest.

"I'm jealous, OK," he says, which is enough on its own. It really is. I could die happily if he stopped right there and never said anything to me again—but he keeps *going.* "I know I shouldn't be. I know what's gone down between us—I'm not a moron, Allie. You fucking hate me because I was a douchebag in college who didn't appreciate how amazing you are, and now you want to punish me. Well that's fine, OK, that's fine—go ahead and make me do any crazy fucking thing you want. I'll fuck some guy's ass, I'll be your little bitch—whatever, OK? Whatever."

I think I kind of seize up. As though I've just eaten a tonne of ice cream, only it hasn't just given me brain freeze. It's given me all-over-body freeze. I can't feel my toes. My good sense is melting.

Did he seriously just shove all of that out of him? It sounds like the ravings of a lunatic, not the smooth moves of an impenetrable stud.

Which Wade was. Until right now.

I don't know what to do. It's like he just compressed everything I always wanted to hear him say into one twenty-second babble—I should feel exultant, vindicated, relieved. So how come I just go limp, and lose the ability to speak?

And apparently this limp inability is bad enough that he has to comment on it.

"You're not going to say anything to that?"

He turns around at the same time, so I can see the expression on his face. Unfortunately, it's no more explainable or readable than the things he's just said—which is probably how I end up going with: "It was definitely better than a shrug."

Is it weird that I actually feel the relief I need to when he laughs at that? He looks like himself again too—like the guy I used to moon over, with the curly blond hair and the eyes like electric sparks, and everything about him so easy and charming.

"Why didn't you ever ask me out?" I ask, because it's easier, now. Of course it is. I'm looking backward through a telescope at the person I was, and suddenly she seems very small and very foolish.

So what if he turns around and says to me, now, that he just didn't feel anything for me. So what if I wasn't enough. *I'm* enough for me.

Only he has one more surprise up his sleeve. One that I don't account for and can't prepare for.

"I don't know," he says, and as he does he hooks a lock of my hair over my ear—the way he used to sometimes, when we were busy poring over stories and all of my curls got in the way. "I guess I just thought you'd always be there."

Of course I know what he means. I was his spare—his just-in-case girl. He got to sleep with everyone under the sun, while I lingered in the back of his mind as some far-off and completely safe possibility. Like maybe we could have finally gotten together and had the marriage and the kids he'd always sort of imagined himself having.

Something like that.

"I almost was," I say, because that's the truth. It's what I came here for—to finally be with him. It's just that it all looks so different now, like something I need to escape from rather than something I want to run toward.

He assumed I'd wait, and that assumption feels stifling, sticky, not like me at all.

"But not anymore, huh?" he asks, and I don't even have to nod. He does it for me—a slow up and down of his head.

"I'm sorry," I say, though it sounds kind of stupid coming out. He seems to know it too, because he snorts out a laugh and waves his hand, then finally manages to get out a few more surprising words.

"You're not the one who has to be sorry. I need to be sorry."

I think that's the sweetest thing he's ever said to me. And it definitely lessens the impact of his next confession.

"I knew, you know. I knew Cameron loved you."

I don't know what's more troubling about him saying something like that. The fact that he obviously kept the truth from me for his own nefarious one-day-we'll-have-a-picket-fence purposes, or that he uses the word *loved*.

Though I do know that I can't focus on anything but said word, for the next eight thousand years. He has to snap his fingers in front of my face to bring me back to reality, and away from the sudden image of me and Cameron, frolicking through fields of daisies, hand in hand.

"Did you just hear my nightmarish confession?" he says, and I try to break it down. Was it really so nightmarish? I mean, one guy wanted to keep me as his spare so didn't tell me that another guy possibly loved me. That's not so bad, is it?

"You're an ass," I tell him. Mainly because it probably is so bad. I just feel less bad about it due to this weird swelling sensation in my chest.

Cameron, I think, *Cameron*.

"I know. But you forgive my ass-i-ness, right?" he asks, and oh he grins that shark's grin of his. It makes me want to punch him and hug him, all at the same time.

Instead, I go with a verbal mixture of both.

"Can you give me back the seven years I lost, mooning over you?"

The punch doesn't hit too hard. Only about 20 percent of the light goes out of his eyes, and when he bounces back he does it with the same easy charm he hooked me with, all those years ago.

"Probably not. But I can do other things—write you a sonnet. Finish packing up this insane room while you lounge around in another man's bed. Do some more ass-fucking."

Is it wrong that I kind of love him all over again for ending on those words?

"I've got to confess—I thought you'd be more troubled by the ass-fucking."

He lifts one shoulder, like *Hey, what can I say?* And then the look on his face…dear God, it's so *filthy*. As though he's just packed full of all the things I never knew he could possibly do, and now they're spilling out of him.

"I got to see you, didn't I?"

Oh Lord, why is *that* the thing I blush over? I mean, I was aware prior to this conversation that he'd seen most of my boobs and my pussy. It's not as though you can watch another man eat out the girl you want to fuck without getting an eyeful.

But even so. I'm bright red.

"At this point, I'll take whatever I can get," he says and then oh,

I blush even harder. I blush all over, even though I swear to God I don't feel the same way about him as I did. It's just—*man alive*—hearing Wade be this full of affection for me, hearing him be so open and apologetic…it's like seeing the face of God.

"Plus, I've got a lot of things to make up to you."

And that's before we've even gotten into his sudden need to be generous.

"No, really," I tell him, but I know that look in his eyes.

It's as dirty as the expression he gave me a moment earlier, and it makes my mind go to all sorts of interesting places. Like Hamin-Ra, where everything is always sultry and dream-like, and pleasure is the greatest aim of any day.

"You sure there's nothing I can do for you?" he asks, and this time I think of Cameron. Cameron saying *This is my favorite part.*

"Well, actually…" I start.

And now *I'm* the one with the shark-like grin.

⁓

I go to tie his wrists loosely, pathetically, but of course he has something to say about that. His hooded gaze hangs all over me, and he pulls at the scarves I'm using to secure him. As though to show me how easily he could get free.

Though isn't that the point? Corin gets free easily, in my story. He tears away the bonds and takes the Queen for his own, roughly, and it's all I can think about now—even as Cameron tells me: "Come on, Allie. You're going to have to do better than that."

I know it. This whole thing had seemed like a good idea when I spoke to Wade and Kitty about it, earlier on, but now I just feel knock-kneed and weak through the stomach. What if Wade's promise to make it up to me were just the ramblings of an insane person?

It certainly sounds like it, when I replay the whole conversation in my head. And when I watch him pull his T-shirt off to reveal that rock-hard body beneath, I can't help remembering how smug and arrogant he sometimes seems.

Smug, arrogant people almost never agree to something like this, do they?

"Tighter," Cameron says, and I obey. I get him right up against the bedpost, arms linked behind his back, around it, and I cinch the scarves so hard I can see the backs of his hands turning white.

And then, just for good measure, I run my tongue over somewhere sweet on him. The heavy curve of his bicep, maybe. The smooth shape of his shoulder. Of course he moans and wriggles and tries to get away, but that's the beauty of this one last lovely tale.

He can't.

"You're getting good at this," Kitty says to me, from the place she's found, all curled up at the head of the bed. And it doesn't sound anything like the words the Queen's little sylph-like assistant says, as the Queen prepares to torment Corin. It doesn't sound like anything the Queen needs to hear, because she is already flawless and fully formed and so aware of her own power that I'm envious of her, even though I created her.

But it's something *I* need to hear. And especially so when Wade saunters over to me, and gets me by the back of the neck.

He doesn't do it roughly, exactly. But I hear Cameron's intake of breath, behind me, and when I glance over at Kitty she has this deadly, dangerous look in her eye. Like the one she got when Wade demanded her cunt, and she offered him something else entirely.

But it's OK, it's fine, it's all totally fine—even when he kisses me with that same rough, almost proprietary sort of pressure. He forces my mouth open and his tongue fucks over mine, and this time Cameron makes a deeper sound. A lower sound, caught somewhere between a sigh of protest and a moan of deep pleasure—of the kind I can't hope to understand.

Does he really get off on seeing me with another man? Or is it something else, something hot and twisted and all mixed up in this story I didn't even mean to write? I didn't know what I was doing when I first blasted out "Hamin-Ra," and I still don't, all this time later.

So I just hold onto Wade and let him kiss me, while Kitty voices all the things I can hardly bear to hear.

"She looks good, doesn't she?" she asks, and I know without turning around that she's talking to Cameron. It's almost the exact thing that the little assistant says to Corin, as the guards maul and kiss and lick the Queen.

And though I'm not sure it applies to me, I sure do appreciate her saying it. I just feel so naked right now, so exposed, even though I'm wearing a cotton nightie and it hardly shows anything at all.

Though I've got to say—I'm pretty sure anyone would feel naked, with one man's eyes all over their back and another man's hands all over their body. Wade gets a handful of my ass, briefly, and I think I go up on tiptoe, but then I turn a little and I can see Cameron looking. I can see him wishing that those were his hands, that he had hold of me in that same way, that he was as bold as Wade suddenly seems when he pushes me back onto the bed.

"Hold her wrists," Wade says to Kitty, so hoarse and breathless seeming—and with this look on his face too. A mean look, I think it is, while that stomach-twisting feeling comes back to me.

I didn't know things were going to go this way. In the story, no one pins the Queen down. But then I think in a bleak flash—*I'm the Queen of nothing*—closely followed by something else. A sweeter thought, that stings as much as it turns me to liquid. It's one I had not long ago, and it's just as powerful as it was then: *This isn't a story. We can do whatever we want.*

And Wade does. He has Kitty pin my wrists to the bed, and once she does so I can see her hovering above me. I can see how long her blonde hair looks, dangling around her face, and how pretty her mouth is, curled into that devilish smile.

But more than that, I can see how easy it is to trust her, and I know that no matter what Wade has planned she'll always be there for me.

Even if being there for me means she gets to lick one wicked, pointed tongue over my right nipple.

Of course, I buck immediately. Not because it's a woman touching me in such an intimate way, or because it feels good, but because the two things cross at some unholy intersection inside me and I can't stand it, for a second. A great bloom of pleasure swells once, sharply, between my legs, and the moment it's died down she licks the other nipple.

You know. Just for good measure.

And I'm not even embarrassed about the fact that after she's done it, both of the little tips of my tits are standing out proud beneath the material of my nightie. You can even see where she's marked me, you can see the wet circles over my stiff buds, and oh it's a sight that doesn't just impress me.

It impresses Wade too, who moans and cups his rigid cock. And it impresses Cameron, even though I'm sure he doesn't want it to. He strains against the bonds he made me tie, and his great chest rises and falls, raggedly.

But oh, it's his prick I can't tear my eyes away from, his big, swollen prick, curving up so steeply that it's almost kissing his belly. It makes me want to beg for it, to squirm on the bed and beg for them to let me go so I can climb him like a rock face and slide right down over that stiff pole, but that's not what this is about.

It's about tormenting *him*, about making *him* feel it, and so I turn back to Wade with some effort and beg for what he's got instead.

"Fuck my cunt," I tell him, and I don't do it just because I crave it, because my sex feels shivery and achy and I need it to be filled. I do it because it's the opposite of everything I ever imagined saying to Wade—no *Make love to me*. No *I need you so badly*. Just those raw words, and oh…I think he knows it.

Some of the greedy light goes out of his eyes—the way it did when I told him about mooning over him—and he hesitates for just a second. But then I spread my legs for him, as wide as they will go, and as I do so my nightie rides up until he can't fail to see everything I've got down there.

And, oh God, I'm so wet already. I'm so messy—all over my thighs and down between the cheeks of my ass. His face goes slack and I know he can see it, but it's Kitty who brings it all into sharp focus.

"Is she all slippery?" she asks, and as she does so she pushes her hands under the flimsy neckline of this stupid cotton thing, to cup my breasts.

More than cup, in fact. She rubs over my stiff nipples and squeezes the abundance of flesh in her two tiny hands, making me moan and writhe on the bed in a way I completely didn't know I was capable of.

But I writhe harder when Wade replies with even dirtier things.

I mean, of course he does. Him and Kitty are practically playing a game of sex-upmanship, by this point.

"She's so wet I can see it glistening, on her inner thighs. And her clit is real, real stiff."

Oh God, oh God, I don't think I can stand this. And him saying those words isn't even the worst thing about this scenario, because after he's said them he turns to Cameron with that shark-like grin on his face, and says: "What do you think, man? You think I should stroke her little bud?"

Cameron doesn't reply, naturally. I think all the muscles in his lower jaw have locked up, and for a moment I feel almost frantic inside. Like I'm just bursting with the need to put a stop to this, and bring him into the fold.

But the thing is—he hasn't said the safe word. He hasn't said anything at all. I can't do anything unless he tells me, because to do so would mean I was letting him down in some way. It would mean I don't trust his judgment of what he wants for himself, that I don't trust the limits of his own fantasy, and I can't have that.

Not even when Wade continues, in that same teasing tone of voice.

"Think I should lick her? It looks like she could really do with a tongue through that hot little slit of hers, tasting all of that honey she's produced. But then again, could be she needs something more than that…"

He lets the words trail away to nothing, though I'm guessing there's no one in the room who can't guess what he means. He means his cock, of course he means his cock, or at least I think he does until he takes us all on a little trip down memory lane.

"I mean, you wouldn't believe what I caught her doing the other day."

Uh-oh.

"Apparently, her fingers just weren't enough for her. She was using a big, thick plastic cock, and oh man she was riding it like she just couldn't get enough." He pauses—for extra impact, probably. "Weren't you, baby?"

I glance at Cameron, then, to see how he's reacting. But the problem is, I can't get anything from his expression apart from *Fuck, I really need to tear Wade in two, then take you roughly against something.*

There's no specific, I-don't-want-to-hear-about-that-time- you-and-Wade-did-stuff-together type resentment on his face. But that doesn't mean it isn't there, and the longer Wade talks the more panicky I feel, until I don't know where arousal ends and a full-on mental breakdown begins.

I just squirm, and blush, and listen to him saying how tight I looked, spread around that plastic cock, and how hard it had made him, to see me so lusty, and abandoned.

He must be having a great time of it now, because I've never felt so lusty and abandoned in all my life. I think I scream when he touches the outer lips of my sex with just the tip of his finger, and I definitely babble something, once he's made one long, slow circle around that soft mound.

"Please, I need it," I say. "I need it."

And then when he refuses to give it to me, I force myself to go ruder.

"Rub my clit, rub it, oh God, yeah—pinch my nipples."

That last one's for Kitty. Her fingertips feel all wet, and she's somehow caught my stiff buds between thumb and forefinger, and every time I push into her touch she twists them, she plucks at them, she makes me groan.

I think I may well come just from the feel of a fucking *woman* touching my breasts.

"See how excited she's getting?" Wade says, and this time Cameron replies.

Though he does more than that. He echoes Corin almost exactly, in a voice that has a core of steel. Even if it's kind of wavering, at the same time.

"Give it to her," he says. "Give her what she wants, for God's sake."

As though I need someone to have pity on me—which I suppose I do, in a way. I feel almost lost in this, so turned on I can't move or speak or do anything without feeling a great swell of intense sensation go through me.

And though I'm sure he doesn't mean it, Cameron's words only make things worse. He sounds so hoarse and desperate himself, and I can see how thick his cock looks, how swollen—but he's busy thinking of *me*. Oh, he always thinks of me. He always has.

Unlike Wade, who just circles and circles with the tip of his finger, now on the inner lips of my sex but still nowhere near all the places I need him to be. And he's laughing too, as he does it, because I'm so wet that the sounds his slight touch produce are obscene. The room fills up with all of this slick, wet clicking, until my cheeks are aflame and my body is shaking and another noise drowns it out.

The harsh grate of my breathing, followed by a whole host of guttural moans.

"I think she's going to come," Kitty says, so full of teasing glee that it's unbearable—but I can't say she's wrong. I can feel it winding up inside me, even without a finger on my clit or in my cunt, and I go with it.

I let it wash over me in tight waves, one after the other until I'm sure I'm going mad and all I can say is "Oh God, yeah, make me come, make me come, rub me there, yes."

But it's good, because it persuades Wade into that final soft touch—the one that pushes me over the edge and tears an orgasm from me. All he has to do is slide the tip of his finger over my bulging clit and I go rigid all over, twisting beneath the restraining hands Kitty has on me while all the sounds in the world try to pour out of my mouth.

With little success. I think I manage a long, drawn out *Fuuuuccckk*, and that's about the most of it.

And then I just lie there, spent, every muscle in my body twitching and every little bit of sense I have telling me to open my eyes. To pay attention to the things going on around me. I mean, it's not as though I'm in the middle of a pleasant garden party, during which I can sporadically doze or maybe just drift on a haze of warm happiness.

I've got a shark on one side of me and a tease on the other, and any second Cameron's just going to burst out of his bonds like the Incredible Hulk, and then where will we be? In fraught foursome land, that's where. There's just no time for bathing in the afterglow.

Especially when I can already feel Wade trying to turn me over. Not even trying, really. He gets two big hands on my hips—oh God, the way he did to Cameron, the way he did to Cameron!—and wrenches me around, so I barely have time to catch my breath or make sense of anything before I find myself face down on the bed.

I don't even get a lot of time to acclimatize to this position. He yanks and then I'm up on all fours, ass in the air and everything spread open for his viewing pleasure—a fact that does not escape Kitty.

"Tell everyone how she looks," she says, and Wade obliges. Of course he does. He's the new, generous Wade, who's only too happy to share the sight of my clenching cunt and my come-slicked asshole with the rest of the room.

I don't think I've ever been so mortified or so turned on in my entire life. He uses the word *rosebud*, for God's sake. Kitty claps her hands!

I'm dying, I'm dying.

And then Wade says: "What do you think, man? You think I should fuck her there, the way I fucked you?"

And I do more than die. I die and then decompose and turn to dust, every little particle of me blowing away on the slightest breeze. In truth, I think Cameron *breathes* and I blow away.

Mainly because I don't know what's worse—that Wade said something like that to torment us both, or that it doesn't seem the slightest bit cruel. His tone isn't even smug, the way it was for the reveal about me and the sex toy. It's just kind of matter-of-fact and a touch teasing, like an old friend punching another friend on the arm.

And when I look at Cameron, he seems… not relaxed, exactly. But certainly untroubled. Wade isn't trying to be an ass about any-thing. He's trying to reach out and shake Cameron's hand, in the middle of a foursome.

Which is absurd enough on its own—or at least it would be, if Cameron didn't shake his hand back.

"Go on," he says, voice grating. Body almost trembling, all over. "Fuck her ass. Take it. Make her scream your name."

It's like some kind of fucking gentlemen's agreement, about asses. I don't even know what to make of it, or understand how I feel about it, and this continues until Wade quite suddenly slides something between the cheeks of my bottom, and every nerve in my body wakes up and goes nuts.

"Oooh, you like that, huh?" Kitty asks, and when she does I make the mistake of looking up. Though really, I suppose it's not exactly a mistake. Seeing someone spread out on a bed in front of you, legs open and a hand working busily over a very wet, very bare pussy…it's not exactly something you never expect to see in the middle of a foursome.

It's just that it's really in my face, and really jarring, and yes, I'll admit it—really arousing. It trumps the glimpse I got of her pussy to the power of eight million, and I can't help marveling over how it looks, so close up.

I've never even seen my own that close up. And she's circling her clit in slow, easy circles too, so it's not as though I can just pretend we're in the locker room together, soaping ourselves down.

I have to face this, in the same way I have to face Wade doing another thing I've never actually experienced before.

Something very slick runs between the cheeks of my ass and I balk. Partly because of the sensation—so tingly and liquid and rude—and partly because I know what it is, and what it means. He's lubing me up before he puts a finger or a cock in my ass, and I don't think I can take it.

It's just too sensitive. I can feel every groove and fold, distinctly, and even more so when he runs a finger down over my clenching hole, again. Or at least, I *think* it's a finger. For all I know it could be the vibrator, his cock, the handle of a hairbrush, and oh Lord I really can't take that.

I lurch forward, unsteadily, and suddenly I realize why Cameron was bruised the next day. I understand, because Wade immediately puts one hand on my hip and drags me back, so hard I just have to gasp aloud.

"Keep still," he orders me, and I shudder to hear him. *Kitty* shudders to hear him. Hell—I'm pretty sure Cameron shudders to hear him, though I only get vocal confirmation of this when Wade finally, finally presses the thick head of his cock to that tiny, tiny place.

"Oh Jesus fucking Christ," Cameron says, even though it's Wade who's getting the sensation of this. Wade who's working and pushing and jerking his cock into my tight hole, until my whole body feels like one big burn and I'm so shaken, so disturbed by the feel of it that I need to tell him to stop.

"Don't," I think I say, and he actually obeys me. He eases up, that red hot pressure leaving me for just a second.

Only then…only then…

"Make her take it."

I think I go rigid. Wade *definitely* goes rigid. And I understand why, completely—because it isn't either him or Kitty who gives that one cruel order. It's Cameron—seething, shaking Cameron, my lovely guy who couldn't so much as ask for a blowjob, a few weeks ago.

But he can do this now, it seems.

"Make her take it," he says, again, and this time when Wade rubs the swollen head of his cock against my clenching hole, it gives. I think of Cameron saying words like that and of maybe him behind me instead of Wade, pushing into my yielding body, and I let it happen.

Wade just sinks right in to the hilt, groaning all the while.

I can't blame him, however. I groan too, so loud it's embarrassing. And I keep groaning, because just the feel of it, just the sense of being filled so completely and the rough, stretched sensation it pushes through my body… it's unbelievable.

Was this how Cameron felt, when Wade did it to him? Could he feel every little part of that greedy, grasping hole, rippling around something so thick, so solid? I'm pretty sure Wade wasn't as patient with him as he is with me, but the feeling remains the same, I'm certain.

Like a million nerve endings are waking up, and firing through my body.

"Fuck, you're tight," he blurts out, and I can't help it. I have to imagine all the possible differences between me and Cameron, and how I now feel compared to him. Do I clench harder, around Wade's slowly working cock? Am I smoother inside, slicker with lube, do I tremble and groan more loudly than Cameron did?

It's a perverse series of thoughts, but I let them come. They make it easier when Wade finally, finally starts pounding into me, because just the idea of him doing the same to Cameron makes me moan with unchecked arousal.

"Oh yeah," Kitty gasps, high and tight. "Oh yeah!"

But I don't know what she's shouting it about. I've got my eyes screwed tight shut so can't make out if she's coming or not, and there's something so random about her cries that I can't pin them down to anything that's happening. Is it the sight of Wade, fucking into me hard? Maybe his face is red and his mouth is tight, and she can see by the pressure he's exerting on my hips that he's almost past breaking point.

His cock feels even bigger in that narrow channel, now, and I know he must be close. He must be, but he's not saying anything or showing me anything, and it's only Cameron and his little filthy outbursts that give me any indication of how this is going.

"Yeah," he says, brokenly. "Fill her ass."

And I turn over inside. I call out his name—I have to. I can't stand to hear him saying things like that while all of these strange, dark feelings barrel through me. It's not just the actual physical sensation of it—the way the thick ridge around the head of his cock is rubbing and rubbing over that tight ring of muscle; how slick and slippery and rude it all feels, as he ploughs in and out—it's the feeling it gives me inside.

Of being debased, and used, and oh God I'm sure Cameron mentioned something like that in one of his stories. I'm sure he did, I'm sure, oh Lord, why didn't he tell me how good it feels? How good it feels, to just give myself over to this wonderful, glorious, down-and-dirty pleasure.

"Harder," he tells Wade. "Fuck her harder."

And then Wade says the magic words. The ones I've been waiting for, the ones I didn't even know I wanted until Wade gives them to me.

"Is that what you want, baby? You want me to go harder?" he says, and in reply I tell him the very thing I didn't fully understand until right now, right this minute, with my orgasm cresting through my shuddering body and everything streaked with unbearable pleasure.

"Don't ask," I tell him. "Don't ask."

Chapter Fourteen

NOBODY MOVES FOR A long, long time. Probably out of necessity, if I'm honest, because I'm pretty sure Wade has broken me. And I've *definitely* broken him. He doesn't move when I ease myself off his softening cock, and he doesn't move when I put a hand behind me to see if he's died, and when Kitty rubs her boobs on his face and says *Hey, hey, Wade, check out my amazing rack?*

Yeah, he doesn't move then, either.

But at least I know that Kitty's still living. In fact, she seems to be doing more than just simply *living*. She seems to be buzzing with this newfound energy—one that prompts her to rub her boobs on me too—until I realize with a little guilty start why that may be the case.

Me and Wade have just had incredible orgasms. Hell—I've had *two* incredible orgasms. And she's had…maybe one? Possibly? By her own hand?

I know nothing about foursome etiquette, but even I understand that this is not acceptable. Cameron's fine—he *chose* to be in this position, and even though he looks like he's been hooked up to the mains and his face is redder than the heart of the sun, he continues to choose it.

Whereas Kitty…well. She hasn't chosen to have zero orgasms. She chose to partake in this bizarre mingling of bodies we decided to embark on, and she deserves more than two people passing into a coma while a third remains tied to a bedpost.

In fact, she probably deserves something more than anyone else here. She's the only one who hasn't judged, or brought her own deep-seated issues to the party—and she almost never seems to demand anything for herself. It's really no wonder that she manages to get involved in so many group sex sort of situations.

She's so *generous*.

"You like that?" she whispers in my ear, and I manage to get an arm behind myself. I hook it around something on her—I don't care what—and squeeze her tight, just to let her know that I did.

To let her know more than that, in fact. I want her to be sure that I don't feel weird about anything that just happened, that I'll never feel weird about it, that she touched my boobs but so fucking what?

She's my best friend, and my best friend can touch my boobs if she wants to. I'm not even going to quibble about how awesome it made me feel, or do any kind of weird *Oh no I'm a lesbian* sort of thing, because I'm not, and neither is she, and oh my God the whole thing was just so awesome.

I can't feel conflicted and weird about something so awesome. And neither should she—not ever, no, never. I just want her to feel fantastic about everything we've just done, and more than that, I want to be as generous with her as she was with me.

I want to give her stuff, and do stuff for her, and what she says next gives me the perfect opportunity.

"Damn it. I really *wanted* a turn."

Of course it takes me a moment to process what she means. But then I turn and see Wade snapping the condom off his cock—a cock that's now as soft and sleepy as he looks—and I understand perfectly.

And though I can't give her a turn myself, I can *offer* her something. Something that looks down at me with this strange mixture of trust and frustration all over his gorgeous face.

He's sweating, I notice. Perspiration has slicked the hair down at his temples, and it's given his body an almost heavenly sheen. Like he's been dipped in honey, then presented for our delectation.

It's too good an opportunity to pass up.

"Why don't you try out our little slave?" I say, and by God I struggle to get out that last word. Not just because of its meaning, but also because of how silly it sounds in my mouth. I'm so nothing, I'm so *not* a Queen. What right do I have to call anyone my slave?

But ohhhh, the way Cameron looks at me when I do use it. His eyes roll closed, briefly, and his lips part, and even as Kitty squeals and squirms down the bed toward him, his gaze stays locked on mine.

It doesn't even shift away from me when Kitty runs a couple of fingers up over his bare chest, and says to him in her low, teasing voice: "You sure you're ready for this, big guy?"

Of course I know what she's doing. It's as close as she can get to asking permission, without breaking the spell of this little game. But to her credit she doesn't wait for an answer—she just takes the condom the moment I offer it to her, then clasps his thick, leaking cock in her two tiny hands.

It looks almost comical, I have to say. But the thought of that big thing plunging into my little bird-like Kitty…yeah, that's not quite as comical. It's arousing and disturbing all at the same time, instead, and it only gets more so when she struggles just as much as I did, with the rubber.

Maybe even more than that, because oh *Lord* is Cameron ever on edge. Every squeeze and push of her fingertips over his clearly sensitive cock makes him tremble, and I can't get over how much strain he's now putting on his shoulders. He's leaning so far forward that his arms are practically at right angles to his body—though it heartens me to see Kitty forcing him back.

She does it just the same way I would have done it, soothing him and stroking all over his gleaming body until he leans against the post. Of course, he pants and shakes while she does it, but that's understandable.

He's too far gone. Way, way too far gone.

"Use him up," I tell her. "Get yourself off on his cock."

And it sounds cruel, I know it does. But it also gives him what he wants and needs, quite obviously. His face changes and his body thrums, visibly, and then she just turns around on all fours like a bitch in heat, and works herself back on his cock.

It's a sight to see, I tell you. I try my best to remain cool and aloof—in perfect keeping with my story, and his fantasy—but I know I shake with newly blooming arousal. Her expression alone is enough to get me going—so shocked, suddenly, so full of that same thing I had felt, the moment his thick cock stretched me open—but oh she does more than that, so much more.

She asks me to help her. Actually asks me to, just as I think she's finally notched his prick to her little slippery hole, and oh Lord how can I refuse? I can't, I can't, even though the idea seems to make Cameron go absolutely crazy.

He's shuddering almost constantly now, and it only gets worse as I slowly make my way back to them. By the time I get to the place where his body is almost joining with hers, he's letting out those little broken *ah* sounds, and straining at the shoulders again.

I can't help kissing him. Just a little, just a glancing brush over his lips, while he grits his teeth and tries not to rage for more. Corin didn't rage for more in the story, after all. He held out to the very end, to the very edges of his limits, and oh God it makes me wonder just what Cameron's limits are.

"You want to fuck her, baby?" I say, and then I put my hand on his cock. Which I'm sure is going to be a mistake, but no, no. He holds his pleasure in and only lets me have a hot, bursting gasp, just before I angle his cock and aim it at her tight little cunt.

"Talk to me," I say, but he won't. Not even when I press my open mouth to the side of his face, and slide the head of his prick through her soft, slick folds. It must feel like heaven—I know Kitty sure thinks so—but he remains on this trembling precipice, body stiff, eyes unseeing.

And then I lay a hand on Kitty's back, and just ease her down over his hard length. Just slow, just syrupy slow, Kitty moaning and rocking all the while, and when he's seated fully in her and all I can see is how much he's stretched her tight hole, I tell her to fuck back on him. I tell her to do it hard, just as Wade says, "Fuck yeah," and adds his own series of sounds to proceedings, and I sigh under the glorious weight of it all, and Cameron turns his face toward mine.

He looks at me, then, all heavy-lidded and too desperate, but I don't give him any respite. When Kitty seems to flag, her cries of pleasure almost verging on sobs, I get hold of her hips myself and yank her back on his prick.

That gets a moan out of both of them. It gets more than that from Kitty, in fact. "Uhhh yeah, I'm gonna come," she says, then hotter, dirtier, "God, his cock feels so good, oh Jesus, Cameron, you fill my pussy so good."

It's the first time I feel a spark of jealousy, just remembering how that same cock had felt in me. Like it might split me in two, like I could come from nothing but the feel of it, shoving into me roughly, and oh I think Kitty is experiencing almost the exact same thing.

"That's it, oh God, just like that," she moans, and then her body jerks, and spasms, and Cameron stiffens under my touch as though he needs to communicate to me exactly what's going on.

She's coming. She's coming and clenching tight around his probably bursting prick, and the effect on him is electric. His body stiffens and his jaw tightens and he squeezes his eyes shut. I'm almost certain he's coming himself, until Kitty gives one last long sigh of pleasure and slides off him.

And then I can see that he hasn't. He's still rock hard and he hasn't filled the condom, but more than both of those things is how strung out he seems. Like he's just going to go insane at any moment—and I'm sure Wade's comments aren't helping any, with that.

"Jesus, man, you're still going?" he says, and then I glance at him, and he's just doing the lewdest thing possible. He's stroking his already-hard-again cock, fresh lube all over everything so the tip and his hand fair near glisten, and while he does so he sucks long and slow on his middle finger.

You know, like a little hint at all the things he could do, if Cameron was feeling adventurous, and wanted to ask.

I don't mind admitting—it sparks a little light in me, to think of Wade sucking Cameron's cock. But then Wade kneels up, suddenly, and goes for the box of condoms still rolling around somewhere, on the bed, and I know he's going to try for something different.

"Bet you're wanting Allie's pussy now, huh?" he asks, and I have to say—I think he's going to be kind here. In fact, I'm so sure of it that I snap the rubber off Cameron's cock, in anticipation of the new one Wade is obviously going to hand me.

Obviously.

Only then he says: "But I dunno, man. I'm not sure you're in any fit state to give her what she needs—do you? Seems like a much better plan for me to take her, don't you think?"

I would find him almost unutterably cruel, if it were not for the questions he puts in there. The constant stream of questions, like he's just waiting for Cameron to answer, to do something, to step up. But the thing is—Cameron isn't going to answer, or do anything, or step up. His limit is clearly on some impossible horizon that I can't even imagine, far away in the honeyed land of Hamin-Ra.

And even if it isn't, he's just not Corin. Not really. He doesn't want me enough, and I can tell that's the case when Wade just pulls me away from him and stretches me out on the bed, hungry mouth on mine before I've even had the chance to say, *Hey, I think it's Cameron I love.*

I know we did that thing earlier, but it's Cameron I love. Even though Cameron maybe doesn't love me. I'm sure he doesn't. In fact, I'm so sure that I feel it all the way up to the point of hearing those scarves rip, I feel it right up until his hands are on me, yanking me, shoving Wade, everything suddenly brutal and too good and oh, yes.

"You're mine," he growls, right down into me. "You're mine you're mine you're mine."

And oh it's better than any story I've ever imagined. His grip presses a bruise into my thigh and I feel his teeth graze my cheek, my throat, my shoulder, everything hot and desperate suddenly. I barely have chance to get the condom on him before he's fucking into me, hard and frantic, those big hands splayed over my ass and my lower back until I'm sure he's just dragging me onto his cock.

I'm aware, faintly, of Kitty or Wade or maybe both of them saying *Fuck* in a shocked sort of voice, but that's OK. I get why. I feel like I'm being mauled or pummeled and for a long moment I'm just clinging to his shoulders, holding on as he takes me in a way I never in a million years thought he would.

And oh God, it's bliss. It's unbelievable. His cock *grinds* against my G-spot. His body shoves against my stiff clit. When he grips my ass and pulls me into his arms, legs spread over his thighs and everything in me just holding on tight, he leaves marks, bruises, evidence that he was all over me.

I think I pull out a clump of his hair. I think I make a noise like a wild animal, snarling at an intruder. But I *know* that I look right into his perfect, amazing face just as he starts to shudder uncontrollably, and my own pleasure spirals out of control.

My climax works its way up through my body, cunt tightening almost unbearably around his still working cock, and I say the words I've wanted to for a while now. I don't just think them. I let them out.

"I love you," I tell him, and then he presses me so tightly to him that I can't breathe, and oh God he comes, and comes, and comes. I feel him doing it, in spasming jerks and the tense swelling of his cock inside me. In the way he grunts in a protracted, abandoned sort of way, right into my hair and the side of my face and, oh Lord, it's so good.

But it's only when he's shivering in my arms, slick with cooling sweat and completely broken apart that I realize something.

He might have groaned and lost himself in pleasure and fucked me like a maniac. But he didn't say it back. He doesn't say anything like it back. And he continues to not say it, long after all of this is done.

Chapter Fifteen

I'M STARTLED WHEN HE finds me, under the stairs. Though not because I haven't seen him for the better part of twenty-four hours and was starting to wonder if he'd undergone another minor freak-out. More because I'm in the middle of my own minor freak-out, and didn't realize it until he looms over me in this dark little space, torch in hand.

I've got the light on in here, but it's still spooky when he suddenly puts said torch to his face, and says, "Mwa ha ha, I guess we didn't all die in here."

Just like he used to, only with that little extra kick of awareness, of nostalgia, of something else I can't quite name. Like the way that everything is now, on the eve of saying good-bye. Tomorrow we'll all be getting into cabs and going our separate ways, though none of us have actually really said it. We haven't said: *Well, I guess the month's up. Let's get out of here, Scoobs.*

It's just going to happen. I know it is. And that's probably why I'm in here, rooting through bits of old bicycle under an old lamp that doesn't work while praying for as few spiders as possible.

"What are you looking for?" Cameron says, after a moment—but only because he's smart. And because he's either grown to know me or knew me all along, and doesn't have to open with something lame and leading like *Hey, what are you doing in here?*

He knows what I'm doing in here. He knows I'm looking.

"Nothing," I say, but he's smarter than that too.

"You know, I doubt you're going to find a secret note from Warren in here, explaining why he did all of this."

I put the bit of old bicycle down. Clap the dust off my hands. Give him a *look* that he probably can't see, through the semi-darkness. So weird that my memories of this little space are now clouded by him, by the blind feel of him and the way he said my name.

Christ, I think this whole place is now clouded by the blind feel of Cameron Lindhurst. I won't be able to go anywhere in here without first remembering all of the things we've done together—though such a problem may be moot, soon enough.

Wade's already got a buyer for the place, and it's more money than I ever imagined having in my life. Just like that, courtesy of Professor Warren. All we have to do is say the word.

"I wasn't looking for an explanation," I tell him, but the exasperation in my voice makes it sound like even more of a lie. In fact, it's so much of one that he doesn't even acknowledge what I've said. He just plunges right into: "You should face facts, Allie. There probably isn't one."

And I know he's right. I know it. Professor Warren left us this house without a word about why, and we stayed here without any understanding of what drove us, and now I'm standing in front of Cameron with all of these feelings inside me, and I don't get any of them either.

I look up at him and everything just kind of swells inside me, the memory of him saying *You're mine* swells inside me, and then suddenly I'm blurting it out just as I did before, only this time there's almost no excuse for it. I'm not in the throes of passion. There's no more reason why he should say it back now, with only a month between this and barely knowing each other at all.

But I do it anyway, because that's what the occasion calls for. No more waiting five years to tell someone how I really feel. No more panicking at the last moment, frantically searching through old rubbish for an explanation or a clue or just anything, really, anything at all.

I want him to know now. I want it to be clear. No subtext.

No secrets. No hiding behind sex.

"I love you," I say, though I only fully realize how much I mean it once it's done. I think of all the times I never dared to say it to Wade and my stomach flips over, my mind goes blank, briefly—but it's OK, isn't it?

I mean, Cameron's not like Wade. It's not as though he's going to laugh. It's not as though I'm really shoving myself out on a limb here, even though the seconds tick by and it's really starting to feel as though I have. I can feel the tree branch, bending. I can feel myself slipping, slipping, and Cameron's not saying anything at all and, oh God, I'm a fool.

I'm a fool for feelings that don't exist. I was sure they did, but what do I know about anything? I pined over a guy who gives me a shrug about it, after five years of painful waiting and longing. I really have to wake up, you know. Life isn't a fairytale that ends with the handsome prince sweeping me off my feet.

It's just Cameron in a cupboard under the stairs, looking all tense and weird before he finally kisses me on the cheek, too hard.

That's what my life is. Being kissed on the cheek too hard. As though I'm some elderly aunt that everyone kind of likes, and any second now I'm going to give him a boiled sweet and a pound coin, then never see him again. He'll come to my lavender-soaked funeral, and look down at my powdery dead face, and that'll be it.

I really don't know why I ever expect anything more.

Kitty goes first. For some reason she's packed another suitcase full of Professor Warren's old cardigans, but hey—I'm not going to question her on it. Yesterday I was busy looking through broken bicycles and old lamps, searching for the secret behind yet another impenetrable man.

We all deal with things in different ways.

"We'll speak tomorrow," she says, as she gives me a one-armed hug. Mainly because that's the deal now. We have to call each other every Tuesday without fail, and say all the things we always meant to before.

Things like: *We're best friends. Let's not ever stop talking to each other, again.*

"I'll call you," I say, and I mean it. It's not just some little placatory thing you tell somebody, to smooth a good-bye. It's real and it's good and even if there's nothing else I get to take away from all of this, at least there's that.

Me and Kitty are good, whispering-through-the-darkness-of-the-dorm-room friends again. I don't even have to worry about it, with her, or hang myself out on a limb. She just comes right out with it before she gets herself into the honking cab that's waiting on the driveway.

"I love you, my little friend," she says, and I get to say it back to someone. I get to say it back!

God, I don't know why I'm suddenly crying. Though luckily, Wade steps in, so it's not as though I have to embarrass myself any further. I just wave as the car pulls away and Wade waves too, and then even better he puts an arm around me.

Or maybe it's even worse, because it's just not him I need to do that to me anymore. Once upon a time, maybe, but not now. Now I just love someone else, another person to add to my collection of people who don't love me back, who don't put their arms around me, who don't feel the way I do.

Who just gaze at me from their too faraway place on the driveway, and don't say anything at all.

Wade goes next, and it's fine. It's really fine. It's funny, in fact, because I don't cry the way I did for Kitty. I just hug him extra tight and when he says, "I wish things could have been different," I actually laugh.

"No you don't," I tell him, and then he holds my face in his hands. He kisses me, lightly, on the mouth.

"I wish *I* was different," he says, and yeah, OK, I almost cry over that.

God, I hadn't thought that this day would be so hard. It hadn't seemed like anything as it rushed up to meet us. It just hadn't felt like some moment when we'd all get in cabs and go our separate ways, as though the only thing keeping us here was a strange set of terms courtesy of Professor Warren.

Just one month, he'd stipulated. And we all stuck to that like glue, for reasons unknown to the universe.

"Good-bye, Wade," I say, and that's it. The Candy Club is no more, once again.

I mean sure, we've all vowed to meet up again—probably somewhere around Christmas, or hey, maybe in the New Year! But unlike the bond that me and Kitty have re-forged I know that those are just empty promises of people with busy lives and things to do and oh, we'll never have this again.

This time next year, the house will be sold. We'll have all moved on, and only the fondest, faintly embarrassed memories of actually acting on our insane sexual tension will remain.

I think it once I'm in the cab, with everything getting smaller and smaller behind me. I should have hugged him. I shouldn't have let things be the way they were with Wade, all bitter and clumsy and not knowing what to do with feelings that have no return.

And then I realize it, with a great gush of something that isn't quite sadness: it doesn't *matter* if they have no return. My life is shaped by feeling those things anyway. By being full of love, even when it doesn't come back to me.

I'm glad that I'm this way. I don't want to be any other—too scared to run the final race. Too afraid to really feel anything, in case or because of or is it OK if I do?

It's OK. It's OK if I do. The Queen has found her heart, and all is well in the land of Hamin-Ra.

Or at least, I think it is until I go through my bag, searching for tissues. And then I find it, the thing he probably intended me to discover once I was home—a story, I think it is. He's folded the sheets of plain paper in the middle—five pages thick, I think, which just makes me thrill from head to toe—and I open them slowly.

Because you know, I'm not excited or anything. It's not as though I think this is going to be some tale of hidden feelings or a story about how much he secretly loves me, and even if it is, well. Well. Maybe I don't want a story anymore. Life isn't a story. I want the real thing, you know, the real thing.

Only then I see the words. These words from my strange, still, lost at the bottom-of-a-lake Cameron. So closed down and careful about everything he says, until right now. Right at the last second when it's almost too late—but not quite.

I ask the driver to turn around. I do, because it's not a story at all—or maybe it is. It's the end of one, the end of my story, and it says: *And then he told her how much he loved her back, truly and madly and deeply.*

The end.

Awakening

by Elene Sallinger

He will open her eyes to the ultimate pleasure…

The minute Claire walked into his shop, she aroused every protective instinct Evan ever had. She looked so fragile, so lost. He ached to be the one to show her a world she'd never dreamed of, to awaken within her the passion she was so ripe to share. It only takes one touch for him to see how open and responsive she is to his dominant side. But the true test will be whether he can let go at last and finally open his heart…

Festival of Romance Award Winner

What readers are saying:

"If *Fifty Shades of Grey* intrigued you, *Awakening* will take you to a whole new level of desire, submission, and unforgettable romance."
—Judge, Festival of Romance contest

"One of the absolute best BDSM novels I have read. (And I've read quite a few.) This one is absolutely amazing!" —Autumn Jean

"Finally! A well-told story that shows the characters' vulnerabilities and how they learned to trust and love again." —A. Hirsch

"Exquisitely beautiful, touchingly heart-wrenching, and hedonistic enough to keep your body on fire." —*Coffee Time Romance*, starred review

For more Xcite Books, visit:

www.sourcebooks.com

Control

Charlotte Stein

Will she choose control or just let go?

When Madison Morris wanted to hire a shop assistant for her naughty little bookstore, she never dreamed she'd have two handsome men vying for the position—and a whole lot more. Does she choose dark and dangerous Andy with his sexy tattoos? Or quiet, serious Gabriel, whose lean physique and gentle touch tempt her more than she thought possible?

She loves the way Andy takes charge when it comes to sex. But the turmoil in Gabe's eyes hints at a deep well of complicated emotions locked inside. When the fun and games are over, only one man can have control of her heart.

What readers are saying:

"Forget *Fifty Shades of Grey*...take a look at this and see how long you can stay in control!"

"This is honest to god, hands down, the best erotic fiction I've ever read."

"Highly addictive!"

For more Xcite Books, visit:

www.sourcebooks.com

The Initiation of Ms. Holly

K D Grace

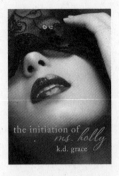

The stranger on the train

He came to her in the dark. She couldn't see him, but she could feel every inch of his body against hers in the most erotic encounter Rita Holly ever had. And now he's promising more…if she'll just follow him to an exclusive club where opulence and sex rule. She can have anything she's ever dreamed of—and more—but first she'll have to pass the club's initiation…

What readers are saying:

"After reading *Fifty Shades of Grey*, I didn't think I would find another book as well written, but then I read *The Initiation of Ms. Holly*, and I was immediately taken in. This book is sexy, erotic, and explosive. I didn't want to put it down." —Dani

"Very, very erotic and sizzling!!! Wow, I could not put it down." —Theresa

"Everything you want in a romantic, erotic, sexual novel." —Jean

"For a fast-paced read with enough twists and turns to keep the story fresh and entertaining, you couldn't ask for a better book." —Christine

For more Xcite Books, visit:

www.sourcebooks.com

About the Author

Charlotte Stein has written over thirty short stories, novellas, and novels, including entries in *The Mammoth Book of Hot Romance* and *Best New Erotica 10*. Her latest work, *Addicted*, was recently called "salaciously steamy" by *Dear Author*. When not writing salaciously steamy books, she can be found eating jelly turtles, watching terrible sitcoms, and occasionally lusting after hunks. For more on Charlotte, visit www.charlottestein.net.